ROUGH
ANIMALS

ROUGH ANIMALS

A NOVEL

RAE DELBIANCO

Arcade Publishing • New York

First Edition

This is a work of fiction. Names, places, characters, and incidents are either the products of the author's imagination or are used fictitiously.

Excerpt from "In Adjuntas" from *King Me* by Roger Reeves. Copyright © 2013 by Roger Reeves. Reprinted with the permission of The Permissions Company, Inc., on behalf of Copper Canyon Press, www.coppercanyonpress.org.

Arcade Publishing books may be purchased in bulk at special discounts for sales promotion, corporate gifts, fund-raising, or educational purposes. Special editions can also be created to specifications. For details, contact the Special Sales Department, Arcade Publishing, 307 West 36th Street, 11th Floor, New York, NY 10018 or arcade@skyhorsepublishing.com.

Arcade Publishing® is a registered trademark of Skyhorse Publishing, Inc.®, a Delaware corporation.

Visit our website at www.arcadepub.com.
Visit the author's site at raedelbianco.com.

10 9 8 7 6 5 4 3 2

Library of Congress Cataloging-in-Publication Data

Names: DelBianco, Rae, author.
Title: Rough animals: a novel / Rae DelBianco.
Description: First edition. | New York: Arcade Publishing, 2018.
Identifiers: LCCN 2017061147 (print) | LCCN 2018004637 (ebook) | ISBN 9781628729740 (ebook) | ISBN 9781628729733 (hardcover: alk. paper)
Subjects: LCSH: Twin—Fiction. | Brothers and sisters—Fiction. | Ranch Life—Fiction. | Violence—Fiction. | Self-perception—Fiction. | Utah—Fiction. | Psychological fiction.
Classification: LCC PS3604.E427 (ebook) | LCC PS3604.E427 R68 2018 (print) | DDC 813/.6—dc23
LC record available at https://lccn.loc.gov/2017061147

Cover design by Brian Peterson
Cover photograph of cut box elder: Rae DelBianco

Printed in the United States of America

TO DANNY DELBIANCO

If the dirt beneath this valley slides into the river,
as it surely will take the lives above and beneath it,
forgive your son's ghost for fighting the moonlight coming through the pines. He understands
very little of the fire you put his body in,
the ashtray you fill with sorrow, the priest
filling the church with smoke and tongues.
The dead are a rough animal with very little grace.

ROGER REEVES, "In Adjuntas"

Part One

CHAPTER ONE

Box Elder County, Utah

It was before dawn when Smith walked out, and a full two hours before the sunlight would be high enough to strip across the tops of the cliff beyond. A flock of starlings pulled out from a scrub oak as he passed and went tittering across the sky black-winged, like bats or demons borne back to hell before daybreak.

He held a .10 gauge horizontal in his right hand, too big for birds, but that was what the old man had left him and so he had to make do with taking the harder shot and blowing the head off supper.

He spat and shuffled his boots through the wheat, or rather stepped large but the reeds still made a swish against the oiled leather as if he'd scuffed them along. Blades of yellow grass for gods or giants.

The cattle grazed up ahead. The sky was melting from black to clouded gray, like an exhaust pipe being wiped clean.

He'd been walking for the better part of an hour now. It was not quite light enough to see the beasts along the edge of the hill but he could feel them there.

He slung the shotgun over a shoulder as he waded in the dew-washed crop. Ran his hand over the thin suggestion of a beard in a face that was wind-marked hard and tanned dark as his boots, but still young, twenty-three. A face with a seriousness that belonged to the rock and those fossilized within it, marred in its earthiness only by the blue glass eye in his left socket. It was the color of a bird's wing, fit badly, and clashed with the soil brown of the right.

The dew was mounting into the air with the coming warmth of day and the mist was now knee-high, and flies rose behind his steps, lost hunters awakening from whatever patches of dark they are made of or wherever flies sleep. He lifted his flashlight half out of boredom and half out of a sense of something else, and one of the steers turned its head and gave him its eye, flashed back as an amphibious green glow. It lowed and shifted on and the others started to low and shift.

He deadened the light. No sense in illuminating what he knew was there. Put the flashlight half in a coat pocket.

Ferric smell as he approached. He'd closed in the last few hundred yards and the cattle steamed a bit in the gray as if it emanated from their hides. But a damp iron smell; burned the nose.

He crossed over the top of the ridge and the animals lumbered on even when he stopped dead and lost his breath.

One of the herd, a midsized steer, down with a bullet in its forehead.

He laid the barrel of his shotgun over his left wrist, holding the flashlight with that hand, his right hand on the trigger. Stepped closer. Saw movement at the underside of the steer, where the hide was peeled back from the meat. He turned on the flashlight and a figure leapt back and the stream of light was instantly met by a flash of something else. Gunshot. Not his. He flinched as he heard a hiss follow the shot and he pinned his shotgun to his side with his elbow to put his hand to his sleeve where the bullet had mangled it and the canvas jacket torn in spikes but mushed ones as they soaked fast and he clamped the hand on his tricep and threw himself back a few feet to drop to the ground at the cusp of the ridge.

The shotgun's action-piece hit him in the back of the head as he fell and rebounded against just the part of the base of the skull to mute the pain of his arm for a moment. He took the gun with his good arm, right, and pumped it with the stock heel against the ground in front of his face.

The figure was gone. Watched from the fallen steer to the ground behind. Gone. His breath was becoming labored now, and he imagined for a moment that his lungs were filling up with blood, and goddamn it's only your arm but goddamn I'm shot but shit man get it together and shoot and he threw his chest upwards to pull himself onto his elbows and wedged himself there and aimed the gun.

Aimed it at what. A line of trees lay beyond the herd of forty, and beyond that, the forest in which at least one man and countless animals had been felled and into which the herd never ventured.

He tried to slow his breath like theirs and picked a spot of brush that looked guiltier than the rest in the depth of its hunter-green color and fired.

The blood was running down to his elbow now.

He had not bled like this before and with it came the shattering understanding of the body as a machine, the warm sludge running down like oil and with it flecks of canvas jacket, the casing for the mechanism. He crossed a hand over the top of his gun to clasp the wound shut and his index finger slotted perfectly into the missing part of the arm, sticky and almost suctioning, realized there was no hole to plug shut, realized with even more alarm that he'd taken his hand off the trigger. Corrected that and fired again at the damned spot of darkened green he imagined as something inexplicable and festering, and the green seemed to intensify and he reloaded, hefting onto the wounded left shoulder to dig in the coat pocket for the ammo that had been ruminating there for months in brass and red plastic, unused.

The shot was answered this time, screeched past his right ear. They could see him.

Another answer and a steer moaned like the sigh of a braking truck and tilted into the ground. A two-pronged heaving into the earth of a four-hundred-pound shoulder and then a nine-hundred-pound hip; it took more than one shudder to ground a creature of that size. With the second concussion he saw that he had never realized just how large they were.

Why didn't they run; they should have run.

A bullet sang above his head and he ducked to the ground, strands of grass pliant but warm like the fur of some beast greater than the one that had just fallen upon it.

Another shot and another animal dropped, ribs emerging like teeth from its side. Three cattle down, enough to make everything go. His stomach rolled.

The sights of his gun blurred from black right angles to static before his eyes and he turned toward his intact arm to vomit. The relief in staring for a moment at the placid wrinkles in tan canvas. And then back again to dark green targetless depths.

His knees yanked him backward instinctively as the herd's breeder bull rolled to the ground in front of him. He grabbed its head as one of the blunted horns met with his sternum and he saw the cloud of buckshot holes in its forehead as the shine of the eyes went from raven's feather blue-black to the dullness of shoe polish. So there was more than one of them, two guns—this was from a shotgun and he'd been hit by a slug.

Why did they still not run!

He dug his elbows into the back of the bull, the sacrilege of propping his gun on a warm body. The flesh pulsed forward and back a final time like the propulsions of a massive jellyfish, and in its last exhale he leaned into it and seated the shotgun atop the ribcage.

A few birds tilted to the south across a sky that was just starting to leak orange across rot-colored clouds.

His chest ached from the blow of the horn.

He aimed slightly to the left this time and fired again. He carried only two extra shells with him and the next would be his last. Shots for foxes, vermin.

He stared hard at the spot of green and then at the trusses of dark trees above it and then back to the low-slung brush that wrapped the trunks in snarled olive lace. Hoped staring harder could make him see through things that couldn't be seen through. Come on, come on, damn you come on.

Waiting to take the shot, waiting for something to emerge. He'd never before been down to his last shot, his last match, and he wanted to curse himself for not carrying more shells but it would have made no sense. Coyotes only required one to the chest, with his aim.

Perhaps he shouldn't have fired at nothing. Was that block of deep foliage nothing? He could almost see it breathe, pulse, as if it had formed the barrel to throw the bullets, as if leaves could cock back and shoot through a cylinder of vine.

The arm was still bleeding but more slowly now. He'd

forgotten about it and was surprised to see the red sleeve. He gave it a cursory grasp and stood.

"Alright goddamn you show yourself!"

Another shot sputtered out like an objection but there was a sense of halting behind it. The shots had been coming at a rhythm and this one was merely a beat in time. A heifer grunted, shifted her weight, then kept walking after the buck-shot grazed her quarters.

Then silence.

"You'd be wise to give it up now!"

He shouted harder and the voice came out deeper than he'd expected, a boom that rang out against the bars of the tree trunks and reverberated against the bull's side to throw itself back up against his ears. Adrenaline was a hell of a drug.

The shots had ceased. There had been nothing more since the spit of buckshot on the heifer but still it was in the air that they had ceased. He kept the butt of the shotgun lodged against his shoulder and stepped around the bull's head. The left arm burned but he raised it to level the barrel ahead of him.

The woods were thirty yards away and he strode toward them slowly, as if he had more cover than the knee-high lumps of cattle that had fallen like flies. All that property, and they were too still for the loss of livestock to crash upon his thoughts now.

The mud weighed heavily on his legs as he measured each step with listening, watching. A slow crack of wind came from across the open field behind him, smelled like morning. The cliff-tops had not yet seen their sun.

The treeline lay ahead, stretch of dark for a few hundred acres and shearing mountains beyond them. A moldering pocket of damp green in a basin bordered by rock and snags of salt cedar nudged between the open hands of a hungering desert.

The shotgun grew heavy and he placed most of the weight of it on his right arm. His hands were lurid with blood and black mud.

He cringed at the first crunch of his boot in the forest's leaves. He was in; the air above him went splotched in shadow as the coming sunlight was scattered by branches. A toad crossed over his boot to the right and the movement made him drop his eyes.

There was a scrambling some yards before him and he froze and looked up.

"Show yourself! Now!"

Nothing. Just the meanderings of birds among the brush.

You've walked yourself into an ambush, that's what you've done. You're down to a single shot and that will only get one of them if that and then you're done for.

No, you know these woods better than any other could. Know where every tree lies so you can throw yourself backward without looking and get cover if you need it.

But still, too many of them and you've got nothing and goddammit how has a single shot ever felt this futile.

He stopped at an oak that had a chunk taken out of the side. Height of his kneecap. So they were much farther back or they had shitty aim or both.

Sun shifted and a ray ran across his shoulder and into the ground. But no more visibility came with it; he'd given them the perfect cover, here on his own land, and had delved into the wooded dark without thought.

The boots crunched in the groundcover and he tried sliding them to stifle the noise but it only slurred the cracking sounds and at last he took them off. Stalked across the forest floor in wool socks like an artificial wolf.

He kept his breath shallow and his arms locked. A line of sweat ran down his temple, tunneling through the dirt that had collected there from explosions of cattle and explosions of earth.

And then he saw it.

Not ten feet away, folded under shadow the way a fawn hides itself in the undergrowth and dark air and seems to cease even breathing until one is nearly on top of it.

The shooter looked up and he re-hefted the gun against his shoulder to tilt the sightline down to the stock-still head.

It sat cross-legged against a maple tree, a piece of black hair caught in a seam of bark like a vein of dirt in the calluses of a ranchman's hands.

A creature with mud plastered to its face, dried and cracked around the eyes and in chunks of dirt upon the small forehead and cheeks, excepting a broken black slash of a mouth bordered in stain from the steer. A creature the size of a child in the posture of a monk. Its face was rendered browless by the caked mud, and the wild crop of hair was ridden with leaves and twigs and other flotsam of the woods in that river-rapid of matted black. Fevered eyes of yellowed tan rode below lids that were leveled, flat as earth, as if the gunfight had not stirred their expression. He lifted a shoeless foot as if to take cover behind the nearest tree but instead against his own will pushed it forward to make his stand. It held a TEC-9 in the left hand and a worn shotgun in the right.

"Drop them!"

The thing lifted its hands and let each weapon fall to the side, and they made the moist sound of a few snapping twigs as they went down into the brush. He nearly choked with relief that it had not acted on his being outgunned.

It wore a dirty black T-shirt with holes across the shoulder and along the edges, a pattern of wear he'd never seen before but was clearly from having carried a pack long enough and far enough to chew through cotton. Through the mud it had child's legs, in that muscleless slenderness like the belly of a gar, these in jeans rolled up to the knee, and a mismatched pair of hiking boots—one construction-tan and with a sock, the other black and clearly much too large.

He checked his six to look for others before stepping forward but there were none.

"Who are you!" He shouted as loudly as he had in the field.

The eyes widened and then narrowed, and he could have sworn he saw the pupil grow thinner as would a cat's. Eyes he was sure could see in the dark.

"I knew you weren't gonna kill me." The face unfolded with its speaking, through the opening faultlines in the surface of the mud, and revealed itself for a moment before hardening again. It was a young girl.

"Who are you!" He panted outright now.

"Does it matter so much?" Coarse accent, but measured, that slunk over its English, a snake sliding over the angles of trailer-porch steps.

The filthy unlined hands rose and gripped her shirt collar as she peered at him more closely and he shrank from them, knew they were something of a place that was not like this one.

"Who are you."

Softer now.

She looked at her discarded firearms, first the shotgun and then the TEC-9. And then at him, until he saw his own dirty face and torn jacket reflected in the glassiness of the retinas.

"If I told you, you wouldn't know what to do with it anyway."

Eighty yards out, a starling traced the progression of a beetle across a cow's gunblack dead eye, the set of six steps trackless over the surface of the sphere that had gone matte and become a dark and unbounded world of its own. The sun was up.

He hauled the child furiously through the woods by the elbow and it followed limply. The shotgun was balanced in his left hand with his elbow locked and the barrel against his shoulder.

Halfway out he stopped and toed back into his boots without letting go of the girl or of the firearm and the soles sloughed in the leaves beside the girl's mismatched pair, the set of four feet shuffling through dead-leaf detritus like four drunken invalids. Her guns still lay at the bottom of the tree.

By the time they emerged into the field the cattle had begun to bellow, as if death was intangible until the puffs of flies began to swell.

The girl stumbled with her head down and the dirty strands of hair fallen over her face, like the heavy veins of a dark disease.

The day was hot and the blood from his arm had turned to brown on the jacket.

Lucy's running figure became visible in the wheat a half-mile out from the house.

"Wyatt!" Her voice and its echoes were gone by the time she reached them.

Lucy his twin, lighter than he. Blonde hair past her shoulders and a sharp brow that kept the sun from the skin above her cheeks and left it soft and paperwhite around the impassible blue eyes. Sister with unmarked hands that had butchered a hundred chickens and done far worse but should not have to do this. He stepped forward to stop her but she took the thing's other arm anyway.

The two of them pulled the girl up to the house together, she playing ragdoll now and falling in their arms as if her violence was spent. Lucy's grip slipped once and Smith saw the flash of mud on her palm before she replaced her hand on the girl's forearm.

In half an hour they reached it, the old pine-shingled box with two floors and too many windows and half of them shedding their shutters and a porch to span the base of it all. Peeling white paint and a screen door that frayed wire like a corset used too hard. And the dead cattle behind them heating under the sun and under the hungered rotations of flies.

In the kitchen he dropped the girl's arm and leveled the gun at her again. The room was of a style not redone for sixty years, and the walls so spotted with fly waste that an unfamiliar eye would assume it was the pattern of the wallpaper. His sister stood there, thin under one of the thrift store dresses, this one blue. She wore them every day and nipped them in at the waist with a line of safety pins like a metallic scar.

"Lucy, get the rope from the pantry."

She came back and cut a length of it.

"Hold your hands out."

The girl's hands were black but the index fingers were wiped clean from trigger-pulls. She watched him as Lucy bound her wrists, with eyes far too light for her and more animal than human, as if she had pried them with a knife from some wild thing's skull and replaced her own.

Lucy cut another length.

"Bring it with you."

He nudged the girl's shoulder with the mouth of the gun to turn her and then pushed it against her spine and marched her upstairs.

Lucy looked to him when they got to the hall.

"Your room, the bolt still works," he said.

It was bare, for living at least, with a bed of dust-stained sheets in the center and an unsanded desk and empty vase on its top. It was a room that invited decease, heavy with the sense of gone adolescence, though one could not imagine anyone young having run to it, carrying denim-blue bird feathers and silken cicada cases and walnut shells shaped like raccoons' masks, things that shouted of being alive.

A lone window with a crack in one of the panes was the room's single expression of the weight that bridled the air within it. A room for dust to heat and then dance up in the sunspots on the floor like sporal ghosts only to fall back down again. That dust lay undisturbed in most places, staked out corners and territory along the walls around the tracts laid bare from pacing in an outline around the bed.

Lucy waited at the door for a moment with a stricken expression, wary of something revealed in the others' seeing it. Then either realizing the room was no more hers than the grounds outside, or as much hers as the grounds outside, the look slid off her face and she came in.

Smith pulled the chair out from the desk with his foot and pushed the girl into it and Lucy bound the girl's torso to the back and he set the gun on the bed and checked that the rope was well tied.

"Who are you?"

No answer.

"Wyatt, your arm!"

"It can wait—who are you?"

He gripped the child's shoulders and shook her.

No answer. The T-shirt seemed to have become its own entity rather than something she wore, oversized and clinging more to the back of the chair than to her, like a splotch of tar melting over the wood.

"What's your name?" He was shouting again.

"It's not gonna matter to you any more than it's mattered to me so far."

Again the accent like thick rope lugged over a dock edge and he felt Lucy wince at it without seeing her do so.

"Where did you come from?"

No answer. Knew then that he wasn't going to get one.

"For god's sake Wyatt the blood's runnin down your arm."

A chunk of dried mud fell from the girl's cheek and shattered on the floor.

"Where."

Regardless where was not here.

"No name worth tellin us?"

"Lucy, don't talk to her."

He took a breath and clutched his arm and spoke again.

"Where are your parents?"

The girl turned her hellion's face and looked directly into his working eye before she answered. "Where are yours?"

At that he turned and snatched the gun from the bed-spread where it left a white stamp in the drifts of dust. Went and checked the ropes at her back once more then went out and Lucy had already run out and he bolted the door behind them.

When he turned to Lucy in the hall she was crying.

"What is that? What happened?" She asked it as she tried to wipe her eyes but her hands were shaking and she merely pushed streaks of blonde across her face.

"I don't know." He shook his head. "Goddamn I don't know. Gotta be on the run from somethin. She killed a steer to eat and took a shot at me when I put the gun on her."

"I heard the shots. . ."

"Lucy, she shot out the bull and three others."

She held in her breath, waiting for him to say more, then passed her gaze from his glass eye to his working one as she realized.

"The ranch—oh god—"

"Stop crying." He could feel his consciousness starting to go.

She looked up at him in watered blue.

"Just stop cryin til we stop me bleedin."

She ran for the kitchen and called out for him to wait but he staggered slowly down the steps after. His brow was washed in sweat and he wanted to kill the thing upstairs.

<hr/>

In the kitchen he took the jacket off and handed the bloodied and muddied canvas to her while he unbuttoned his flannel. It stuck on his arm and he nudged a finger in between the layers of fabric and plasmatic muck until he winced and it broke free.

"How bad is it?"

"Surface wound. Nothin lodged."

She held his discarded jacket over one shoulder now and the bloodstained sleeve fell over her left arm to replicate his.

It still pumped slowly, and the arm was wet and red down to his wrist. He took it under the sink and let the water run, twisting his bicep beneath it. Lucy passed him a towel and a glass of whiskey and he dipped the towel then prodded it into where the missing flesh had been.

He sat down in a kitchen chair and she brought a sewing needle and he shook his head even though she had made no offer to stitch his arm. He took the needle to close it himself, the metal already stained with dried blood. It unspooled itself in skeins and clouded inklike into the whiskey as he dipped the needle in.

He sat there with thread to close a hole but found no hole, only a void chalked with flakes of canvas frayed or curled tight in the deep cardinal mess. So much more like a hole in that it could not be closed. He used the needle to dig two pieces of cloth from the wound. Soon he stopped and let all fall into the whiskey glass, the needle sinking along with its quarry and the unhunted still in his arm, and he stood.

She was cutting a bed sheet and he took the strips from her hands and wrapped the arm and it bled to make a leech-sized spot in the linen and then stopped and he was already buttoning himself into a clean flannel.

"What are you doin?"

"Can't wait no longer."

"The cattle?"

She looked up into his face and immediately looked down again.

"Here." He took the pistol from the top of the china cabinet and thrust it into her hands so hard that her back hit the kitchen wall. "She could kill you."

"I know."

"So watch her."

"I know."

"Promise me you'll shoot if you have to."

"Wyatt what is she?"

"Mexican cartel maybe. The kid had a TEC-9."

She stood there holding the pistol to her chest, her skin blanching to milkglass in the shadows of the house.

"What if they're after her?"

"She didn't have nothin of value with her, just a bag full of rocks. I checked. They wouldn't care."

"What do we do?"

"I don't know." He turned to go out but she stepped to block his way.

"Did it happen near the old place?"

"No, not the old place."

She nodded and bit her lip. He reached out a finger as if to touch her forehead but instead touched the gun, then turned and went out the door.

⸻◈⸻

The meat was as good as lost the moment he left the field with the girl but he could still save the hides if he worked quickly.

In the barn he adjusted the bandaged arm and took down the ax from the inside wall and a jug of gasoline from beside the tractor. Money there too, but no other way of doing it. The barn swallows waded in and out of the sunlight above the open door like feathered bats to watch what felt so criminal. He looked up to their fevered gathering along the ceiling beams and they eyed him from black-beaded faces.

"It wasn't me!"

No answer nor forgiveness, only a scuffling among themselves, and he trudged on.

It was half a mile more to where the cattle were. He reached the fence and untied the barbed wire gate and cried a loud "Haw!" so that they would know a fresh pasture had been opened. Heard a low and then the heavy shifting as they rose from folded limbs onto hooves and mutilated the earth into small mountains in the mud behind their steps. He left the gate open and went through.

After a few moments he came to where they were, and they hefted by without looking at him, and he stood still for a moment. Let them pass, counted out thirty-eight subtracting the fallen four and marked the heifer that had been buckshot-skimmed but saw that the skin had not been broken and then shut the gate behind himself and went on.

Finally he came upon the downed cows, the reluctant butcher with Abraham's knife. Ax such a crude tool but there was nothing else to do this job with. Things borne from hell must've come better equipped.

The four lay in twisted disarray, the second steer still propped upon folded legs as if it were still alive, and he realized now it might not have died straightaway. The air smelled gray with the aftertaste of blood and the gunpowder had thinned back into the dust. No smell of rot but the flies dove and a few sparrows picked along the red shores lining the bullet wounds. Had to remove the heads and legs before he started to skin.

He took the head off the bull first. Seemed fitting. Some semblance of honor in the funeral pyre. In his first swing his left hand slipped on the grip and the blade landed on the ground beside him and he cursed but the next swing met its mark.

He turned his face when it hit though he'd gutted elk before and this should have been no different. Let its head and legs lie and pulled his knife from his belt and peeled back the skin starting at the shoulders and then cut on.

The one killed in the night had bled too long for the leather to be salvageable. Pounds from the flank were gone and he shrank from thinking of how the girl had managed to eat that much of a leg on her own. Fleeting suspicion of her having had help but knew she had somehow as god or as monster done it herself. He chopped it into pieces without craftsman-ship or design.

It was grisly work, skinning then taking off pieces of a hundred pounds or so and dragging them to where the bull had fallen, and twice he thought his arm had started bleeding again. Thirty or so parts and three hours later he had amassed a pile. Three complete hides splayed wet in the grass and uncomfortably human in their having four limbs.

He lowered the ax and straightened to wipe the sweat from his brow as he had a dozen times and his hand came away red. It was good that Lucy was not watching.

He took a breath and stared at the mound of meat the height of his chest. And sister I suppose this is the end of it all being ours and only ours.

The smell in the field was digestive now of half-fermented cud and of raw things that had never seen daylight nor air before. He threw the ax into the final gut and did not flinch when it splashed. That part was done. Laid the ax aside.

He emptied the gasoline over the banks of cattle spines and dropped in a match.

Nothing to draw the coyotes now and put those still alive at risk.

He staggered back from the blaze and watched one of the eyes go up in yellow and then run in a gluish paste over a velveteen cheek. Why hadn't they run.

Smith crossed his legs and sat down in front of the bonfire. Took a handful of grass and tossed it futilely in that direction for good measure.

He'd killed a thousand times on this ground before. Chickens and cattle and deer and squirrels and an Appaloosa gelding that snapped its leg seven summers ago. This ground had seen innards before and maggots had painted it like patches of snow more than once. But the waste, was it different? Just called attention to it, weren't nothin more than that. But when you counted it all out . . .

A lone spider crawled over the tops of the blades of grass

and chose the unfortunate direction of the base of the fire. Felt
the heat and scuttled under the drying nose of the heifer in another poor decision, another set of carbon parts to crinkle and
collapse under the heat. Like the snakes that propelled themselves through the wheat only to fall under tractor blades, and
the insects that chopped across stems like calcium machines,
and the worms that hooked and churned and overturned again
and again in bovine guts, over and over and dead dead dead.
A land that was built to consume them and to consume their
descendants over and over once again. To consume him, and
he pulled his hand away from the wild oat strands he held as if
they were hot and then sank his hands back in.

He killed on this land like a duty, and perhaps it was the
land itself that did the killing, growing all of them only to
eat, swallowing without chewing, and eating their house
in bites of sinking peat and snatches of mold. And toward
what—toward what underground underworld river was he
supposed to go, if he were in fact the determinant of his own
fate and had a boat with which to navigate his own direction
upon it, with all of it sinking. But what could be harsher than
the dried-out sky of Utah that whitened skulls and beat sand
up through pastures and offered nothing to fight the chaotic
downtaking of what floated on the irrigated mud above the
southern deserts as they swallowed by the century. He kicked
a skim of dirt toward the flames. Certain there were somethin
more to it.

In the face of the bonfire he stood and shouldered the smaller
two of the hides, folded in half and hung across him like a
giant's lapels. Walked back to the house and held them with a

hand on top of each as he hiked through the wheat and then left them on the porch railing.

When he returned to the fire it had lessened, a few pieces of muscle still rising ridge-backed like fans as they unwound from the bones and the occasional spit of flame as the bits of fat caught alight. He waited for it to go out and did not look at the remains, sat and rested until the light died behind him, then turned to the hide of the bull.

It was too large and too heavy to fold over a shoulder and so he took a foreleg in each hand and then stumbled forward. The thing fell upon his back like a cape, and he dragged it over the ground, blood in a smear below his false eye where he'd pushed away a fly and his shirt and jeans going dark with the viscera. Hunting knife between his fingers and for his mantle a thing going marbled blue with arterial blood nicked and running down the back of the white alien underside of the skin as he staggered through the fields like some filthy prince of corporeal nightmares.

At the house Lucy was waiting behind the shell of a door and went to grab a hide but he put an arm out to stop her and she stumbled back. He did not want to see her with blood on her hands, not now.

She brought a sack of salt from the pantry and struggled with it behind him on the stairs and followed him to their parents' room. It was devoid of furniture; they'd had to sell it off. A graveyard, pillaged of the marriage bed that had brought them forth, their own marauders. But here the floor was bare and there was space to stretch the hides flat. He felt the air of the room change when he entered and it could have been a smell from years before or the smell of meat when he laid out the skins.

She dragged the salt bag and left it there in the middle of the floor then retreated to a corner of the room. Three impish outlines the size of beds framing it, and Smith watched the flickering light jostle the reflection in her eyes so that within them it looked as if the hides still stumbled, alive. He limped back into the hall even though it was only the arm that was wounded. Lucy stayed.

The girl in the room beside had made no sound since they had left her, and Smith took up the shotgun again and slowly opened the door to look.

She was where they had left her, sitting with her head bent so that her hair obscured her eyes, and it took away that sense in the gut that there was anything else alive in the room with him. He knew she was watching him from below the flats of entangled hair with a gaze like a scavenging bird's. The hair was parted by the nose and her mouth was taut, concentrated, lips drawn into twin chapped railroad ties to span the tract of her face and he half-expected their repetition to continue down her chin.

He did not approach her and instead fastened the hand of his shot arm around the doorframe. She stayed motionless, but a strand of her hair lifted with each nasal exhale until the breathing increased and it lodged under a chip of dirt on her cheek and stayed there.

The cattle dead and the ranch soon to be gone, because in a land where a hailstorm or a snowmelt flood or a bout of blackleg could take out a year's crop, somewhere in those years you'd have to mortgage the ranch, and then someday you would reach a point where you could not lose a single steer if you were to keep the place. They'd reached that point a year ago.

It should have been wild storms that licked them after all these years, torrents of black rain and hurricanes of wind and ice shaped in spikes that sloughed from the sky like armored scales of a creature you'd never see. There was altogether too much feeling in it for the only mark of the end to be a muddy kid tied to an antique chair and cattle that did not know to run from gunfire.

He wanted to say or shout something at the girl but could think of nothing and she did not move and so he shut and locked the door again and went out to feed the remaining cattle and the half-broken mustangs and hogs and cluster of chickens in the encroaching dark.

Smith took the gas can and ax from the expired fire and gathered the guns from the woods and the plastic bag of effects that the girl had left and went to the barn. As he worked, each of the animals watched his silhouette, bloodied to the waist as if he'd waded in it, and they skittered from his lamplight.

Behind him in the house upstairs, Lucy was flitting back and forth above bared skins with a skirtful of salt, tossing crystals like a flower girl sprinkling petals for a wedding march or for a grave, dancing in circles with bare heels as the room went from the spoiled pink of sunset to dark blue. And whose grave it was whether it were the cattle's or their parents' or the grave for the death of their safety in a fugitive communion here away from the world was uncertain, but here in the dark and iron smell he was sure she was again the child she once had been.

CHAPTER TWO

The Black Steercalf

Night fully fell and he came in exhausted and still thinking of the meat that was burnt up now and he went upstairs. The hides were crystalline with salt and the light shivered across them through the open door and Lucy was gone, had likely disappeared to an arbitrary dark corner as she did most nights since the father died.

She would sit in a chair or on the floor and watch night slide by, doing nothing or with her sewing in hand, sightless fingers stabbing at patches and tears with needle bent and when the sprinklings of red had stopped showing up on his socks he had wondered if she had learned to darn blind or if her fingers had merely run out of red to bleed.

Silence beyond the locked door still, but a more true silence than before, as if the animal finally slept. He left the shotgun in front of the door. It would lie there, a watchdog for the man who is without one, set of bolts and wood that he was sure had a mind of its own and would awaken like a hound with buckshot teeth when necessary. He turned and descended the stairs.

The kitchen was lightless now but there was a single lit bulb hand-wired to a beam on the porch. Its light fell through the unshuttered window and onto the table in a dust-tinted gold, and the moths that batted around it outside were reprinted in little black shadows upon the oak like ghosts suspended in the plane of a different underworld than this. A horned owl lowed in the woods beyond in a bass of something too large to reside in trees.

He walked through to the sitting room. There was a low ceiling scarred across with beams in warped faultlines and a frayed rag-woven rug the only thing to keep his boots from the floor. He slid them off even though he always felt weaker unshod.

He ran his hand along the sideboard and wondered at what point splinters wore smooth. It was quiet now and there was no owl. Was no longer sure there ever had been. The air empty with chill and tangibly without voice.

Photographs on the sideboard. The father at the back of the portrait of three, with two pallid children, one of dark eyes and one of light. He pushed the frame down to lie flat. Behind it a cameo of the father that had come before and one of the father before that, who had come from the East and into the desert, exploring too late for adventure but too early for towns or civilization, so that life for his descendants was a series of unremarkable struggles against nature with neither triumph nor end.

What to do when the father was gone and they were too young, too young but had been born old and youth had been nothing but a season in which calves were new and then butchered by the next fall. He withdrew his hand and looked to the answerless dark of the room, felt the force locked in the room above it lend the darkness a compressive weight.

But there were no more photographs to show that only two remained, after the gun went off in the woods and Lucy had killed the father.

———

He was eighteen and still a boy and was halter-breaking a steer on the day the father died.

It was a black steercalf, born the spring before and the thickest of the herd. In the heat of the sun its hide was sleek with sweat that ran like oil and the light reflected off the sheen on Wyatt's arms and neck and face in blinding white. Six hundred pounds, and he'd faced it down in the steel-bar corral and manned the halter over its head.

He'd worked it in circles, tight in against its right side so that he could dig in his heels if it made to run. They'd been going for an hour already and the blue rope frayed against the calluses of his palms as if to braid into them like veins. When the shot echoed from the woods the steer had bucked, hind legs first and then the stabbing toes of the front like a lever and boy-Smith had been thrown against the wall of the corral.

They'd gone hunting. Before first light. They would be three miles out now at least and Wyatt dusted himself off and circled the steer in the corral, half-bent at the waist, as his father and his twin would be circling the shot elk if it were not yet dead. The rope hung from the steer's face and its end followed in the dust, raising taupe clouds that stuck to the sweat of its legs like the powder on moth's wings. It went on like that, drudging a groove into the circumference of the corral, every now and then tossing its head to loosen the trailing rope from about its feet, Wyatt a few steps behind and unable to close in any faster else the steer would run. Eyes down and the ground gone shattered gold with the glare.

The sweat was streaming into his eyes and he pulled it from the crease of his upper lip and had paused to crouch in the dirt and rest one or two or three times and he didn't know for how long and each time the steer waited, a few steps ahead of him and just out of reach, and he'd trudge after it again, and then at last he got a boot toe on the end of the rope. The steer had felt the line on its mouth go taut and was just beginning to test it when Wyatt saw her at the edge of the woods and she was not hauling an elk but a man. He stepped off of the steer rope and opened the corral gate and the steer stormed past him into the field as he walked silently toward the barbed wire fence that would let him out to the woods.

When she looked up, it was the first time her face ever wore real fear.

It wasn't your fault. And it wasn't your fault and the steer had gone out to pasture and bucked against the dying light and he never got a halter on it again from that day on—wasn't your fault.

The sweat had dried on him then and turned to brown and his forearms were like slicked with clay and he made his way toward the sister in a sundress with a man at her feet. Wasn't your fault.

And Lucy had broken that day.

The blue rope carried off into the twilight.

They'd buried him on the ranch, a hundred feet from the forest in which it'd happened. And never reported it, because why report it when she never meant to do it. When he could never let her be a patricide. When it was an accident. But the man had not been an elk.

The darkness in the room shifted.

"Wyatt."

She was in the armchair in the eastern corner. He turned toward the voice.

"I aint know what to do."

He walked over to her and the proximity pulled her features out of the darkness. Her lower lip protruded beyond the upper, and the shadows turned their natural pink to the sepia of something in the photographs. Her feet were bare, half out of the pair of steeltoe boots squared in front of her, toes toying with the boot tongues as if deliberating whether to run. The leather upholstery behind her shoulders was tacked tight with metal that echoed the safety pins at the waist of her dress, and her hands lay upturned over the arms of the chair like two fallen horses.

He reached out a hand to one of hers but did not touch it. She rose and followed him to the kitchen table, and he lit a kerosene lamp between them as they sat around it in childlike conference.

Twin faced twin, a single face mirrored overtop of the brown-tinted light. Same cheekbones, same brow and mouth, and the reflections deviated slightly with the flame. The lamp was soon encircled by gnats that expired in winged sparks after a moment in the heat. Then his eye adjusted to the light, and some of the deviances remained.

Just stared at one another for a moment. Had been truly twins until twelve years ago, when in boyhood he still had that angled stubble-less jaw. She'd worn her hair short like his then, hadn't given it up until she was eighteen.

In the lamplight she was still that figure of eleven, with wing-thin shoulders and untamed eyebrows that would furrow

and nearly meet when she butchered livestock. His face was ir-
revocably its age of twenty-three, and he could feel it as age,
the wear and losses of the past half-decade across his temples
in a sunburned and weathered mark of misfortune or decay.
But she, she was unaffected, and her face showed nothing of
losses or storms.

She spoke first.

"We caint call the police, can we."

Smith shook his head. Not with a father buried in your
land.

"I weren't so scared by her til I realized she really is just a
kid," she said. Whispered in a place that was too remote for
anyone to hear had it been a shout.

"I know."

"So young, barely into her teens young."

"I know."

"And the cattle." Her voice ran cold.

"You know we aint had enough stock to take that loss."

She bit her bloodied sewing thumb. They both knew what
it meant.

"How much more we need?"

"To keep them from seizing the ranch?"

She nodded.

"Forty-six hundred dollars. What we woulda got from the
ones that died, minus the hides."

"You mean that she done killed."

"Yeah. That she done killed. We needed every one we had."

The skin between her eyes and cheeks buckled.

"God . . ."

" . . .Damn it all to hell."

"Yeah."

She sat back and let the smile leave her face and took a

breath. He hunched forward in his chair as if it were not already all silence and he would not be able to hear her. With his
lowering of stature their eyes aligned and she watched both
of his as if one were not dead. An errant strand of blonde
had fallen against her cheek like a snapped piece of straw. She
touched it for a moment then let it lie, and spoke again.

"What do we do?"

He picked at a smudge of manure caught under a thumb-
nail and considered as if he had not been considering it these
past ten hours. Her finger had begun to bleed again and she
laid it between her lips, the blood dappling the anemic pale of
them as she waited for him.

"I've got nothin. I don't know. All I know for now's that we
caint just let her go."

"Until we figure somethin out?"

"Until we figure somethin out."

"We aint gonna be able to make it up. We're gonna lose
the ranch."

"Don't, Lucy."

The thumb dragged to her cheek now as her hand envel-
oped her face.

"Wyatt, we can't leave it now."

"Lemme take a day to think. There's gotta be somethin.
She aint got nowhere to go. No food, no money. She can't run."

Lucy put her hands on the table and made as if to push it
away from her.

"We shouldn't have done it this way. We shoulda called it
in, even if we had to leave, even if I got in trouble—"

He looked at her.

"But you didn't mean to do it," he said. "And this is our
family's land. We do not leave. We did not leave then, and we
will not leave now."

She looked down and the forget-me-nots shadowed to nightshade on her bodice. He put a hand over his shot arm and stood but went no closer to her.

"We'll figure it out, I promise."

Lucy started laughing. She fell back in the chair and her face flickered as she rocked into and out of the plane of the lamplight and the impressions of the insects outside the window scattered from the table below her shadow. She did not stop and grew hysterical and when she still did not stop he grabbed the arms of her chair.

"What?"

She shook her head.

A moth caught itself in the lighter fluid of the kerosene lamp and combusted. Its remains stuck to the ceramic base like floral tar. She looked up at him as if looking at the darker half of herself.

"You aint talked that much in a damn long time."

⸻

He let her laughter echo along the blackening walls, a weak raised ghost of the sounds they had made in that house as children. There was no moonlight and he went down the hall and up the stairs in the dark. Went into his room and left the door unlocked, as she'd have to sleep there too tonight. The reinstating of those nights of their childhood, when she'd crept into his bed for comfort or for courage or the semblance of it in seeing your own face on the pillow next to yours. The hall lamp would be out and the sheet pulled over their heads and they'd watch spindles of light pierce a battery lantern and touch their fingers to it when too frightened to grasp one another's hands. They'd lain awake when the cold ran under the windowsill and their sameness was the only thing to keep them warm. Twins like sharing the same body and same metabolism, organs, to heat them both and perhaps even redeem them both merely by existing for the other.

But after the father died they had grown too old for that, or she had had to gather the courage up and was unafraid now, and he would send his fears winging as thoughts through the wall that separated their rooms. Believing that, in some capacity, somehow, she was sending something back, be it comfort or secret fears of her own.

He fell asleep to the surety that what was locked behind her bedroom door was indeed locked there.

Lucy came in an hour later and he woke to the disturbance of the bed but did not move. She was clad in another thrift store dress that was a nightgown merely because it was white, and for whatever unspeaking reason it was she never wore white in daytime. She lay down and rested her head on only the edge of the pillow, as if she did not belong there and had not grown up there. Her silhouette falling into goose-down like a cartilage ghost, his blood-copy with sun-bleached eyes.

She was far from him but her warmth streaked across the sheets toward him like something like frost but like something dark and from out of the earth. Would only come into his room once she believed him to be asleep.

"You never would let it be my fault, would you Wyatt?"

He knew he could not answer, let her see he'd heard. She talked to him most nights, and it was always "tell me I didn't do it Wyatt," or "we're still the same aren't we still?" or "if you're still me then I'm still you." She'd sit balanced on the edge of the bed, face steadied at the blank wall ahead. There were no more battery lanterns, it was not a conversation, and she would never stay. Save tonight, when she had nowhere else to sleep.

He held his breath and waited for her to say something more and at last turned his head to look at her. But her eyes were closed now and he did not know when she had closed them, and so he turned his own eyes up and fell into ragged sleep, as the creature in the room next door heaved nightmarish breaths into the floorboards and shadows of Lucy pinned themselves to the ceiling.

Hours before dawn he awoke and rolled out from the bed and dressed in another flannel and jeans, the house and the room still fully dark and his hands on the walls and on the closet door.

In the hall he turned on the light and with his finger still on the switch he looked back at Lucy through the doorway to his bedroom. A collarbone bent out from the neck of her dress and curved upward with her breathing, a structure under milk-translucent skin that seemed too insistent, too strong to be a part of her but rather something she had grown onto, her skin and her capillaries and their blood and her hair like lichens wrapping stone. Between inhale and exhale there was no sense of life about her. He turned away, then closed the door and went to sit in front of the locked door where the shotgun already lay.

He sat there for a while with his head in his hands, breath creeping through the quiet, then leaned back. There was a voice from behind him as soon as he set his head against the door.

"You're alone here, aren't you?" It was muffled through the wood between them but the intonation was detached, moving, as if it rode the darkness feathering from the crack beneath the door. The hall empty and the lamp excising all shadows, and the voice could have come from below, spoke for the land instead.

"I don't think I've been in a place like this before. This is a strange place," said the girl.

"Don't talk." She had to have been calling out for him to hear her through the door but he spoke as if she were whispering behind his head.

"It's a different kind of alone, I think. The two of you."

"I said don't talk, dammit."

"Is it?"

"Is it what."

"A different kind."

He grimaced at having answered.

"A different kind, a battle with the land every year, and no eyes for your war," she said.

He said nothing and could not hear her breathing, knew she was holding it to listen for his reaction. He did not move, and she spoke a minute later.

"I want my bag of rocks back."

The shotgun had warmed to the temperature of his skin and he felt only its weight on his lap now. Through the door behind him, the child's voice began to run without stop, a hum from within the throat or from the air within the walls.

"The rocks stay so long in one place, take so much heat and rain and time and rising and falling with the ground, and they endure and they're untouched, only for you to come and pick them up and put them in your pocket. This place, just you two and . . ."

And the land, and the father, and the cattle bones. Smith slammed his fist against the wood above his head and the voice stopped. The girl muttered and ground her teeth now and then, then at last went quiet enough for the previous words to pass out of the air.

When he fell back to sleep with his head against the door the light in the hallway was still on—a solitary flare sent up from that square-mile-sized cheek of Box Elder, gold and alone in the dark, to confront the impudent bonfire of Utah stars.

———◦◦◦———

The sunlight broke first from the narrow windows to the east and melted across the floor to claw at the butt of his gun and he did not move until the heat had conducted up the barrel to burn his hand.

Lucy was up and gone from the bed; as he passed the open door he did not have to look.

He laid the shotgun against the bathroom doorframe and went to throw water onto his face from the basin with both hands but had forgotten the stiffness in his left arm and caught it halfway to his chest and the oat-colored water ran down his sleeve. He lowered it and then with the other hand wedged a finger under the rim of his right lid and let the glass eye drop from the socket.

It landed with the sound of something hitting rock as it caught a pocket of air between the oblong curve of the glass and the surface of the water and then overturned and sank and overturned again. Landed on the sink bottom to look up at him in periwinkle blue, from a deep sea populated by invertebrates consisting only of misshapen eyes.

He looked up at the flaking mirror on which the image of his scarred-open face wavered thinly, the seam of muscle where the eye had been like a misplaced thread. Or like a plow line raked in the clay of the field, deep enough to swallow the cattle, and his hands went to the sides of the sink at the flood of loss from the day before.

He pulled the plug and stayed a finger in the drain to keep the eye from going down and waited as the water washed over it and the glass started to dry in the air. He heard Lucy on the stairs. She'd have a cup of water for the kid, the girl, no name for it that didn't sound strange mouthed in the back of the head, but she'd wait for him to go in.

He was fitting the eye back into place when he heard the latch and he grabbed the gun by its mouth but wasn't fast enough and he heard Lucy say "shit!" and the china implode against the floor as the door was kicked open from inside. Then he was in the hall and Lucy turned toward his sound and the dark arm came across her face as the girl barreled past her from the room. He lunged to knock her away from Lucy with his shoulder but the girl rebounded to the right and flung herself down the stairs. She tumbled down not stepping and not even using feet any more than hands or elbows or hips, a hellborne flight in which she seemed to morph to fit the handholds as she fell.

He started after her but was slow and four steps down he turned and ran back up. Looked at Lucy on the floor, feet sprawled holding her hand over her cheek, but she gestured him off so he ran on into the empty room.

Among their footsteps in the dust and silt of the day before were the wormtrails of the chair's feet, gone black in smears where the wood had tunneled far enough through the dirt to scuff. The chair was by the window, too narrow a space to climb out but enough glass to smash the finial of the chair through and cut the ropes on the jagged edges.

Smith kicked the chair aside and held the shotgun readied to the window and watched the ground in front of the house. Before he had exhaled the girl was out from the floor below and running across the yard and he punched the gun along the splintered glass in the window and she sidewinded for a few strides at the noise but did not stop and he lowered his eye to the gunsights and waited to see if she—she was going for the truck, he would have to do it, and he dropped to one knee and aimed dead in front of her to scare her off it. Half the buckshot shattered the sideview mirror and the other half rang out against the metal bracket and the girl flung herself underneath the truck.

"Son of a bitch!" She was too close to the tires now, no good.

He bent the gun up and loaded in a second shot with the barrel balanced against the broken shards of the window, the rope strands still frayed on their edges like clusters of spiders frozen in place.

He slid the barrel back through to a hollowed ribcage rattle of broken glass. He stared hard at the distance, trying to judge it from the mouth of the gun. Knew exactly how wide the cloud of shot would spread in the time it took to get there. Lucy appeared at his shoulder. The sister in a brown dress lowered the hand from her cheek expecting to see blood but instead the wet was the involuntary tears from a blow to the face and she stared ahead as the bruise flushed maple red. The brother with a wounded arm held his breath and took a shot that landed perfectly in the ground far enough from the tires but close enough to convince the one between them. And the girl-child with matted hair and glass-bloodied forearms was at a dead run to the road.

Lucy was at his heels as they ran down the stairs. She skidded on the kitchen floor in her boots and grabbed the pistol from where she'd left it by the sink.

"Keep it ready," he called over his shoulder.

"You afraid for me?"

"Course not. Cover the house and the truck."

When he reached the door he saw her turn and get her back against a wall, both hands on the gun.

"You!" Out in front of the house, and his voice echoed through the unanswering flagellum of wheat fields.

It was a quarter mile to the road, and with just two pairs of hands to tend it the front field had long gone to wild brush and seed. The screen door shuddered like an old nag behind him as he ran out into the sand flats of grass with shotgun in hand. Birds screamed in their circling above the grain and he did not realize until a thistle sheared against his ankle that he was barefoot; she'd beaten him there as well.

He tore through the undergrowth past the bramble-choked wheat and it went green for the last hundred yards with something sleeker, more slippery than the bur-ridden tangles of the field. Something sickness-colored. He put his hands on his thighs heaving from the run and stared at the roadside, that half-paved snakehide that went on empty in either direction. No vehicles coming through, and with him close behind she could not wait for one.

Too much wild grass and it had erased the path behind him as if he'd waded through water. Too many directions to go and too many thousands of acres to cover. He could not stalk and hunt her out. But if she hadn't left, if she'd merely doubled back—

He turned back toward the house and forded the field again, turning constantly to check behind him with his gun. The birds were silent this time. The strands of wheat tangled and burst in little explosions of grain behind his calves as he ran.

He wanted to fire a shot as warning but knew not where to aim and the bottoms of his feet cracked over old silage and went numb but it distracted from the sear of the arm against his shirt. Cows lowed from a distance and cicadas wore through the air in a heady tenor lull and he was coming through the crop and the locusts cried out and at last he was at the steps. Lucy met him at the door.

"You're okay?" He panted it.

"Why. What happened." She held the wet white shards of the cup in one hand and the pistol in the other.

He hefted the shotgun back to his shoulder.

"Nothin. I thought somethin might've happened in here."

She exhaled, ribs lowering dangerously toward the safety pins, but did not relax her grip on the pistol.

"You know she's gone, Wyatt."

He followed her in and slammed the door behind and she startled.

"We gotta get it back, somethin back so we don't lose this place."

"She's gone."

Smith rested the shotgun on the edge of the table and did not reply.

"There's nothin she could want here," Lucy said.

She dropped the shards into the trash and turned to him again. Her eyes were something melting.

"What are you gonna do?"

"I don't know." But he did. "I gotta go out after her."

"I know."

"It don't make no sense. But the sellin it off in crumbs, gettin the mortgage—I can't let it go so easy. I gotta do it. Something."

"I know." She said it to the hole in his arm.

He thought of the steer the girl had eaten from. Nearly half a flank missing and he'd never found the remains. A bottomless, wall-less, fetid hunger that had a face different from the one that carried it and a dragging body elsewhere that held the poundage consumed. That much gone overnight and a chunk of his arm, but no perhaps she didn't eat it all but fed some gray force in the woods that had always been there, but no it was just a girl. You have to go.

Smith went to the pantry and ripped a few cans of food from the shelves and threw them in a feed sack from under the sink. He began filling jugs of water then glanced at the countertop once more. He'd left the girl's guns and plastic bag there the previous morning. The guns were untouched but the bag was gone. He set upon them and disassembled them with the same clinical deftness with which he would a shot rabbit, then gathered the pieces in his arms and carried them into the pantry. Came back with boxes of ammunition and spread them on the table.

Lucy sat down and laid the pistol on the table before him, and not understanding that she had meant to give him both guns he shoved the shotgun toward her. The bolt dragged in the surface of the table and left a war trench in the resin and she flinched from it but stayed in her chair. He stuffed the pistol in the back of his jeans.

"You've got the ammo for it."

Lucy stood but said nothing and he ascended the stairs again, boots on and ringing in leaden collision on each step like a buck's dull and half-bored cry and he pulled another box of bullets from under his bed and the wool blanket from above it. He paused for a moment by the bed, the pistol heavy in his waistband. The palm-sized Winchester they'd gotten for self-defense though the father was never without the shotgun anyway. It'd never been used besides target practice in their fields, Lucy shooting out empty soup cans with a smile that twisted toward the eye she closed when she aimed.

He turned from the room that had encapsulated his boyhood or lack thereof and if he did not return would remain as soulless as it had always been. White room with flannel shirts hanging in the closet with their various tears stenciled in with misaligned stitching, glued by sister's finger blood. Because she never did any sewing to create, and bled only in retrospect, to repair. Would still bleed while he was gone, the land still tearing and wearing out cloth, or might stop bleeding if they were forced off the ranch, and that would be worse because that would mean forgetting. He left it behind him.

When he came back down she'd sat again, patterned dress slumped in the spindled wooden chair. Smith put on his jacket with the left-arm gash and as it warmed it felt like it bled anew.

Her eyes were wide but without emotion. Tangles of blonde framed her face, the color of wheat as if it had been made from the fields or they from it.

"You'll be okay?" he asked.

"Will you?"

"And you'll tend the cattle?"

Cattle too few in number now, animals that had not known to run from a world exploding.

He told rather than asked.

"I'll tend the cattle," she said.

She was staring out the window toward the corner of the woods, and he knew what she saw. Two hundred yards out at the base of a hill lay the sunken six-foot-long divot in the ground, a grave with only a hand-nailed cross to mark it and her rabbit's jaw necklace hung across the planks.

He looked back at her. The shotgun was still on the table.

She glanced at it with her hands behind her back as if she wanted them tied.

"Wyatt, I can't."

Hadn't touched that gun since it'd been used to kill the father. Father buried without a gun because they couldn't spare it. Thing that couldn't save him here and so couldn't be expected to save him in the next world over, if there was hunting there to be done. He saw it in her eyes and immediately took it back and laid the pistol where the patricidal gun had been.

"I shouldn't have. Sorry."

She looked down.

"I aint gonna be gone for long," he said.

He loaded the shotgun and put two shells in his pocket.

"You gonna be alright without me?"

"Wyatt—"

"Yeah—"

"You aint gone away before."

He took another step back and turned to face her fully and for the first time realized how the wounded arm had broken his posture. He wanted to say that it wouldn't be nothing, but found that he could not voice it.

She laughed and it turned to something like a shriek, and she lifted her chin as if to free the sound from her, the skin below washing ruddy tan from the sun reflecting up off her dress and the cheeks burgundy, excepting the darker stripe from the bruise.

He felt something of his skin shift and put his hand to his wounded bicep and it came away clean.

"Shoot if you need to. Promise me you will. You don't know what she'll do."

The one whose last trigger-pull had quit the father from the earth.

Lucy held a box of bullets flat in her palms like a Bible in oath and nodded again.

He looked over his shoulder once more as he walked to the front door, at the dirty hair like the wheat strands in the field, at the dress that washed to her ankles in papery mauve. Tried to forget the wide eyes even as he stared at them; they would look like this again if he came back to say that they would have to leave, and then even more so in the dark of roadsides and nameless woods where people without homes or histories go.

"Won't be long," he said.

"Aint nothin," she said.

She turned away and went back to staring through the window. He felt himself pale and the blood that had deserted his face found a home in pulsing about the wound in his arm and he looked out at the truck, the splintered side view mirror half hanging off the metal shell of burgundy and silver paint that ran like a tractor, waiting there. And he was at a run toward it.

⸺◦◦◦⸺

Mandrakes grew there now in the shadow of the hill though the man had not been hanged. He did not know how many years it would take until the roots twisted deep enough into that earth to pierce the body below or perhaps it was the guts of the body whence they had sprouted to begin with, or perhaps there were nothing there at all and perhaps this land really did swallow them all without mastication or digestion and were they to go out there with a shovel would find nothing. An empty space, or if he was to dig deeper and did find the father then maybe he could also find his eye, in that cavernous throat deep in the ground of which the desert was the eczemaed skin, that cavern filled with the myriad things they'd tossed down, chicken bones like cross-stitches strewn across discarded leather and the almost floral twistings of unrolled barbed wire and steer after steer, find it somewhere in the soiled hay or perhaps still stuck to the piece of baling-wire that had extracted it, still waiting for him and still seeing, still watching in the manure-heated dark where even here flies turned, would always turn where there was decay. This fever of hungering earth outside their door and under it and they'd fed it something that made it so that now they could not leave it but in doing so had bound themselves to be consumed by it someday as well, had maybe even given it a taste for it. But it is his family's land. They had belonged to it from the beginning.

CHAPTER THREE

The Man from Box Elder

The decade-old F-150 started with a sputter like the cracking of ribs. Shotgun in the passenger seat serving as witness to his pursuit. He went south. There was nothing much in either direction but there was Salt Lake City to the south and he knew she knew that.

Kept his speed low and watched the ditches at the side of the road. Slim chance at hitchhiking; she wouldn't be far. Wasn't reckless enough to risk a hundred miles of foodless wilderness by going back into the woods, or the pantry window of a house when not a one was without a shotgun in this country.

No, he didn't know that. Had to see, had to be sure.

At the edges of their seventeen-hundred-acre property there was a trailer home left on one of the crumbs of sold-off land, the last ones that hadn't abandoned their single acre to go south seeking cities for better work. He pulled in and a small wave of children surged around the building toward the back of the lot. Closest place she could go if it were vehicle or food she was after. Smith dismounted into the gravel, shotgun in hand.

He caught one of the children by the shoulder, one who strayed too long gathering his younger siblings' plastic toys from the dirt. The boy was white-blonde but tanned a deep red, with eyebrows that stuck out at odd angles like salt crystals and matched the flaking skin of his sunburnt ears. He was wearing only athletic shorts, with a handful of the waistband balled up and tied with baling twine and they were hemmed with the dust that had been kicked up the back of his calves and now the dust settled as he stood and gaped at Smith crouched before him.

"Got a job for you, boy. Give you a dollar."

The boy's lip ceased trembling and he nodded, nearly smiled.

"Good. You see the rock over that way by the end of the drive?"

The boy nodded.

"I need you to sit out there, and if anyone comes down the road lookin this way you run like hell inside and git me. Got it?"

The boy nodded profusely and Smith took his hand off of him as if suddenly stricken by the closeness, and the boy sprinted to his post on reddened legs capped by white heels.

Smith turned toward the trailer. Shotgun barrel nosing along above the gravel like the muzzle of a hound as he walked. He went up the nailed two-by-four steps, bent the shotgun up readied because he knew they'd have one too. Rapped twice on the white aluminum door. There was mold in its casing.

"What ya want?"

"It's just a neighbor."

"We aint got no neighbors. We aint want yer business."

"No ma'am. From over ways. From the Smiths."

A pause.

"The Smiths?"

"Yes ma'am."

Another pause. And then—

"Aight you hang on."

He stepped to the side of the door in case there was something he was not expecting and the two-by-fours groaned and then the woman appeared in the doorframe. Mid-thirties and in a dressing gown and hair racked in antithetic neatness in larval pink plastic rollers.

She looked him up and down and stared longer at the badly fitting prosthetic that he knew looked like a stone in his head in the dark of the entryway, and still she did not step to the side to allow him in. Her eyelids were bordered in day-old mascara and a scar ran from her lip down across her chin that twitched parallel to her eye movements.

"You'd be Sinclair's boy, then, wouldn't ya?"

"Yes ma'am. It's Wyatt."

"Well aint you grown. Come in, come in."

The trailer was a thing the width of a pickup truck's cab but a cab's length replicated several times over, and no more decorated than such a truck's cab would be. In its waxed stiffness the carpet made louder protests against his boots than the wheat or even the leaves on the floor of the woods had, and he followed her and she did not object to the fact that he had his shotgun barrel pinned awkwardly against his chest by his right hand. Sights to the ceiling at least. When the door rattled to a close from her yank on it she turned away and shuffled through a floor brushed with discarded newspaper and forded her way to a woolen couch and he sat down beside her.

A child ran across the floor in front of them, pushing a yellow plastic wagon.

"That's Bryson Horace there."

"Okay."

He held the shotgun between his knees. Watched a thick black fly traverse the two-inch window above the door.

"Wyatt, you said?"

"Yeah."

"I'm afraid Bo aint back from the shop until seven."

She thought for a second.

"We got milk, you want some milk? Or some moonshine? We got apples for it."

She rose to her feet and Smith blurted out, "No—" and she sat back down, keeping her hands in front of her.

"No," he said it more softly and shook his head. "I'm lookin for someone—"

"What happened to yer eye," she burst out, voice frightened.

"Dumb accident."

"Ah."

She was shifting nervously and took a toothpick from behind her ear and stuck it in one corner of her mouth and started picking at the scar on the other.

"You seen anyone?"

"Caint help ya there. Aint seen anybody outta place in these parts besides yourself."

The woman bent and flung a hand ineffectually at another child that was now writhing across the rancid magenta carpet before them, then turned back to Smith.

"Who is it yer lookin for?"

Her gaze still worked across his dead eye, ignored her offspring scattered around the floors.

"A girl. Youngish one. She stole somethin from us."

"I hope it wasn't nothin irreplaceable."

Smith laughed then tried to choke it down and the woman slid further from him on the couch. He recovered himself and wiped the glass eye with the back of his hand. The shotgun gaped at the ceiling.

"But how's your pa? Your sister? She must be somethin real pretty now. Aint seen you since your old man had to borrow tools to fix that tractor."

Smith stood.

"She is. And it were the baler."

"What?"

"It were the tractor hitch on the baler. Broke again the week after and I tried to fix it without him seein and the wire tore off the pulley and took my eye. Broken end right through to the top of the socket. You be careful if you see that girl around these parts."

He was halfway to the door.

"But what do I do? What am I s'posed to do if I see her?"

Smith looked at her as he opened the screen, then turned and went out, leaving her standing in front of the couch, one hand clutched to her collar and a dislodged pink curler in the other.

When he threw the truck into reverse and started to back out of the drive he saw the boy still there on the rock, his white hair scrawled across his face, forking a stick between his bare toes. When the boy heard the engine he lifted up the stick and Smith saw that he'd broken it in places to make it look like a rifle. He pretended to cock it and aimed it toward the road. At the mouth of the drive Smith passed the kid a dollar through the window, one of his last, and the boy leapt down from the rock and snatched it and made off for the trailer home or for the woods behind, back to sisters whose hands had never killed.

——◦◦◦——

Smith watched close in the ditches for some fresh break in the low branches as he drove, but there was no point tracking in this country without a lead. Altogether too much land, and she or he or both would be dead before he ever found that fine line of human passage in the leaves and dirt. He'd have to go by the landmarks, the places where she might think she could get something and hitch or steal a ride. Cutting his options already, and the feeling settled weightily into his stomach.

He let himself think about heading back, to confirm that she was not flat out on the pavement of some hick's drive to their shoddy hunting shack. Knew she had to be smarter than that. He went on south like on instinct but in it was also sense. Weren't nothing to the north besides abandoned lots and thousand-acre farms in which she'd find no more hospitality than she'd found in the man who had fired at her over the back of his own bull.

Twenty miles out, at the forked exit for the road to Salt Lake City, he found the abandoned truck. Pale turquoise blue with a black deer antler decal in the back window, and he recognized it as an old one from Bo Anderson's yard. In the opposite lane, headed north. Slowed as he came up beside it but did not cut the engine in case she'd wrecked it and was waiting in the undergrowth to try and take another. But there were no skid marks on the pavement behind it, and only stamped down grass where the right wheels had gone into the ditch, no dug up mud as there would have been if it'd been braked quickly. Axle probably bent from going half off the road but would still run.

The driver's side door was open and the keys visible on the seat. He stopped his truck and got out. Listened. Could sense what a deer felt like when it was standing frozen in the brush nearby, that featureless presence of something breathing. He knew he was alone.

The patterns of the trees here were strange to him, even though they were of the same stock as those rising in his woods. Had been known by the men that came before the roads did as all part of the same wilderness. Miles upon miles of forest that was strange, always morphing. Before the man had died in his woods and they somehow became no longer strange. Because in a forest in which you do not know which tree your father was killed behind, your father has been killed behind every tree.

Smelled the air and was smelling it for her. Hunting her out like an animal, because that was the only thing he knew how to hunt. It was silent but the false silence of woodlands, the slurred or barked calls of featureless birds and the rustling of their wings through the brush like skirts and if you removed their sounds you would hear the sandpaper legs of the insects they preyed upon and if you removed their sounds in turn there would still be the maddening ticking of grubs in the heartwood of the trees, perhaps even the groaning movements of the trees themselves. And if there were a true difference between the trees of that ranch and the trees of this road the sounds made no discrimination.

No tracks in the grass. She'd gone on the road. And he remembered—the gas station a mile ahead. Hadn't wanted the stolen vehicle seen, had turned around to leave it. He got back in his truck and went on.

When they were children, the trees and the cattle had made equal giants to their size. They would race among both in the same, ducking sideways between close tree trunks in the woods or crowded shoulders at the trough, or vaulting hands-first over a fallen log the way they did over bedded-down cows.

They were so small then that it seemed they could run below the bellies of the cattle by just scarcely bending over, and Lucy dared Wyatt to do it then volunteered to go in his stead before he could answer. She chose an older one stamping at flies, and she imitated it with her boots in the field and then she ran, and before Wyatt could follow she'd gotten cow-kicked in the knee.

She had been laughing and he had carried her up to the house on piggyback even though he was no taller than she then. In the kitchen he'd wiped the mud and manure off her knee and cut a bandage. It was bruised good but no more than a scrape, that of a child who's fallen on pavement.

"I aint gonna let it scar," she'd said.

"Nah?"

"We're the same, so the only thing that can make us different is scars. So it's only outside that can make us different from each other. We just have to make sure not to get scars."

"You gonna get scars on a ranch."

"Nah, I'll git better at doin things. I won't get kicked again. Not by no steer or horse or nothin."

"Shoot. It's not like that anyway. You're a girl and I'm a boy. Time and the world are gonna make us different."

"Change and scars?"

"Yeah."

"So we just gotta quit time and quit the world."

He was staring out to where the woods began beyond the

hill, so far that they appeared only in a blurred black-green line like the bruise on her knee.

"You in, Wyatt?"

"What?" He'd let go of the bandage and looked back at her.

"You'll come with me?"

—◦◦◦—

It was a place that looked as if it had been erected for the edge of a swamp, and now acted like a sponge, with moss bristling in emerald fur on the eaves of the roof and the gravel-mixed dirt around it all dried and dusted. Gas station that functioned as country store in a tract of land too remote to have one.

There were two young men in T-shirts standing on the porch in the morning gloom, one with a waxed straw cowboy hat lowered over his eyes and the other with his jeans funneled into his boots like a bullrider and when Smith parked and got out of the truck they eyed him and split wordlessly and went to lean against the front of the building. For a moment he saw himself as they saw him, gaunt and raggedly clothed and with one discolored eye and shotgun in hand, and knew more than anything it was that he was not often seen around these parts that had spooked them, and he went in.

The proprietor raised his head from where he leaned over the counter with a newspaper fanned out in front of him, a portly man of over fifty and in sun-stained overalls who was balding unevenly and had not shaved for at least a few days.

"Wyatt?"

He smoothed his hands over the newspaper to make the gesture of putting it down but without having anywhere else to put it and looked up again.

"Wyatt Smith?"

Smith did not look at him and instead walked among the shelves of cellophane-wrapped pastries with dust upon them. He stared at the goods with a sense of alienation, pushed at a package of donuts with his finger and when the pastry didn't budge he wiped the finger on his pantleg.

"Wyatt it's been what, three years? Five? We aint seen you here in a damn long time."

Smith rounded a corner of wire racks and at last met the man's eyes.

"Somethin like that."

"Was gettin to thinkin the winter must've gotten yall, way out there."

"Nah."

The man shifted uncomfortably and set his left hand on the corner of the newspaper.

"Well . . . what can I do ya for?"

Smith approached the counter.

"You seen a girl around here? Short, dark hair, 'bout fourteen. Black T-shirt."

The proprietor ran a hand over his skull as if to push hair back but only succeeded in moving too-long strands of gray over his baldness from the overgrown hair at his temples.

"What you searching her fer?"

Smith stopped in front of the counter.

"You seen her then?"

The proprietor took his hands off the newspaper and held them up in defense.

"No, nothin the like. I'd just wondered who she is and why you searchin her."

Smith turned and went back among the white-painted wire racks.

"It aint nothin."

"Alright."

"You sure you aint seen her?"

"I'd swear on the god almighty."

"Alright."

"Say, how's your pa doin these days?"

Smith looked up at him.

"He's doin right fine, thank ye."

"Tell him to stop in sometime, say hello. Yall caint be getting by just off your land and mail orders that well."

"I sure will. But we are."

Smith went out and the door clattered behind him as its decade-old bell smothered itself among flyers for lost dogs and horses for sale.

The teenagers were standing on the porch still and the one with the tucked-in jeans hacked and evacuated a mouthful of tobacco spit in front of Smith's boot. The boy was all-over dun-colored and had a missing canine tooth and wore two heirloom rings on his right hand.

Smith stopped.

"What you doin way out here." The boy shifted the pack of chew from one side of his mouth to the other with his tongue.

Smith turned to look at him with the good eye.

"Aint 'way out here' comin from Box Elder."

Smith stepped over the grease-slick of spit and continued down the stairs.

The teenagers closed the gap between themselves at the edge of the porch, one inadvertently sliding his boot heel into the mess.

Smith stopped at the beginning of the gravel wash and turned to them.

"You two seen a young girl round here? Black shirt black hair."

"Yeah we seen her," the one in the Stetson hat jawed. "Yer ma make off with a Mexican or somethin?"

"Somethin like that."

The other one had been about to elbow his friend in the ribs but stopped mid-motion. Smith handled the shotgun into the passenger seat and started the truck. Was on the right path.

As he backed it from the lot, the one with tucked-in jeans called out.

"She went on with a crew of bikers. Not from here but there were a half dozen bikes and one of them had tan saddle-bags with matchin tassels on the handlebars. Went on south. Hope ya find her."

Smith nodded. When his truck had edged into the mouth of the road the boy who had spat turned to the one in the Stetson.

"You don't mess with Box Elder people you dumb fuck."

———◦◦◦———

It was no longer necessary that he slow to look for her between the trees that lined the road. There'd be nothing for another twenty-six miles and that was short time in their terms of square-mile ranches, lands of no name with trailer parks littered in between. He caught his eyes in the rearview mirror and thought they were just tired enough for twenty-three. One eye that had seen things and one that was unseeing now but had enclosed the things seen in seventeen years behind it, to keep forever. Six years without the eye and five years without the father and an hour and a half without Lucy.

The fury had risen up again if it had ever abated. It was a

live thing now, a worm stretching the tops of his arteries and smashing itself against the hole in his arm.

They had never been away from one another. When they had still gone to the country store they had gone together, and on the ranch you were never apart. There was an intercon-nectedness in those family grounds, wires laid by the burying of the hopes or the bodies of the men who came before or the bones of the cattle they raised and killed, and he could feel her move across the fields and through the barns and flit along the edges of the woods as if he could reach out a hand to know for sure. Because it had always been that—that we are the same, that I am she and she is me.

And if I am she and she is me then I did it also. If my hands are her hands also then I am a patricide. When I awake in the night tearing the sheets off of myself to see if the blood is on my hands and feel the pounding all the way to the vertebrae at the back of the throat. And when it is dark you can see the dark on your hands as if it is there, like there would have been blood on her hands that day if she had held him close as he died. But there was not and she had not. And so you'd check your hands to see if they were covered in blood or holding the gun while she lay sleeping in the room beside yours dressed in white, ex-haling hushed breaths because now she does not even breathe like she did before.

She would never be a patricide because it was an accident, an accident and she could never be one, so I would play patri-cide to take that guilt away from her. I am patricide and I killed my father and I shot him dead. Because in a tract of grain tilled over dried bones she is everything right in the world. Because she is me and I am she and blood on her hands is blood on mine.

He blew through the twenty-six miles and killed a squirrel as he sped because there weren't enough cars on that road to teach the wildlife to keep off of it. And when he saw the place he slowed.

A motel, the type that smelled of vice more heavily than it did of vermin. A signpost peeling yellow among the cacti splayed around it spoiling from being too far into the north, too much in the wet, and the sign was blank. He knew there were some things that couldn't be made any better or any worse by giving them a name.

He parked behind a semi truck beside the leasing office and watched the proprietor look up at him through the window and then down again at a livestock supply catalog.

The motel was sloughed in the same yellow paint as the rotting signpost. Flat roof, only a dozen rooms. The remnants of his sideview mirror shot light at his back, shards hanging onto old glue like a glass anemone. A breeze passed across the parking lot and it bristled, went silent.

He walked over, gun in hand, and fingered the nubuck tassels of the wrappings on the motorcycle parked out front. There were another eight bikes propped in various angles and the single semi truck and a few pickups. Looked up to the room directly in front of the tan-wrapped motorcycle and decided that that could not have been the one. People who posted up in places like these did not want to be so easily marked.

He flattened his back against the wall starting there, and worked his way down, flannel catching in the rough bits of stuccoed clay. Three rooms down in the acid heat-quiet he heard a voice.

"You, come on over here, you aint had none of this."

And the reply:

"No ice. I said I want ecstasy."

There it was, the measured accent that was like nothing

else he had heard in all his life before. Studied and overly formal and misshapen in a mouth not raised on it.

He slid to the space between the door and window of the room. Back of the head to the wall so that he could fade into the dull of the paint and see sidelong through the window. The curtains were half-drawn, in the way that shows those within are hardly aware there are windows anyway.

"You sure you don't want any a this?" The first voice.

There were two men in the room. The speaker was a dirtied miscreation of a man. His beard grayed down to the lapels of a leather jacket that looked rusted and was taut against the muscle of his neck. One of his ears was studded along its edge and his skull shaved and tattooed solid with multi-colored snakes like rotted laurels bestowed from the ruler of a place buried far below this one. His eyes moved slowly, a pair of mottled driftwood rafts in veined white gel.

A much younger one sat at the shaky table by the window, probably still in his twenties, with stark black hair and green eyes a vulgar green like something printed onto the cellophane wrapper of a gas station sandwich. He wore only jeans and a leather jacket, shirtless under it, and as the girl walked by him he took a glass pipe from an inner jacket pocket and the movement exposed a jagged tear in the leather, directly over the heart. He caught the girl in her appraisal of him and poked a finger through the hole.

"It was my big brother's, but he aint needin it no more." His fingers shook as he pulled them back.

She had wiped most of the mud from her face and it showed that she truly was a child. The complexion underneath was so close a color to before that it gave the impression that the muck had emanated from beneath her skin to begin with.

The bathroom door opened and a third man entered, equally worn as the first yet older, a biker with a whitewashed beard and hollow blue eyes as if they'd been wind-bleached the same way, and a facial expression that was altogether one for staring down rogue horses or rogue men. He closed a flip phone in his palm.

"Your E man's on his way."

The snake-tattooed man held out a one-inch bag of crystal to the girl.

"You sure?"

She looked from the older one back to him.

"I only speak when I'm sure."

The man came closer to the window to take the pipe from the boy, and in the light Smith could fully see the tattoos, teeth bared above his brows and at his ears and twisting backward into a scaled nest furred with his patching hair.

"Did Guillermo say where he was?" she asked.

It was meant for the older one but the snake man answered.

"He'll turn up soon. We're aimin to let loose a bit in the meantime."

He put the pipe behind his ear and went over to the bed-side table.

The old man on the other bed tapped a rhythm on his knee, fingers vibrating in a silent hysterical violence.

Smith stayed against the wall, gun upright against his chest, the butt of it rested on a bent leg. Wait, had to wait. He worked his weight back and forth in the flexed boot and his foot started to go numb. Wait.

He watched them fashion the device from a water bottle; rolled-up postcard pierced through the side for a straw and pipe inserted just below. The pipe's end was jagged, looked as if it had been snapped from a piece of high school chemistry glassware.

The snake man went first, the leader, and took a butane hand-torch to the end of the pipe. Breathed in and the pupils rose against the tide of eye fluid. The air was seeping through the rotted sideboard along the windows and smelled like burning plastic.

The man leaned over to pass the mechanism to the other old one then fell back on an orange bedspread gone paisley half with its original print and half with burns or blood or tar. There was never enough seating in these motel rooms given what they were really rented for.

The smoke-stained ceiling ticked away minutes. A quarter-hour as the ones inside numbed and Smith's heartbeat bored away at the underside of his sternum.

The girl sat with her legs crossed, meditative-faced, as the three men dropped in turn. She was fully lucid but adjusted her gestures when the men looked at her to assure them it was otherwise.

An hour might have passed, the girl waiting. And it was a waiting, from the unaffected patience on her face. A strip of black hair was sweat-plastered across her forehead like an asphalt-lined scar. She stayed motionless, balanced there on the edge of the bed, and watched the tattooed man's exhalations with a cocked head like a venom-eyed chimera dog. Smith against the wall remembering to breathe when the old air began to ache in his lungs and the untiring adrenaline numbing away the heat, his arm, the concrete below his boots, all save the crags in the stucco behind his back. At one point someone had turned on the radio but none noticed it now. Old country, Conway Twitty singing with a Nashville accent over "Hello Darlin'," while the static in turn numbed the flat notes. The three heads watching the ceiling, punctuated by a turn of the face, an undead rising for another hit, then throat falling limp again, landing on the bedspread like with a snapping of the neck that bled through internally and up into the eyes, black blood.

Outside the lot was silent. Smith watched a lone crow hook its toes into the buckshot holes in his truck mirror. No one out here but him. His own mind a desert with the unbounded time, watching the world that wasn't his. Waiting for her to break through it just once more so he could make a last stand, with hands or teeth or buckshot to hang on and hold together the place that let his life exist.

The man sat up after Smith didn't know how long and lit a cigarette. The smell roused the other two a bit and the old one rose up onto an arm on the bedspread and lit one too. The young one's head lolled as he sat. The tattooed man let the ash drop on the carpet and it blended with the rakish polyester instantly as if it were of the same material, and the cushion of the room merely layers upon layers of years of thousands of different sinners' cigarette ash.

The old one spoke first and broke the rhythm of the room: the faltering revolutions of the off-center ceiling fan, the pulse cracking from the muffled radio, the fevered tap of yellowing hands on lacquerless chair-arms and moldering bedspread.

"Where you come from Jane?"

She wasn't any Jane.

"Just around. Nowhere worth noting."

The man set his half-smoked cigarette on the edge of the bedside table. The girl watched it as the paper flaked, then reached over and caught the cylinder of ash as it fell. She crushed it between her fingers then drew a gray line from her forehead down the bridge of her nose and one beneath each of her eyes to her jaw.

The tattooed one slipped the bag from his breast pocket

and loaded another dose into the bowl of the pipe. The boy's pupils were gaping badly now, dark but wide like the mouths of carp and as hungry, soft-walled and limitless in their green void, as if one could throw a breadcrumb in and then reach to grab hold of them. Black fish to sell in an unthinkable underworld market.

The pipe was passed last to the old one on the bed and it was empty and he nodded to the boy in the chair.

"Hey kid, throw me some more of that stuff."

The boy straightened in his chair and the leader's eyes batted open.

"I aint got no more."

"The hell you aint, you got a bag right there."

"Not for you I aint."

Smith slipped his hand down to the trigger guard.

"You." The old man stood shakily and reached along his belt for his knife, fingers discoloring in aural red, and the boy jumped up and in less than a second the leader stood and tore the glass pipe from the water bottle and shoved it jagged-end-first into the man's left eye.

Smith was down in a crouch with his hands balled at his temples before they all heard the glass splinter against the bone of the eye socket. He dropped the shotgun but the sound was lost to those in the room as the man made a "guhh" noise as if punched in the gut and then started to shriek.

Smith shut his eyes and the sound kept coming and the space below his working eyelid was red against the sun and the sound was like a calf screaming. He could see the animal and it was dark and then the blue murk of the eye running like his had and he knew it would be running down the man's face like half-cooked egg and it was all animal, so animal, and to anyone who had stumbled across the scene it would have looked like nothing but a solitary boy yoked with shoulders that looked broken, below a fogged window in the heat-wet pavement lot of a dilapidated motel.

At last there was the sound of agitated springs as the man fell onto the mattress in the room behind Smith and the shrieking stopped.

Smith lowered his hands but stayed on the ground. Glanced up into the window. The wounded man was flat on his back; a lusterless red froth foamed across his cheek.

The leader let loose a single cough then reached over to the amputated pipe still in the man's eye and scraped the remnants of powder from the bowl, spread it along the base-joint of his thumb, and snorted it, then added more from his bag and took that too and the boy bent, awkwardly deferential, to take the residue off his leader's finger.

The man pushed a nostril closed and inhaled harder to pull whatever was left in the nasal passages deep into the lungs.

"Motherfucker."

The girl looked at him. She had shifted onto her knees but had not moved from her place by the head of the bed nor changed her expression.

The younger one rose half out of his chair and grabbed her by the waistband of her jeans and pulled her into his lap.

"Git over here."

She twisted loose from his grip and was standing in front of him before he'd realized he'd let go. Her face was corrosive.

"You said that Guillermo was coming."

"Guillermo-whoever will turn up, whatever, les have some fun first." The young one waved a hand in dismissal and reached for her wrist but missed it.

The girl turned to the snake-tattooed man and held out an ash-stained hand.

"I changed my mind."

He handed her the remains of the water bottle pipe and the butane torch and he and the young one leaned back, staring at the ceiling and breathing slowly, watching the fan limp through its repetitions in dusted off-white. The wounded one sputtered, his non-violated eyelid shut loosely like the unattached flap of an old scar.

The girl looked to each of them for a moment then went into the bathroom and closed the door. When she came back into the room she pulled the door closed again behind her and soon there was the smell of burning.

The smoke in the room began to grow and the two men that were still conscious stirred at the vague stimulus but in their state did not notice it more than that, and would not have been able to break through the drug-induced apathy if they had.

"You're amateurs."

The girl lit the corner of the dying man's shirttail then unscrewed the butane canister and emptied it onto the bedspread. The leader's eyes were still on the ceiling and she stood and watched him as his hand began to twitch uncontrollably and the air went mottled like the back of a rat snake.

<hr>

She must have stayed as long as she possibly could have, barring the door and watching the orange carpet blacken to polyester magma and the paper peel like gnat wings from the wall. Soon the window went dark and then the blackness was no longer arctic-gray waves of smoke but a powder that stuck.

Smith stayed crouched below and watched the door, his shirt pulled over his mouth. A hand came through the window above him; it turned over from its punch then went limp. The leather sleeve about its wrist was curling with red edges and the hot glass showered into Smith's hair and down his back and he pitched forward and his face almost met the concrete but then he was up on his feet again, stumbling into the heat of the day, his arm going warm from bracing himself in the fall. The asphalt rocked in the heat mirage and the plane of it bent upward and the parking lot felt the same temperature as the blood coming out of the arm and then they blended together and were the same substance and then he caught himself again, one hand outstretched into the air and the other hand on the shotgun.

He staggered and turned around in time to see the girl walk out from under the overhang, the door closed behind her. The proprietor had run from his office and was standing there shouting and the girl passed him without a word, walking on like a wraith with melting rubber smoking from the soles of her boots. Her eyes were red from the ash-choked air. The proprietor looked from her to the flames that were now breaking through the roof and then back again and back again still shouting and not knowing what to do.

Then Smith was striding toward her, shotgun readied.

"You!"

She, in a trance, did not answer, had stopped and was staring toward the road. The rubber of her boots had cooled and no longer smoked and was smeared in a trail of stalagmites on the asphalt behind her.

"You!"

There was a noise like cracking and a figure came screeching from the room where the fire had been set. Jacket in flames and beard already crusted black, the tortuous snakes recognizable even on the reddening effigy of their owner. He ran toward her with arms outstretched, burning fingers, and suddenly her focus shifted and she turned from the road and made a quick rotation to hook a foot behind his thigh. He went down onto the pavement and fell to rolling in an attempt to ground the fire out.

The proprietor was screaming now at the smoldering man on the ground and a few more of the indistinguishables that had holed up there for sand or for ice had stumbled from their rooms. They watched from under the overhang with hands shielding their eyes, clothed in various items for the day and for the night, a mudstained T-shirt with stolen sneakers or a clubbing dress under a canvas construction jacket. Whispers over dried gums.

The proprietor stood beside the burning man and would not stop screaming and the girl turned his way and pulled a penknife from her pocket as she ran and punched it into the side of the man's neck and he too went down as the carotid artery sprayed up onto his chin and jaw.

Smith watched the man fall and rushed after her with the shotgun aimed.

"You!"

But her gaze was trance-like again and she ignored him and mounted the motorcycle with nubuck tassels, toed it toward the woods, and fired the engine into the undergrowth.

The man lurching on the ground was clutching at his face, the heat of his rings branding it further, and then he was rolling more slowly and then stopped altogether. Smith threw himself back into his truck and overshot it and the middle console hit him in the gut and he spit out onto the floor of the passenger seat and scrambled up. Got his foot on the accelerator and the truck kicked gravel as he swerved and he hammered down the road parallel to the direction in which she had gone.

CHAPTER FOUR

Hanged

He could see the smoke until he was a mile out. It chalked his rear windshield, went up in gunblack like Cerberus panting.

Down the road his heart attenuated in its pounding and he slowed the truck to a crawl. She couldn't be moving that fast in the woods. Police would be there eventually but she probably had forty minutes at worst in these parts before they arrived.

He opened the window a crack but heard nothing. The smoke was still lolling over the treetops, and the sweetness of its smell exposed the violence in it.

She didn't have to come back to the road but to her left was the Great Salt Lake and beyond that fifty square miles of desert and if she didn't know that now she'd figure it out soon enough.

He eased the truck over to the side of the road and put it in neutral and got his hunting scope from the glove compartment and propped it on the dash. Stared into the trees, his hand on the gearshift and his foot readied at the gas pedal. Deciduous and thickened here, bristled with sheets of chloroplast veins. Clear enough ground that she could make it through on the bike but too much brush to be able see the road from more than twenty yards in.

A rusted Bronco came down the other lane but then it was silent again. Smith got out of the truck and lifted the hood and pulled the spark plug wires. She'd figure it out eventually if she tried to make a break for it with the truck but he'd hear her and it would give him enough time to get back. Kept the scope and the shotgun with him and when he broke through the tree line he got down onto his stomach and crawled.

When he could no longer see the truck over his shoulder he stopped, worked himself by his elbows under the canopy of a newly fallen oak. She was either going to hunker down and wait this out or cut and run for it. The ground was fleshed with too much green to focus the scope. He put it down and listened.

Cicadas kicking out wingbeats like shouts. The tree line had knocked down the breeze and nothing moved. He had not realized how hard he had been breathing. Took a longer breath and held it.

Fingernails dug into his palms to stay quiet. And then, the near-silent purr of a motor in the blind distance ahead of him. Ten seconds he listened, and it seemed to get no closer. He was up and at a sprint over wrecked tree limbs back to the truck. She was going for it. He'd overtake her in the south.

—◦◦◦—

There is an unmarked line in Utah, somewhere among the flatworm lengths of invisible county borders, past the point when you can say you're headed south and are now already in it and just going further down, where the plain opens forward and the plateaus are too high on either side for you to see the sun and so the sun seems to come from the ground itself. He watched the earth shed its green skin and dry into tan bruises of acacia bramble and sand—the top fingers of the desert, spread upon the map from below like a callus on the earth.

He was still on top of it; the plain spread as a valley before him and the highway cut to the right before switchbacking down into the lower country. The mouth. Where time and land swallowed up the green of his ranch and ejected it dry, as blasted quartz and trilobite fossils and a hundred millennia older. He stopped here and got out and kicked his legs over the guardrail and sat. His arm hurt now and the pain made him hold it piked against his chest but he was glad for the reason to keep a tight, balled posture. Felt too exposed for one used to hunting by flattening himself against the leaves and dirt.

He'd wait, as long as he had to. He thought once about striking it out on foot and picking his way among the boulders down the cliff face in case she had trouble with the bike and he could catch her with a broken wheel somewhere in that mile-wide of rough slope and rock, but decided against it. Not enough of a guarantee.

Flies picked along the old manure on the leg of his jeans and he rubbed the bad arm with his hand. The heat was making the socket around the glass eye sting and he blinked it out of turn, mirrored the disjointed flicking of the insects. Out in the sky before him was someplace where the birds stopped. Dead air, where there was nothing below to give it life, like a certain point too far from shore where the gulls stop and as if a colorless gas rose up from the ground to say no more, no more here. Dead in a different way from the burned cattle with white sparrow footprints parting the ash down the nose of the skull.

He'd never been this far out before, but he knew what it was. Where the sheets of sand were not the color of dust, but the color of light. His forefathers had seen it, and he cursed them now more that he had seen it himself. What that man Wyatt Sinclair would have seen, whether he would have seen its blankness as a place to hide or to run or a clean slate so clean that even the hand of a god could not have made a forest grow there.

And to settle upon the tract of land that fed it, in the North. And had the men that came before and died before intended for their sons to die upon the same land or to excise themselves from it as the first Sinclair had done from the East? But had only a son and daughter left behind them, two who were one and the same, grown up without a mother and perhaps the father had simply made them grow out of the land himself. That a mother meant no more than photographs on a side table and no more than the wrinkled portraiture of those men who had come before and perhaps there was no history and they were each other's own mother, and had willed one another into creation or existence in the dark of the woods themselves, as nothing was more true than that they were a remnant of those woods and carried a darkness of leaves that blocked the sun from their hearts. She is me.

He shook with it, that the place that belonged to them now or that they had always belonged to could already be lost.

Waited. Glared at the line where the cliffs hit the sand until his eye blurred.

They were eight years old when the father took them out into the woods for their first hunt. When she'd realized it'd grown past her shoulders, Lucy had asked the father to cut her hair short, so Wyatt had helped in the kitchen with a broom while the father placed a soup bowl over Lucy's head and cropped off her hair with garden shears, and she'd laughed and tried to kick the falling strands of blonde with her boots before Wyatt could get to them. "I wanted to look like you," she'd said. And the father had asked whether she didn't want to look like him and she had held the shorn pieces of blonde to her chin in a beard and Wyatt picked some up and tried it too.

They'd marched into the woods single file at sunrise and Wyatt made her walk in front of him but she let him carry the rifle, a Ruger 10/22 with a maplewood youth stock painted red. The father led, the shotgun that ten years later would kill him and be bestowed upon Smith slung across his shoulders. Lucy called out names of plants and trees and insects while they walked and the father told her to hush when they approached the meadow.

Wyatt took her hand then found that the rifle was too heavy to carry with just one arm so he pretended to be annoyed with her and took his hand back.

Fifty yards before they reached the meadow the father stopped and held his hands out to the sides and his children fanned out behind him, one behind each palm. They could see where the clearing began, the sunlight chewing holes in the block of green that was the woods.

They moved forward slowly, more as one than as three, or at least as two, the father and then he and Lucy. Their footfalls were silent as the small shoes nudged under last winter's leaves and the father's boots bent expertly around the brush. At the edge of the meadow he lowered his hands and the children scrambled forward and went onto their knees and crawled in the yard-high wild oats until they reached the crest of a small hill, the best vantage point. The father came behind them and lay on his stomach and Wyatt put the Ruger in position against his shoulder.

They waited there in the meadow, and a grasshopper landed on the rifle barrel and Wyatt watched it as it moved across it and snapped up into the air and tumbled into the tall grass. They lay there for a while, not speaking, and Lucy began to fidget, braiding strands of oats into blonde shoestrings. And then the father—"there"—and touched Wyatt's shoulder and pointed at a blackbird that had alighted on a branch extending over the far side of the space ten yards off.

"Now aim carefully, think. Distance, wind. Think. Hold yer breath when you pull the trigger."

He squinted and scrunched his left eye shut and took the shot.

He hit the mark, square on the bird, but the thing fell backward off the branch and its wings fell open and it floated as it went down, wafting pitifully in the air until it landed in the grass.

Lucy jumped up first.

"You got it."

Wyatt stood there holding the Ruger, red-faced.

They walked together to where it had fallen and it was so small that it took them a few moments to find it and at last the father saw it and picked it up and held it out to Wyatt. Its wings were still outstretched and the bullet had hit square in its small chest.

Wyatt's lip began to tremble.

"Take it, son."

The little thing and its beak so small and the feet smaller still and the bullet hole like a cannon gone through it at that size and had never meant to hurt anything had never meant to kill and he could not hold back the tears any longer.

"Son. Take it."

And he snatched the bird from his father's hands and went running from the meadow so that they would not see his face or hear his tear-clogged breathing.

He was back in the woods, back in the place where there was no light and he felt alone and it was comfort and he wiped his nose on his shirt and looked at the bird and then held it tight to his chest and hoped with some farfetched shred of hope that because it was still warm it might get better, though its heart was most likely implanted deep in the bullet hole in the tree trunk behind.

Lucy and the father had followed at a run and they caught up to him. Lucy pushed his shoulder.

"Where do you think dinner comes from dummy."

"Not this one."

"Still." She held the Ruger now.

"Why didn't you go first?"

"'Cause you're the better shot, dummy."

He sniffed and she took the bird from him so he could blow his nose again into his shirt and then he took it back and held it once more to his chest. The father put a hand on his shoulder.

"When I was your age, my father made me kill and skin a fox kit."

Lucy took a cartridge from her pocket and reloaded. They went on. Tears still ran down Wyatt's face and none of the three looked at each other. He held the bird to the top of his shirt against the skin.

Just as they were reaching the ranch's pastures Lucy stopped and shouldered the gun. Wyatt and the father froze.

"What is it?"

Lucy lifted the pinky from her trigger hand to point.

There was a gray rabbit in the brush some feet in front of them. It had seen them, but was still deciding its next move and its muzzle twitched with such a fever that it was visible from where they stood.

Lucy pulled the trigger and it flinched then went down on its side.

The father yelled of excitement or pride and then quieted himself and they went to it and he picked it up by the back feet and showed it to her.

"A fine shot. Right in the head."

She stood silently, visibly steeled herself.

"We'll have it for dinner tonight."

The father kneeled and spread the rabbit on the ground.

"You two may as well watch this, as it's gotta be done each time yall hunt."

Lucy still held the Ruger and Wyatt still held the blackbird.

The father pulled the hunting knife from his belt, an antler-handled elliptically shaped thing like a stone, and detached the head and feet and started at the rabbit's back to skin it then flipped it and worked backward from the hip. The tiny viscera went onto the ground in a single movement of the chest cavity breaking and the father stood and lifted up the small carcass and shook it.

"And one last thing—"

He handed the carcass to Wyatt who took it, wide-eyed, and went back to the rabbit's head and pulled the skin from the lower half and broke off the lower jaw and handed it to Lucy.

"You boil that, and we'll get it on a string for you to keep."

She nodded, and reached into his palm to take the animal part, and only looked once at the red that wiped off onto her hand as she turned the thing with yellowed teeth half-covered in fur and half-covered in flesh and then closed it in her fist.

Wyatt left his blackbird at the edge of the woods.

After they'd eaten dinner they had all gone to bed, and once the light was turned off in the father's room Lucy came into Wyatt's room and climbed in bed with him and they joined hands and did not speak for a long time. Then Lucy pulled the blanket over her face.

"I didn't really wanna shoot that rabbit."

"I know."

"Do you have a light?"

"No. Flashlight's out of batteries."

"Oh."

They laid there, her right hand in his left, stretched on their backs and faces toward the ceiling but the covers pulled up over their heads so that the heat from their breath would re-bound off the blanket and onto their cheeks.

"Wyatt?"

"Yeah?"

"I didn't wanna, but somethin told me to do it. So I just did it."

He didn't answer.

"Or maybe, do you think that maybe that rabbit was sup-posed to die today? That that sort of thing is what fate is?"

"I wouldn't put too much fate to where our dinner done comes from."

She turned onto her side and encircled his hand in both of hers.

"My room's too cold."

"I know."

Dusk fell and the desert floor shifted and went mottled rose, like a mammoth carpetfish shaking itself from the reef bottom. The silence tore at his ears, reverberated against the plain so that his breath echoed back from the distant mesas in a sound of something shattering.

And at last there it was. A half-mile to the east, sand tossed up like smoke and drawing a line due south, too far to see the line waver around ditches and brush. He rose, watching, and then ran to the truck; he wouldn't make it down there much before dark but knew she'd be slowed in swerving against the arroyos and snakeholes that littered that type of ground.

No vehicles had passed him since he'd stopped and he pulled the truck back to the searing flat of the road. Each switchback was a sprint to an abrupt gray horizon as the air darkened. The descent felt like one done in a box.

At the head of the plain on flat ground he hauled his truck to the left, off the road. She was a quarter mile or two ahead of him and he'd take it at an angle. The tan upholstery of the motorcycle was invisible against the dust, merely looked as if a louse tunneled just below the surface of the desert's skin, the black of her hair its cretaceous markings as its armored back broke through.

Fifty yards off the highway he had to stop to unwind a barbed wire fence. No gloves but his calluses were enough and he took the loops from around the fenceposts and laid them on the ground and drove the truck through.

He knew she could see him, the space between them closing. Dusk was falling fast, and it was as if the desert took a collective breath and shook the insects from within its surface like a steer shivers flies off its hide.

The highway ran thick to their right, a halved graphite pencil. It fed into the interstate down here, and every few moments he could see the last strands of sun rock off of the metal of the cars that were passing on like dried beetles on a string. The sky had gone bruise red.

Twenty miles out, a grove of dried junipers twisted out of the horizon like browned hands. He was close enough to see her turn back to look at him, her face a terracotta sheet turning navy in the coming dark. The motorcycle dipped in among the trees and was gone. He stopped the truck and got out; there'd be sinkholes and exposed roots to wreck on if he got any closer.

Most of the trees were dead. Their bark was of a sinewed pattern and the same color as the shotgun, trees like discarded cicada shells. He went on. The highway still droned in the distance.

The motorcycle was riderless and on its side; a twisted handlebar coiled against the earth like a quicksilvered snake. The sand was shaded enough here that it was cold and stuck to his boots, formed the fragile constructions of footprints behind them.

He went on through the grove and a thread of green started up among the brambles and dried stalks, ran from the ground to the tips of branches. The ground got wetter and he started to suspect there being old well pipes here, cracked and abandoned.

The grove broke and he reached the output of the pipes. A rusting water trough, the size and shape of a bathtub, algae and red fungus bloomed down its sides, and the girl's face buried in it to drink. Three stone-colored mustang ponies stumbled near her, gums green and agitated from the putrid water but too thirst-desperate to leave. Had the malformed spines of wild horses grown their whole lives in the desert.

The girl was crouched with her shoulders up like a cat's. Three hours in the desert air and the thirsting had already

started. Had a palmful of water halfway to her mouth and he
racked the shotgun. She looked up and let her fingers open and
the water fell through. The ends of her hair had fallen into the
trough as well and slid from its rim to give her a dripping collar. The dust stained black with wet on her chin and jaws.

She stood before he could tell her to. He walked around
the side of the trough and her face was within a foot of the
gun's mouth. She stared at the eclipse it made until she went
nearly cross-eyed then looked beyond it into his working eye.

"What do you want."

He could hear the spit catching on the sand along the back
of her teeth.

"My cattle." His hands were shaking on the gun. "I want
what's owed for my cattle."

"Got nothing to give you for them." Her face was still.

"Then find some way. There's got to be some way."

No answer.

"Forty-six hundred dollars. I need forty-six hundred dollars
to keep the ranch."

The girl's eyes flashed the color of tin as the sky darkened
and a mustang in the background nickered then chewed at its
leg. One of them approached the trough and then fell back
again.

"Just gimme the goddamn forty-six hundred or tell me
how you'll get it so this can be finished and I can go home."

He was almost in tears. Gun still angled down at her head
and finger pressing sweat into the trigger guard.

She lifted her hands out to the side and turned slowly in a
circle. Her unmatched boots sloshed the sand around her in
waves. The plastic grocery bag was tied to a beltloop at her hip.

"I've got nothing. I don't have it."

"Then you find a way—"

"And if I don't?"

"If you don't, I'll kill you."

"Gonna kill me the same way you killed the one buried on your ranch?"

He thrust the barrel of the gun forward so hard that it knocked her head back and she grabbed it with both hands to keep her balance. She regained her step and forced herself forward on it, the mouth of the gun tight against her forehead where its semicircle imprint was starting to bleed. He locked his arms and the two braced like stags ensnared in combat.

Their breathing was hard enough that the pressure between the gun and her skin wavered and with every few breaths the contact would slacken then be shut again, the barrel spraying dots of blood across her face. She would not draw back, and soon the breadth of her forehead was littered with pinprick-sized spots like the hide of a demonic Appaloosa. He glanced at the bag on her hip, saw what he thought he'd seen through the clear plastic.

She had the rabbit's jaw. She'd been to the grave.

"The mandrakes give it away," she slurred through sweat and spit. Blood pooling along her upper lip.

"He wasn't hanged!" The shout echoed against the horizon lines of the desert and through to the tendons of the hands on the gun.

"I can see the guilt."

"He wasn't hanged!"

The girl twisted her hands on the barrel of the gun and he pressed it in further and she looked down toward her chin as she made something of a smile and a droplet of blood slid over the corner of her mouth. She'd been bluffing. Could not have known it was a killing. Her eyes were a pair of black dogs when she raised them again.

"Maybe not. But mandrakes have a certain sense of things. Something in it was not right."

She was watching his finger on the trigger. Two of the horses had come back to the water trough and he considered if he had to cut her down here whether he could catch the horses to sell but knew they were worth nothing.

"Find a way or I kill you right here."

No ranch no home. No way to save a sister. A killer in front of you, calling you one too. The horses watched with gaping, sad, sun-sick eyes.

"Do it then."

He braced his heels. Do it. Lose it all; it's already gone.

She took a hand off the barrel, wiped her brow, looked at the blood on her fingers, then spit.

"Do it."

There was a shot and the horses scattered with a jolt.

CHAPTER FIVE

Trees with Meat Inside

The girl landed on her back like an inkblot crumpling. Smith flung himself back against a tree and yanked open the mechanism to his gun. The girl had her hands to her forehead and was pulling at it and Smith found the two shells still loaded.

"The fuck was that?"

The bark of the tree to his left was torn white across the side of the trunk and she touched it as she scrambled up then looked toward the road as Smith realized the sound he heard was not echoes of the shot but approaching engines.

"Fucking motel junkies must've ratted—" And the girl was at a run from the grove. Smith shouldered his gun and ran after her, past the water trough, and it was when he broke clear of the trees that he saw them.

There were four of them, out from the highway, on dirt bikes and hack motorcycles. Dark faces with rags tied across their foreheads or mouths and still two hundred yards out.

The one in front leveled his 9mm again and the shot cut wide and landed in the sand ahead of the girl.

The sand was rocky beyond the juniper grove and then bowed up into a pair of mesas and they headed there. The horses had sprinted off with a snap of their hips and it made a sound like a prequel to the gunfire that followed. One of them caught its leg in a root and was squealing and the motorcycles were closing in, a hundred feet off. Men with tattooed hands and black oiled guns, a different breed from the dead men at the motel. He could see from the girl's face that she knew them.

The rocks had slowed the bikes but Smith and the girl were in full handgun range. Three bullets passed Smith's temple in quick succession and he twisted to return fire without time to aim and the shot laid gnat-bites in the sand that were quickly washed over in tire tracks. He racked in another shell as he ran.

One of the bikes swerved for the girl from the side and the rider leapt from his vehicle and advanced upon the girl on foot, screaming in Spanish. The man had his gun in the air and did not take a shot and she did not answer the words but turned and ran into him and the two fell into a tangle on the ground. She rolled away from him faster and got her knees up onto his shoulders while he was still on his back. His neck folded as she broke it and in seconds she was up again, running with his gun.

The girl glanced over her shoulder once, then veered away from the mesas, away from cover. She was going for the caught horse.

More shots came and she kicked at the root to free its hoof and when it didn't work she pointed the gun down and shot the root loose. The horse buckled at the hindquarters and slipped and the girl dove low and hooked onto the side of the animal in a parasitic grasp as it flung itself onward.

The men shouted to one another and in response one of them twisted his bike and headed directly at Smith.

The girl made it as far as the feet of the mesas before the horse stalled and began to flail to throw her off. A bullet clipped its flank and it quit its protesting and lunged forward again but the motorcycles had by now closed the gap between them. The first of them skidded into the horse's hind leg and both crashed in a yelping of animal flesh and chrome as the second collided with the animal's front. The second machine reared as it fell and its headlights flashed twofold over the horse's muzzle, the nostrils flared and dipped in black viscera or motor grease, and the fallen lights faded as the glass was washed with blood, bulbs caked dark but still glowing gold at the edges. There was white splinter across the handlebars and then the first of the bikes was back up and gone and there was a thundering that seemed to come from the ground itself as the echoes off the red rock dove and burrowed into the sand.

It was too late for Smith to get out of the way of the man headed toward him. Like running through water, the sand clawing at his boots and weighing them down, and another shot missed. The man on the bike was within arm's reach now, red-rimmed eyes caged by pierced eyebrows, and Smith dove and rolled to the side over the ground, covering his face from the rocks. The man braked and yanked the handlebars over to double back, and drew his pistol for another shot as the rear wheel skidded and sprayed sand. He was too close, and almost above Smith, and Smith outstretched his hand for the shotgun that had fallen in the sand and swung it around by the muzzle and flung himself upward, jamming the butt of the gun into the man's shoulder. The shoulder imploded and the pistol flew and the bike flipped.

The man's tibia snapped as the bike came down and it caught Smith at the hip and pinned both men beneath it.

———∘∘∘∘———

Sand soaked his teeth and the man was pinioned at the knees beside him, the emaciated creature with a brown bandana around the neck and ire in the eyes. Smith's shotgun wedged between their chests with its barrel to the sky, the man's shoulder loose and left arm thrashing and his hands clawing in aimless fury at Smith's throat and Smith tucked his neck to block it. The man's hands went down the sternum snatching for some weak spot and then plunged toward the mechanism of the gun. Smith tried to wrest it back but the man's weight was against him and his fingers reached the trigger but Smith held it tight and the gun went off and the shot broke through the empty seal-brown air above.

Get the barrel down, get the goddamn barrel down, now and do it now or he's going to kill you and the man went again, this time at Smith's eyes with his index fingers and thumbs and Smith turned his dead eye toward him and felt the fingers worming into the edges of its socket and with his working eye could see no more than his warped reflection in the metal of the gas tank, the spreading fungal dark eating into the image as the shadows grew. He rose up to slam his shoulder into the man's chest and it was enough. Smith swung the gun down and implanted the barrel into the pocket of the man's collarbone and fired.

There was silence for a moment and the air seemed to flake in gray then there was the smell of gunpowder soaked in blood and the man had stopped and laid his hand across his chest at the wound which was only a small thing when shot at contact point and the eyes that had rolled about wildly now were fixed and there was screaming far in the background but not his and the rabid calls of chasing motors and muscular collisions of kicking horses that were imagined or still there. And the man's eyes upon him in viral black and Smith's hands were fumbling with a shell from his pocket and digging for it and the depth of the pocket had never felt like this much and he was at once squirming with his legs to get himself backward but the weight of the bike held him fast. And the man was saying nothing and was not screaming and his mouth opened in a black hole to absorb something, anything, or to expel it, but air would do no good either way now and those eyes gaping as much as the mouth if not more and they had not looked down at the wound or at the blood now running down through the man's fingers and Smith finally got the shell in and racked the shotgun and laid there with the barrel shaking trying to align it and his arms shaking and still trying to align it and the man's eyes were suddenly animal. Smith fired again and the man's torso jerked back as far as his pinned legs would let it go, turned up to the darkening sky with the shotgun blow to his chest.

Smith collapsed back into the sand, the emptied shotgun in his arms. Breathing hard. Couldn't feel either leg.

There were no more sounds of horses or engines and the gunshots were gone in the distance, but the world was beating beneath the side of his head and he was no longer sure whether the *tak-tak-tak* was instead the sound of the desert and the souls that must people it, red-eyed and sand-skinned, scraping themselves off of the ancient rock and reanimating from where they'd lain frozen beneath the mesas. The sky had gone from blood red to black.

"In the desert, the skies aint look like this," the father told them. They were in the dark, he and Lucy and Wyatt, but what need was there for a fire on those nights when the sky was shot through with stars like birdshot and if you held out your hands they'd be blue in the light.

"You git the same stars, but the horizon comes all the way to the ground, so it looks like if you ran far enough you'd run right into em."

They watched the father spread his arms to demonstrate then looked to where the mountains lay beyond the start of the woods, like teeth to cut the horizon off. They knew things were different in Box Elder, even though it was the only place they had ever been. It was a place with something wrong about it, you could sense it, and they didn't suspect that all the world was wrong like that because they knew somehow that this place was different, was something else.

The three were sitting on the porch steps and the dog would snuffle around the back of the siding and pull out critters and pestilential things. And the father told them about the trees and they listened and listened and to Wyatt the crickets made it sound like you could never be alone in that world again even if you tried.

After, the father told them not to get too scared without him and went inside for a lip of tobacco and a rawhide for the dog. And Lucy grabbed his hand and said, "Let's go see if it's real," and he said, "There aint gonna be enough light to see shit," because he was just learning to curse and thought it was the thing to say but she only laughed at him. They went anyway and Wyatt took the ax from the barn and he carried it at its head and Lucy carried it at the handle and he dragged it when they got to the woods because there were no stars through the leaves and they were going to have to feel for the kind of bark they were looking for.

He realized there wasn't a chance in hell he was going to be able to chop a tree by himself so he told her to look for something smaller, and it was so dark that he ran into her once and grabbed her arm thinking it was a branch and she screamed and laughed but Wyatt screamed louder, grabbing what he thought was a tree and it turned out to be warm.

And finally he found a sapling that had died and fallen over, the right breed, right bark, and they dragged it out together like they had the ax, and took it to a crest in the field where there was plenty of light from the moon and from the sky that had opened up again and was reflected in the droplets of sweat on her, looked to Wyatt like the stars were sprinkled across her arms.

It took him one chop, and he halved the thing. The father was right. Box elder's just a kind of maple, good for sap and all that. But if you find a box elder tree in the woods that's gotten sick or been scarred or done had anything else bad happen to it, nobody knows exactly what does it, when you chop it open the wood will have a bloody red stain inside.

Wyatt yelled like hell when he saw it and Lucy pulled up her shirt to cover her mouth and just stared. They left the thing out there, sapling so small and no taller than they and what had really gotten them was that the trunk he cut open was no wider than one of their arms.

They went up to bed, and despite the silence neither fell asleep until sunrise, nor said a word about it. And the next morning, Wyatt didn't know if the father must have found it or the dog but it was gone.

The man coughed, and then coughed again and some of the air expelled straight from the perforations in his chest. Smith woke up suddenly to what had gone on and tried to crawl away but the bike held him without give. The man's chest rose with one more expulsion of breath and it looked for a moment as if he would sit up, then the momentum was lost and he fell back into the sand beside Smith.

He landed on the dislocated shoulder with his face to the side, eyes open though one of them stuck with grains of sand and when the eyes watered and blinked to clear themselves the movement was too slow, more a weakened mechanical function than a reflex. The tears of sand ran down his nose and then went unseeable into the shadow on the ground.

The man opened his mouth but blood ran out, no words, and Smith stared at the hole in the man's chest.

"I . . . I . . ."

The man said nothing, stared at him with one eye and the other was turned to the sand now. He was still breathing.

"Oh god, I aint . . ."

The shotgun had fallen between them, like a limp thing now that it was without shells. A slice of the man's lung was visible through the ribcage like a piece of pulsing coral. Soon he would be dead, and soon Smith would have killed a man for the first time.

"I—"

Couldn't say you didn't mean to.

The dying man still stared and Smith did not know if it was with seeing or not.

Killer.

"I . . . I caint get up."

The dying man still stared.

Killer. He shouted and punched his good hand against the

bike and strained against it and could not move and he shouted again and his hand burned and he dropped his head back into the sand. Night had lowered itself and lay brooding on top of them now as if protecting its young. The metal of the bike went cold against the exposed skin where Smith's jeans had torn and he was suddenly conscious of the warmth of the ground.

The dying man blinked once more, but the nether eye was drying out against the sand so the eyelid stuck halfway down and then caught up with the other.

The man coughed again. Smith never would have allowed hunted game to suffer for this long. He raised his hands, one shaking from the wound up the arm and the other with blood-streaked knuckles from punching the bike. Slid one hand behind the man's head, past an ear scarred in an X where a piercing had closed, to where his hair was matted with sand, and gripped the chin with the other. If he got up onto his elbow he'd have enough leverage to do it, but he waited.

Just another minute. Wait a bit longer, so he doesn't die and so you're not a murderer. The dying man was wearing a T-shirt that now read delta–shotgun blast–delta fun run, with older bloodstains on the collar. The bandana had been nudged down around his jawline at some point, so saturated it looked black now.

You can wait. One more minute in the *before*, before the rest of your life is the *after* and you are, you are now and you will always be, forever now, a—

He looked at the man. Took his hand from the chin and held it in front of the open mouth to feel for breath and there was none. Whether you'd been strong enough to put him out of his misery or not, it was over now. Killer. He clawed at his own legs and the bike would not move.

He watched the droplets of perspiration dry into flattened spheres of sand on the man's brow and exhaled, then looked out into the dark. The stars had overtaken the last strands of twilight and he could see a few feet in front of him, all of it cast in silver. Beyond that, everything was black. The mesas huddled on the plain beyond like mastodons at rest and the warmth ran out from the one beside him.

His legs were not moving. He'd dug out around them as far as he could reach but he could get no further under the bike to dig them all the way out. The dead man's body bore some of the weight, but the machine was edging four hundred pounds. The sweat and spit started to run cold down his face and he knew the drops of water gone were successions of minutes lost out here.

There are two ways to die in the desert. Heatstroke and disembowelment. The coyotes would get to you either way, but the dehydration determined whether you were still alive when they did.

He fingered the shotgun next to him in the dark. Wished he'd filled his pockets and socks and waistband with shells. His truck sitting thirty yards off with a full box of them.

He pictured the coyotes trotting through the dark if he stayed conscious for that long and wondered if it'd be Lucy's broken eyes in the faces of the ones that came for him or if they'd have her rabbit jaw's teeth.

He realized he was lying on the wounded arm. He got up on his elbows as much as he could and took the jacket off and laid back. It had gone numb and he watched the hole bleed like a fist opening into the sand. Enough blood around here already that this bit wouldn't draw them any more than they were drawn already. He wondered whether he could put up enough of a fight when they came that they would choose the dead man over fresh meat. Think, man.

TREES WITH MEAT INSIDE

Smith dug at the sand around his thighs until the sand ate the nail beds of his fingers raw. Midway from the thigh down, the legs were still pinned tight. No use, couldn't reach to dig out any farther.

The highway shook awake with the passing of an eighteen-wheeler but he knew he was invisible to it now.

He looked around himself for anything that would work— no tools in the dead man's pockets, none in his own, no sticks or vines under the first layer of sand after he tore it up with the side of his hand. And then his glance came to the shotgun. Empty, half-covered in sand now, gritty and oiled antique thing of his father's.

Reached out the shotgun over the width of the bike to see if it was long enough. It was.

He laid the gun to the side for now. He steadied the left arm at the elbow, put his weight on it, and flung himself up to reach the upper handlebar with the right hand. He grabbed it on the first try and felt something, a skein of tissue or the skin, split in the wounded arm and yanked back on the handlebar with the remaining strength in his torso and the effort made him scream.

Smith fell back into the sand and looked at the dead man as if worried about waking a sleeper, but the handlebars had turned as he had wanted and the angle of the front wheel would give him leverage against the midsection of the bike.

It would take hours upon hours but he might get out of here. Dragging yourself through minutes like Lucy dragging the father through the woods and his fingers crawled into the sand as if searching for whatever reserve of strength her hands must have had then.

He nudged the nose of the shotgun in along his thigh past where his hands could reach and scraped away at the sand. Began to dig.

Looked out once more into the dark as he worked and felt a shift. Knew it was the screen door behind Lucy. It was too late for her to be tending the animals, and he knew what she would be doing. His heartbeat slowed to the pattern of her footfalls as she made her way to the grave. She would see now that the rabbit's jaw was gone, and would perhaps not understand, would think it'd been carried off like carrion by some scavenger far late to the feast. He saw her kneel and sink her hands into the dirt at the foot of the crudely nailed cross that was still soft dirt because she did this every night, as if to hold the fungal things that lived within it and would lift a handful of dirt to her chest, as these things would not communicate by voice but by heartbeat. Telling the decomposers, not yet, not yet, don't take it all away just yet. And would set it down again and wipe her hands on her dress but hands stained with dirt and no blood. In the shadow of where the cross was dug in and beyond what her hands had tilled were the mandrakes, her skirt across them as she knelt, which perhaps was the thing that gave the shade to make them grow. Something that was not right.

Smith made one last whisper beside the dead man.

"I didn't really wanna shoot, but somethin told me to do it. So I just did it."

I know.

He kept digging.

He did not know when he slept but at some point he had or had lost consciousness and when he awoke the air was white and there was no division between it and the sky. The sand below him was soaked and left a cast of his arm when he sat up and the rain had sprayed drops across the canvas of his jacket. He could not see three feet in from of him. His legs hurt, were half-aching and half-sensationless under the beached motorcycle. And the land was steaming.

The man next to him, dead. A weevil crossed from the man's throat to the dried cliffs of the torn shirt and fumbled onto Smith's hand, one of the creatures here that only existed in the moment after rain. He shook it away. Looked at the man once more though the man was graying already with the dew and there was nothing more to see that he had not already seen and he turned back to digging.

He'd worked his wounded left arm to the point of uselessness where the right arm couldn't reach, but he was almost free. Continued on, his brow crusted and caked with gun oil and sand and sweat and he could feel where the grit had edged its way underneath the glass eye from the now-dead one's fingers and he took it out but it burned more without it so he wiped it and put it back in.

At last his right leg felt loose enough to slide it under the steering column, and he twisted until he could pull it back and braced his foot against the engine. Flinched as the weight shifted and put more pressure on his left leg.

It slid away undamaged, below the torn denim nothing more than skinned, like a child's. He crawled from beneath the bike on his back in the motion of an arachnid molting. His legs were numbed from so many hours and it took fifteen minutes' crawling in that flat of ground before he was able to put full weight on them.

There were no birds and the insects still hummed ravenously, and he wondered if the sun had risen. Then realized it would not rise today. In the egg-white sky he would not see it move, and by the time this cleared it was just going to be there.

He walked away from the dead man and took his first steps as a killer.

He went in the direction that the girl and her pursuers had gone. The mesas parted from one another ahead like hands falling from prayer. The heat was a part of the air now, a gelatinous thickness that slid over his face, and he stumbled out into the desert in a zombie's pilgrimage.

Smith passed the motorcycle that had been dropped by its owner when he'd leapt upon the girl. Dead man sprawled near it with his arms spread and rainwater still in the dishes between the bridge of his nose and his eyes. Past the motorcycle there were no tracks; he was unsure whether they had been washed by the rain or the light had bleached his eyesight too much to see them.

At the base of the twin mesas lay the second bike, and the downed horse. A body beneath the bike but it was not the girl's. Up close the horse's hide was windbeaten to the color and texture of cornmeal. Broken upon the handlebars by the forelegs and shot through the stomach. Its mouth white with sand, like a rabid animal in a grainy encyclopedia photograph. A TEC-9 lay nearby and Smith checked the clip and it was empty.

He went on, holding his shotgun flat in two hands like an offering. Ascended the dune that rose between the mesas and stood at its crest. The ground was still white here and the shadows of the mesas were more a feeling than a visible thing.

Slumped against a mesa wall at the far end of the passageway was the final man. Smith hugged the stone and approached with his gun leveled but lowered it as he got close. The man was dried, dead. Shot through the head and a shot in each knee pluming red to leave a pair of eyes in the sand. Bullet holes in the sandstone beside his head like the nests that rock swallows take.

Smith knelt to look at him. Knowing now that someone had sent a team of four after her thinking that that many would be needed and even then had failed.

The sand here was broken up, waves made from spinning tires, and he walked further out. Ten feet from the dead man he saw a new trail of blood, someone else's. It went on for another five feet and then the tire tracks of the bike became clear and straight, and the blood was gone.

He stood there upon that hill, staring out at the Utah desert into which she had vanished. It stretched endlessly, and he wondered whether it were a trick of his loss of depth perception that did it or if the emptiness really was that long. The mesas rose to either side of him, trilobite fossils locked within them, stacks of millennia in red and gray to make the towers of some alien city. And she was out there, dead or perhaps evaporated into the dust of motorcycle wakes and had never existed at all, or perhaps there were horses, more horses that she willed up out of the sand and that ran their course across the endless flats of desert, cast into purgatory merely by the cruelty of the geography.

He watched it for a long time, then turned back toward his truck with violence on his mind.

<hr />

Smith grabbed one of the water jugs from his back seat and poured it over his face. Stray bits of sand stung at his eyelids.

He knew she was wounded and would die out there. She belonged to the desert now and it was a definite thing. He'd gone so far and she was probably dead already. He looked at the road that simmered in mirage to the right. Perfectly straight as it cut through the dry country. Lead-filled vein in a wash of skin.

A road to nowhere because the ranch becomes nowhere without that money, and a road to make a killer because your becoming makes her one too, in your returning to you-were-she-and-she-was-you. And then would come the leaving, two wandering shadows good as dead, gone from the place where their first dead was laid.

It was all gone.

He put his head in his hands and sat there on the tailgate of the pickup truck for a long time, arm paining him softly and boots suspended motionless over the shaded sand and the red rock cliffs looming in rusted daggers beyond. Had a feeling the girl wasn't dead.

That place that had risen off the plane of the desert in the distant North like Mount Olympus or a floating land—to men standing in the desert, the fathers that came before, a place forested by trees with meat on their insides must have looked like paradise. An empire to raise with cattle and sons. He looked up.

If this was to be the end of that empire, he wanted to see it. He wanted to see the end of his home. He wanted to see the end of his life. If it was going to happen whether he wanted it to or not, he wanted to watch.

Fresh hides had to be salted daily for twelve days, and Lucy circled about the upstairs of the house like a child with nothing to do. She'd salted the hides for their third day, in a room that still smelled wet and was hung with blue shadow for a few unnatural minutes past the arrival of dawn. She ran across it as the rays of sunrise had, snowing crystals over underskin, but that was hours ago and now the livestock outside were bellowing to be fed. They made the clamor of a hangman's crowd, the throats of horses and the tongues of cattle and jaws of pigs. She walked now with her hands over her ears. Circled again and again. Stopped once and addressed them.

"Be quiet. It's all ending."

At last she gave up and went to see what Wyatt had done to the cattle.

The wheat field ended with a cliff of air that no longer smelled like it. The herd was in the other pasture still. She walked on a few hundred yards until she hit the site of the bonfire. Had never recoiled at a burnt smell before but this time she knew what it was. Charred ribcages in a pile like blackened springs of an old mattress ripped open to exorcise all its years of sin. Reached past the height of her shoulders, the odd horn spiking toward her throat from black skull faces that shone with white eyes of clean bone inside the socket where the smoke hadn't scathed as much, like mad cartoon expressions to caricature their end. A bird with a clammy-skinned neck was picking at the calcified leather on a tailhead. The bone-eyes laughed as it stumbled and fluttered to catch its balance again where it teetered on a heat-cracked hip. A few wisps of ash caught the wind and cleaved off of the charcoal at the base of the heap and spread into fingers of poisoned lace as they lighted through the grass that was a mockery simply because it lived on. Because it was not like a house that had burned.

She started to gag, mostly with the loss, and covered her head with her hands.

Before she ran back to the house she turned around once more and looked at the dead things.

"Be quiet. Please."

Part Two

CHAPTER SIX

Walmart

He took the road south and stopped when he saw her, twenty miles out.

The figure on the horizon staggered, a narrow black form with the lowering sun beyond it and the ground rinsed white. It took another step to the south and then dropped.

Smith slammed the truck door shut and walked slowly out from it. There was flat sandstone out from the side of the road and he marked his steps across it and stopped where it sank into gravel and then into wind-washed sand.

It was the kind of desert quiet that few men experience in their lifetimes, and the ones who experience it more than a few times start inventing voices to fill the silence. He stood with his back to the truck and his face to the sun. Raised the hand of his good arm to his eyes. The sound of the fall still echoed, with nothing more for the sound waves to rebound against but him or because his mind held to it a little longer,

with no other noise to grasp upon. Sickly warmth of familiar-
ity in that sound. And then he remembered: the sound of shot
game going down.

He shook his head at nothing at all and descended into the
wash.

One would have expected some birds, but this far out they
were scarce and there were none.

A beetle circled a small piece of brush as he treaded past.
Little tracks stamped in a ring in the sand to suggest it had
been circling it for all time.

Walked on, and as he got closer there was sound in the air
again. A grating against the ground as each limb scraped ahead
in turn. Sand rolled away in minuscule waves from the channels she made as she dragged herself along in progressions of
two inches at a time, but still in the desert that makes a sound.

She continued on even when he came to stand above her.
Arm bent at the elbow and two outstretched legs. The other
arm was clutching underneath at the stomach that he couldn't
see but the left pant leg ran red-black down the side, and in the
waning light it only looked as if the black T-shirt had worn out
to the point at which it had simply liquefied. Her plastic bag of
belongings still tied to a beltloop at the back of her jeans. He
stood with his thumbs hooked in his pockets.

"Hey."

She still continued on, moving elbow, foot, foot, and then
again, each in time to a perfect rhythm of maddening slowness
and ineffectuality.

"Hey—" He nudged the thigh with the toe of his boot.

She turned her head in his direction and retched, and it
echoed in the silence so loudly that he recoiled as if hearing a
gun go off. The echo died and he looked at his boot and tried
to scrape the wet that had adhered to it off into the sand.

The sand merely coated his boot and stuck.

Her hair was plastered to her forehead and matted around her neckline where she'd tried to tuck it into her shirt with soiled hands and there was sand on her chin. She moved a final foot and stopped and lay there and looked up at him, found she had to squint, and then just shut her eyes, kept her face in his direction.

"You got a cigarette?"

"What you want a cigarette for?"

"Just to have."

"I aint got no cigarettes."

She turned her face back into the ground. More sand stuck to her cheek. She turned it back up. Eyes still closed and expressionless face tilted his way like one of the figures at the bottom of the pile in a war painting.

"Got water?"

"Nah."

She lowered her face and continued on, heaving herself forward on the lone elbow and trailing it with two little steps in the mismatched boots. As if climbing a wall that stretched for miles. Babylon of sand, and the footholds of its walls crumble, shear straight down.

He followed for a few steps. She stopped as if in thought but then he realized all her movements now were slow and mechanical enough to suggest there was thought behind them and it meant nothing.

"Then what'd you come out here for?"

"Just to see."

She spat into the sand and a bit of mucus ran down her chin. Then she laughed.

"Goddamn it," limply shaking her head. "Goddamn you."

He shrugged and turned back toward the truck.

"You. Wait."

He stopped but did not face her.

"Help me."

"You've taken everything from me. I aint owe you nothin."

"Please."

"I aint owe you for nothin."

He walked back to the truck and when he got there the sun was down and it was night.

He took one of the cans of food from the back seat and loosened the top with his knife and then took the blanket roll too and stretched out in the bed of the truck drinking out of the can cold. Mouth extracting beans from the can that were like glutinous stones.

He shifted to get off the bad arm. It left a wet spot on the blanket and he dizzied. He lay back again and looked up at the sky. It still held a fevered purple at the horizon but bled to blue and then black up above, the stars breaking through as it darkened like holes shot through a canvas ceiling and he thought of the daylight poured through those holes but no it wasn't like daylight and no it was cold, like ice somewhere, and he heard a coyote cry to the north. If they came close it would only be right to get up and shoot her out of mercy but he decided he wouldn't do it.

Perhaps that was the better way to go anyway. So fiercely natural, a tearing of limb then gut with teeth, instead of the sterile physics of another man's finger on a trigger. But too much like cattle, wasn't it. Dying too much like cattle.

A thunderstorm started far out to the east and the lightning touched down with electric hands, melting sand into strands of glass so deep in the ground that no one of these times would ever get to see them. If there was rain with it, it was too many miles from here to make a difference. He settled deeper into the blanket as the wind picked up. Out here the wind could come like something four-legged, like something plodding in drafted rhythm under an ox's yoke, or it could come like an ocean, a body that, if it had still waters, they were beyond your reach and not what you were made to breathe. If it were like an ocean tonight perhaps the girl would be washed away come morning, washed away with the whole history of it all and his tracking out here and his forefathers' footsteps across it years before alongside those of however many of the mules had made it this far into the journey. And if he awoke early enough to still see a bloodstain in the sand where she'd lain, then a few more rushes of wind would surely take that away as well, and then you could go home. You could go home, and it would not be like it had never happened, but in not being able to see it anymore it was still as if something had been undone.

He hunkered down deeper in the truck bed and told himself that it was the noise of the coyotes that kept him from sleep, not the knowledge of what they might do.

He awoke just before dawn, to a blade at his throat.

He drew back, but she had a hand firmly on his shoulder. Was straddling him in the back of the pickup truck and he could smell the blood that seeped from her abdomen. Felt at his belt for his hunting knife and it was gone. Still mostly dark, to an unadjusted eye, but he could see the slash of teeth in a half-slack mouth six inches from his face, half-slack mouth that was laughing. An amputated grin in the desert half-dawn.

"You son of a bitch. Ha, you piece of shit son of a bitch."

He inhaled and tried to pull backward again but her grip held fast and he waited a long time before he exhaled.

She laughed again and shook her head.

"Ah, you stupid piece of shit."

She leaned away and looked off into the west where her dragged tracks lay worm-like in the sand.

"Thank god, ah thank god."

"What do you want?"

Turned her face again to look at him, the gesture apparently as quick as she could muster but in its slowness came off as so cold.

"The hell you think? Give me whatever water you've got then drive me somewhere I can get bandages and iodine."

She rotated herself backward so that he could stand, and she leaned on his shoulder with the knife pointed at his neck as they walked around to the cab.

It was his old deer knife in her hand. Flipped open from the hollowed-out antler handle with a woodland scene carved into the side, a setting expunged from the memory of every animal and man and stone out here. The thing he'd used to gut so many meals and goddamn a four-inch blade why had the father left him with a four-inch blade.

She entered the driver's side first with the knife still to his throat and hoisted herself over the middle console and into the passenger seat without lowering her hand.

"There's nowhere's gonna be open yet."

"Doesn't matter."

She exhaled and leaned back and removed her arm from her stomach. Red and black parts came away with her hand. The shirt stuck to her across most of her abdomen. Bullet had passed flat along the surface from what he could see, and torn through a good portion of the muscle there, the fabric puckered and stuck to the span of it in an eight-inch slash of dark that cut from the center and delved to the left side.

Sand had glued itself to the damp where she bled and where she had sweated, and in the half-light it looked as if the shirt were patched with scales, her own or torn from another creature altogether. No organ damage if she was still moving but still too much blood for it not to be running thin.

He started the ignition.

"Where's your water?"

Smith nodded toward the back seat and remembered as he did it that the shotgun was back there. Lying on the seat, left unloaded. She put the knife between her teeth and hauled herself to lean into the back seat. He thought to lunge for it but knew she'd have the knife in him before he got it racked. Clenched his jaw and bit the inside of his cheek.

She brought up the first of the two jugs with methodical effort. Had not seen the shotgun. She took the knife out of her mouth and held it against the jug as she drank like something starved, then drew back from the opening and let the rest run down her shirt. It started to pool around her on the cloth seat in a darkish placental muck and he looked away.

"Drive."

He pressed the accelerator as yellow light sparked from the east.

He drove south because there didn't seem to be any way else to go. She kept her eyes locked on him and the knife close, her arm outstretched with her elbow rested on the middle console. She sputtered and coughed every few minutes, and the outside of her arm was cracked and blistered from dragging through the sand.

He could feel the sweat running down onto his eyelids. Knew the fever was starting and looked down the collar of his shirt and could see the threads of red beginning under the skin, reaching from the hole in the arm. Couldn't think yet. Just drive, man, drive.

The knifepoint was tight enough against his neck to make an indentation, and he would feel it go a bit slack when her consciousness would falter, and then she'd awaken with a start and dig it back in. He felt a surge of panic that he might die that way, by her jerking her hand like that. Dead because some kid couldn't hold her head up, with his father's hunting knife stuck in his jugular.

Could you kill her, could you kill her now. Leave her in the hot truck and make a run for it or take a grab at the knife at the risk of your own neck. Twist the knife into the wounded gut, make it feel the way he felt the flesh depart his arm and felt the cattle sink through the surface of his earth. He wanted the shotgun.

But his hands were going slick with sweat on the wheel and he drove on, and he leaned away each time her arm went slack. To the left the sun rose and fanned light across his exhausted sullen face and her sand-worn opened gut.

About forty miles out he saw a Walmart. She was still curled in a ball in the seat, watching him, her eyes calcified amber and furious even as the rest of the face hung off her cheekbones, the muscles there too exhausted for expression. She'd left the water jug horizontal on her chest after the last drink, and with each deceleration of the truck it rocked, sloshing a bit more onto her throat. He parked in a handicapped spot at the front.

"We're here."

"Is it open?"

"Walmarts always are." It was seven AM.

She suddenly became aware of the presence of the water jug and set it on the floor and slowly sat up while holding the knife to him, a feat he had not thought her capable of given her state during the ride.

She nodded to the door and he opened it and she crawled over the console to follow him as he got out. She had to hold herself up against the doorframe.

"Untuck your shirt."

"What?" He pulled it from his waistband and started unbuttoning it to give it to her.

"No. Just untuck it."

He did.

"Put your arm around me."

He bent his arm around her ribcage, found a grip away from the part of the shirt that stuck to the skin. Still it was wet and seeped against his fingers, fragmented between cloth and sand and muck and nearly pulsing in its amoebic mix of colors derived from black.

She transferred the knife to her left hand and slid it up under the back of his shirt, hand on his shoulder and blade against the ligaments there. She leaned hard into him and they walked in through the automatic doors, arms entwined and a slice of steel beneath.

The clerk at the entrance, withered woman of over sixty, merely nodded to them. A cadaverous pair spat from the desert was no spectacle to those who worked at a place where deer had been butchered in the parking lot.

They turned in a limp toward the back of the store, though it was not so much a limp as it was the struggling of a spider that was missing several legs. Not the imbalance of a limp but a series of errors in the patterned steps of a creature that still thinks it has a greater number of viable feet than it really does.

The white paint on steel shelves leveled out a sanitary smell, and the fluorescent lights chewed with a tinnitus hum. The tile floors were all washed or at least made to look that way, and the sand between their boot soles and the floor turned into a sheet of crushed glass.

The girl stopped and looked back over her shoulder to call to the clerk.

"Is there a pet section?"

"A what?"

"A pet section."

"There." The clerk pointed and went back to her needle-work.

Halfway to the back there was the whir of an electric motor and they froze. An overweight man in a camouflage sweatshirt appeared past the end of the aisle on a seated scooter, and gaped as he rode along until the next row of shelves obscured him again.

They passed a wall of algaed aquariums, beyond it a stand-alone wire rack of betta fish held in pint-sized cups. A few of them hung still, suspended as if in agar, like so many decorative foods. A solitary red one floated, fantail drooping in water that was slowly rotting green.

The girl leaned forward and started rooting through the white cardboard boxes of tank filters and water additives and fish food. Then she stopped. She shook her head and laughed, and looked about to cry.

"Ampicillin. My god, he was right."

She reached in and pulled an entire line of boxes onto the floor but the last box caught on the ridge of the shelf and she slipped. *Now.*

He yanked his right hand from her side and slammed her shoulder down. The knife caught in the back of his shirt as she fell and when it landed he kicked it but she swung her leg and caught him in the ankle as he did it and he went down onto the floor as well. She seized some final flare of strength and flung herself toward the knife but he grabbed her leg and she left a brushstroke of blood on the tiles as she skidded. Her shoulders crashed into the wire shelf and the cups of betta fish rained down on her and burst open like eggs.

She rolled onto her back to reach the knife and grasped it but he lunged at her and got her wrist and shoved it back and it slashed open a bag of aquarium salt above them and her fingernails went into his hand and he got on top of her and pressed the heel of his other hand into her bullet wound.

She gagged and spit out blood from the corners of her mouth and a bit of bile followed it and he pried the knife from her fist as he leaned in harder and at last got the knife loose and put it to her throat.

She looked up at him with her head against the steel shelving, the salt purpling the cut on her forehead and stuck like rocks to her cheeks and two colored fish working back and forth in her wet hair.

Her face was impassible; he knew she saw the killing in his eyes this time.

Smith started searching out the jugular vein, couldn't see it with the dust and sweat slathered on her throat. He could go through the existing wound into the stomach but this would be quieter, faster. She was saying nothing, clenched teeth and breathing through her nose. He took his other hand from her gut and brought it to her neck to wipe away the dirt, but when he overturned the palm he stopped and held it there.

It was black with blood.

The girl closed her mouth and stared at him. He folded the bloodied hand onto her jaw to steady himself. The girl's eyes flared and she gritted her teeth and tried to turn her face but the knife was still flush against her skin.

Smith looked down at the girl.

"You're dead if I don't get you out of here, and I might as well be dead if I don't get that money."

The girl followed him with panicked, animal eyes.

"You know I'll do it this time. And if I got up and walked away right now instead you'd bleed out within the hour or the cops'd get to you first. I'll give ya the same pair of choices as before."

She stared at him with something that looked like faith and something that looked like disbelief but without overshadowing the something that was always there of violence and she looked at the dying fish and boxes of antibiotics beside her head. Her breathing reverberated almost silently against the cardboard and through the static department store music. She nodded against the knife.

"Get me out of here alive and I'll get you what you need."

<hr />

When they had learned to shoot and excelled at it, and could gut and skin and twist the necks of the geese in the yard and the broiler chickens when they had them, the father taught them to build box traps. Box traps saved time, for you could leave them there in the woods and return to your work, but there was always a risk of capturing a possum or a skunk, and Wyatt and Lucy loved that part of it, that you could open up a box and out would pop dinner or stink-for-a-month.

There were no broiler chickens left this late in the fall, only laying hens, and you did not kill those if you wanted eggs this year or broilers next year.

They brought the Ruger with them, in case they saw anything on the way, and Wyatt gave it over to Lucy halfway in and she passed him the burlap of apple slices they carried to reset the bait. The father had mapped out the dozen traps on a piece of paper and brought it with him, which astounded the children, when the father knew every bramble and leaf and turn of those woods, and they at last grasped that the ranch really was that large.

The first five traps held nothing, the children bending over with their matching hand-shorn hair hanging down over their eyes when they stared upside-down, and the sixth trap was a false trigger.

They moved through the woods and it was far from the march of carrying the gun into the forest for the first time; the children had also learned how to silence their boots in the leaves. The three made a leaderless unit now, and each paused with cocked ears for the sounds of insect wings and bird beaks, backs bent as if they were perpetually about to crawl.

The door of the seventh trap was closed and the father nudged it with the toe of his boot and the inside of the box responded with a thumping against the back panel in blows like a heart against a ribcage.

"Lucy," said the father, and Wyatt knew the father was remembering his handling of their first ever hunting trip, and felt his cheeks burn as his hands went cold from not moving them.

They turned the box onto its end and heard the creature scrambling to the bottom and the father already knew it was a rabbit and not a skunk from the pattern of the thumping. He slid the door away and Lucy wiped her nose with one of her sleeves then rolled them up and reached in.

It was a good one, a cottontail of about eight pounds. She had one hand on its chest, its forepaws between her fingers, and the other hand supported its rump. It made no sound save its whiskers grazing her knuckles as it breathed. Wyatt averted his eyes as she shifted the rabbit's weight onto her hip to get a better grip. No sound came.

"Lucy." The father took a step closer.

Wyatt felt her eyes upon him, and even before he looked up he knew what she would do.

When he met her eyes she threw the rabbit from her arms. It hit the ground on its back legs and sprang into a jump and was gone.

"Lucy." It wasn't a yell from the father but an expression of pain. When one has gone without dinner enough times they learn that the yelling does not change it, and she heard it in her father's voice and covered her face. He put a hand on her shoulder and they went to check the remaining five traps, but all were empty, and the three walked back to the house before sunset, soundlessly not out of necessity but out of the habit that barred them from making noise in the woods, while the Ruger lay horizontal in Wyatt's hands as a dead thing but an inedible one.

There were no broiler chickens nor steers ready for the slaughter, and without a rabbit there was no dinner.

She climbed into his bed that night and had apparently already cried, in what he imagined as a forcing of the tears, choking them out like nausea into the pillow to get them out as fast as you could to get relief, and now she merely hiccupped. She grabbed both of his hands.

"I'm so hungry," was the first thing she said when she caught her breath.

Wyatt nodded. He was hungry too, but by now it was a blameless hunger, and he figured it would pass as the times before had passed and the times in the future would probably pass too.

"I'm so hungry!" Her hands drew back an inch from his and balled into fists.

"It's okay. I don't mind."

She shook her head, and they lay in silence for a moment, no lights on but the moths still sensed the heat from the house and batted against the window with wings like white open palms.

She shook her head again and then was gone out of the bed.

Wyatt awoke past midnight and crept down the stairs in his underwear, and at hearing the father's door he sat down on the bottom step as the father passed him and went into the kitchen and went behind Lucy and gently took her wrists in each hand.

"That's not how we do it."

The hen's neck was snapped and half cut off and she had cut it on the board without thinking and the blood trailed from the sink where it pooled and then dribbled back to the cutting board again. She was midway through plucking it.

She lowered her hands, and then wiped them on her pajamas already filthy with chicken-shit and hay.

The father took the chicken up by the destroyed neck and nodded to Wyatt and Lucy followed and they put on their boots and coats over their pajamas and followed the father to the barn where he took down a shovel from the wall.

"We can't do things that way if we want this to last."

The father was strong and so it took only two shovelfuls, and he laid the dead laying hen in the ground and covered it over with dirt and Lucy understood and took two pieces of hay from the coop and laid them like a cross over the mound. She turned her face away every time Wyatt came close, at last covering it with her hands until the father led her into the house.

There was a cottontail in the sixth box when they went to check them the next day. They could not tell if it was the same rabbit, or whether fate had anything to do with where their dinner came from. But Wyatt reached it first and Lucy turned its neck within his hands without a word.

⟢⟡⟣

Neither spoke in the wake of what had happened, so they went through the pharmaceutical aisle silent in their steps of three, a set of faux and drastically wrong conjoined twins once more. She nodded at the things she wanted as the lights beat upon them, and the gore-mixed black of her shirt was something else entirely in the face of the colored print of pill bottles.

By the time they reached the end of the aisle he'd pulled a half dozen rolls of cloth bandage, a roll of medical tape, a bottle of rubbing alcohol, and a bottle of iodine.

They hobbled to the only cash register open without breaking their connectedness. The cashier was a freckled blond teenager, with a bulge under his lower lip that suggested he was just learning to chew tobacco.

The boy blinked then stared when he saw the strain in the girl's face and then the stomach of her shirt, though it was black with the muck and no red was visible. Smith dumped the contents of his arms upon the conveyor belt.

"Good lord, what happened?"

"She's fine."

The cashier boy still eyed her and opened his mouth.

"Really. Nothin to worry about."

The girl stumbled and fell into Smith and it moved her closer to the cashier. They watched the change in his face when he smelled the wound and Smith realized they had made a mistake.

"I think I should call the police."

The girl raised her head to meet the boy's eyes and put a hand flat on the checkout conveyor belt.

"You don't want to do that."

"Why not?"

"Because I know your name . . ." She leaned forward until the credit card machine bent against her chest, to read his nametag through what was doubtless a blood-loss-induced blur. Sand came off at the base of the machine.

"Paul. That's it, Paul. And I'm not a person you want knowing of your existence, let alone your name, where you work, and that you drive either that 1984 Ford, the Bronco with a cracked back window, or that piece of shit yellow Honda I saw in the parking lot."

The cashier blanched and yanked his hands back from his checkout equipment as if it were that that he were being incriminated for.

"Now please let this man here pay for his items." At the end of her sentence she ground her teeth with the effort of standing.

The cashier nodded profusely and seemed to know the gesture was too much but continued it anyway and scanned the items with shaking hand and was nodding still even when Smith dug out his wallet and handed him a bill and his thumbprint upon it came away red.

"You wouldn't still be standing if you were in my position, would you?" The girl's voice was almost a whisper.

"What?" said the cashier.

"You wouldn't still be standing. Remember that."

Smith picked up the bag of supplies and the girl cast a last look at the cashier and then they went out. The cashier stood there, slack-jawed, the empty conveyor belt he'd forgotten to turn off rotating slowly and every few seconds overturning a child-size handprint of blood.

———◦◦◦———

Back at the truck Smith opened the door and the girl collapsed in the passenger seat. She pulled her shirt up slowly and as she lifted the fabric strings of meat came up as well. She separated her flesh from it with the other hand then yanked it away, looked as if to take the shirt off completely but the pained flexibility in the chafed arms stopped her.

It was a mess. The bullet's path was ripped across the front of the abdominal muscles like a shovel's trail in the ranch dirt of her skin. The tear was an inch wide.

She snapped the top off of the bottle of alcohol and poured it down. Stomach caved inward and she seemed about to drink from the bottle but he handed her the water jug. She leaned back into the seat and so he poured the alcohol again and then the iodine. She shuddered and spilled the water. The burnt sloughs of skin frayed from the mouth of the gash but the gash itself was clean. He pulled the bandage from the shopping bag and she snatched at it, wrapped it around herself with aggression but with a look of something like sympathy in her eyes. The first time he'd seen anything of mercy in her and it was self-directed. Wrapped it around four times and the rising of red through to the uppermost layer mushroomed like dread from underneath.

He passed her the second bandage and she used it as well and this time it stayed white. She dumped the boxes of ampicillin from the shopping bag and nested them around her lap as if they were something of comfort, some of them coloring from the seepage in the wet seat. She ripped open a box and started tearing the antibiotics from the blister seams and swallowing them in mouthfuls. After a half dozen she curled up in the seat and closed her eyes.

When she had not moved for several minutes, Smith took the iodine and alcohol bottles from the floor and held them between his knees, took off his shirt. The blood in the bedsheet bandages had dried but when he unwound them the cutout edges of the skin were circled in petals of inflammation. The moment he saw it he clamped the bandages back around it. Felt infection burning into them below his hand. He held them there for a while until he felt that the seeping had slowed and so he pulled the soiled bandages off and held them out and let them fall into the air through the open window. He rinsed the broken place and cleaned it, each falter of consciousness and grip of fever as much an infliction from her as the initial destruction of armflesh. Poured the disinfectants until it had gone numb with the stinging and bandaged it and replaced his shirt. No visible sign now of the rotting within him save the tracts of gold down his hand where the iodine had run. He reached over to the girl that was dying more slowly now and broke a sheet of ampicillin tablets from their blisters. She had not moved at the touch of the back of his hand when he'd reached for them, and did not move now when he tossed the box back onto her seat.

They sat there for an hour or more, Smith staring out the windshield at the empty parking lot watching sparrows pick at tumbleweeds of trash. The sun ran through the top of the glass and lit the dust in the air of the truck's cab.

For a long time there was no sound and he looked over at the girl. Curled up creature that he hated. There was a moment in which he feared that she was not breathing, that he had admitted so much only to have to bury the small bones in the desert, but then she sputtered and went silent once more. He waited, and as he dizzied again he feared they would dry like that, atrophy into sand in a cooking truck. And then, in a voice as if she had been spending the time gathering it:

"There's a place out there where they taught me to use fish antibiotics for gunshot wounds."

"How far?" His hands had gone numb and he looked at them, their anesthetized vibrato at pace with the turns of light through the windshield.

"Where are we?"

"Halfway down the state. Three hundred miles to the Arizona border."

She sat up just enough to see out to the road.

"Take Interstate 15 south until you hit 70 and then head west. Then the first dirt drive after the seventh cattle guard."

"What is it?" He was still staring out the windshield.

She halted for a half-breath against the bandages then answered.

"I got the directions from the last of the men on motorcycles. I've been looking for this place for a long time."

"The kneecapped one."

She nodded, without any show of reverence toward it, and took another breath, measuring how much it agitated the diaphragm.

"They'll be short on men with the breakup of the Cordova cartel. They might try to turn you away but if you don't let them, and you're as desperate as you seem, you can get it all back in a day's work for them. That's all I can offer."

"What is it?"

"What?"

"What work is it, dammit."

"You're not in a position to be worried about that."

He kept staring at his hands for a long time, looked up and stared out to the road for even longer. Then nodded and started the ignition.

In the four hours that followed neither spoke. His thoughts

were blank and he saw the light skin around his sister's cold eyes in the blankets of sand they passed, and the girl's thoughts he knew were bloodied, repetitions of the slash on her gut imprinted in the anarchic tracks of the cliffs beyond. He'd seen the way wild game looked at themselves when wounded, and knew it was her first major injury. First mortal injury.

He'd repeated the directions in his head until they were memorized and then marked off the landmarks in turn. The girl twisted every few minutes in futile attempts to get her wound comfortable but kept her eyes always to the road, never lapsing in awareness as the serrated shadows of red rock formations hunted across her face.

He hadn't noticed that the radio was on but heard it now. He reached to switch off the dial and realized it was too late to turn it off, that it might signal something. When he didn't want to talk and was damn well sure that she didn't want to either. He kept the truck pounding down the road while Conway Twitty crept again from the radio with that feeble humanness that belongs to songs made for dry country that is inherently without them. "Hello Darlin'" crossbred with static out the speakers and the girl enacted her slow-motion exorcism on the passenger seat.

Far onto Interstate 70 they passed the seventh cattle guard. The landscape had not varied for the entire journey and he would have suspected them of having gone in circles had the road not been so relentlessly straight. Scrubbings of dead brush crowded in the sun, bleaching under the sky, and buttes that split the sand like tumors and nothing more besides the lone man's longhorns that roamed the grainless plains, swinging the burden of their temples with each step across that wasteland like gear-laden men bound for war or dispatched from it.

The pickup truck shifted onto unpaved roads as the directions progressed, raising a cloud of dust like plumage behind it. By the fifth hour the pain was leaching from his arm into white larvae in front of his eye. He took the water jug from her seat and tilted what was left in it into the right side of his mouth without taking his eyes from the road.

It had been twenty miles since they'd passed the last abandoned plywood produce stand and a hundred since they'd seen a living man. The pain clouded in again to blind him and his forehead hit the doorframe and when he rebounded from it the truck was drifting.

Smith got out and the girl swung open her door but didn't move from the seat. The truck like a red beetle in a dish of sand and nothing else.

"Out of gas?"

He nodded.

She gestured at a ridge ahead shaped like a horse's back, darkened with ribs of bat guano in the shadows.

"It's just beyond there."

He climbed into the back of the truck and stood on the roof and looked out past the ridge. It emerged below in the heat—a dark brown line like a strip of bark on the land. A compound of a half dozen flat-roofed buildings.

It would be over a mile and the truck would have to stay in the center of what was still called a road all the way out here, another abandoned thing to add to the compacted millennia underfoot. He climbed down, leaving it.

He did not ask whether she could walk. He put his shotgun against his shoulder and began to stagger on. She waited a moment, then stuffed the sheets of ampicillin into her bag and slid from the truck like something without bones and trudged forward with both her arms wrapped tight around her abdomen.

Three steps into the sand and she was down. She looked at him from below the shadow of the arm that she'd braced above her head, eyes gone cervine, the blacks of them obliterating the yellow-brown. He hesitated.

"Don't you dare." She took another breath but it caught in the throat then dribbled out onto her hand.

He looked down at his arm. The bandages were soaked through with more than one substance and heavy like a weight on the skin. The pain dug in along the nerves like maggots.

She raised her head again.

"They'll kill you for this."

"Shut up." He turned away and began parting the brush with his boot, broken orbs of cacti clinging to it like smaller galaxies. Kicked a trench into the sand with his heel, then bent and used his right hand to dig.

"They'll fucking kill you!"

He laid the shotgun in the shallow grave he'd made then filled it in and marked the place with two rocks laid beside one another. The girl had curled herself into a ball again and he lifted her up coarsely, like livestock you've butchered but is too heavy to sling over an arm. And the newly made killer carried the demon-child with black beaded eyes through the desert, as her hair dried in bars across her cheeks and his arm began to drip rot down his side.

CHAPTER SEVEN

Scalp

The compound wavered in the heat like an ownerless shadow on the breadth of sand and as Smith approached it the main building came into focus, raw in unfinished wood, clearly hand-hewn and not one laid by trailers as most in that kind of country were. There was a cluster of uneven shacks with flat roofs at its right and to the left was a great building of glass, with vaulted ceilings that reflected the glare in an explosive landing of sun.

A man reclining in a yellowed plastic lawn chair below the building's overhang dropped his cigarillo and pulled a pistol from the back of his jeans at their approach. His front six teeth were white but shattered, and in their jaggedness took on the look of those belonging to child, canine, beast. His hair was matted into string-like dreadlocks that hung to his eyes, and stains blackened one of the embroidered skulls of his cow-boy boots. He advanced with the pistol extended by one hand, then lowered it when the girl lifted her head.

"You . . ."

The girl dropped from Smith's arms and landed in a crouch.

"Hi, Guillermo."

He flashed an uncertain expression that exposed the blackness behind the teeth and ran to clap her on the shoulders, gun still in hand. She raised her arm to ward him off then pushed aside the frays of her shirt to expose the bandages. A red fan was beginning at the corner.

"Shit, kid . . ."

She slipped forward into the dirt but he lunged and caught her.

"Yo what the fuck? Are you shot?"

She didn't answer. Guillermo cast a cursory look at Smith, who had his good arm braced against his legs, heaving, then slung the girl into a fireman's carry over his shoulders and ran beneath the overhang and into the front building. Smith hefted himself up and followed.

There was no threshold to the room and the dust pooled in from outside and continued hardpacked as the floor. Inside, the yellow-paned windows were stained by fly excrement and the walls were feathered with dried baskets stacked to the low ceiling, sheets of ribbon pinned and faded down the far wall. A Formica cashier's desk was blotched with sun discoloration like liver spots on a geriatric hand. Back to the left the ground turned dark and arched in muddied footprints below a plastic sheet door, and Guillermo turned there.

"Awan!" He shouted it and turned sideways to push aside the plastic slices with the girl's feet.

As he followed through the doorway steam stuck to Smith's face, his near sand-blindness washed over in green. Massive blue petals, marbled and cracked like the cliff faces of a hallucinatory desert, were crowded on the tables between leaves the size of horses' faces. The sun rifled through the roof in white but was dispersed by the cloudiness of the glass and so the room took on an aqueous glow. Orchids curled along the wall with water-rotted leaves and blooms he had never seen before hung arrogantly or crawled the shelves in magenta and were laid to waste, violet, on the tables sopping with wet.

Guillermo ran down row after row and when they reached the back there was a Navajo blanket on the workbench and he kicked it to the floor and unfolded the girl upon it.

His hand was on Smith's throat and his pistol to Smith's temple before the girl had fully hit the ground.

"What did you do to her?"

Guillermo's boots dug into the mud and Smith's back was against the glass wall. There was blood in Smith's mouth and the hand was jagged in its calluses, running with sweat that smelled like smoke.

"I didn't do shit."

"Then your people—"

"Not my people. She's in my debt. I brought her here to get repaid."

Guillermo was shorter than Smith but had the type of wild eyes that might squint or flinch but did not look away from things and had seen enough not to care about what they saw done henceforth.

"That a ransom?"

"A trade."

"What makes you think she's worth anythin to us?"

Smith jerked the side of his left hand up and caught Guillermo in the larynx and yelled with pain as he did it and grabbed the gun with his other hand and as the man bent over coughing Smith stepped astride the girl and pointed the gun down at her head.

"She worth anything to you?"

Guillermo still coughing and looking at him now with red watering eyes and a hand on the hurt throat. The girl looked up at Smith for a moment, then turned away.

"Tell me right fuckin now or I'll shoot." He could feel the socket flexing along the glass eye as he worked to keep his expression steady.

"I—" The man was visibly unsure.

"Right now."

"Good, good." The voice came from halfway down the overgrown aisle.

Guillermo stepped back against the wall and lowered his hands from his throat as quickly as he had raised them at the first.

The man was limping toward them, with a hand outstretched as if there were a cane that he leaned upon but there was not. The wear across his face was more a mark of weather than of time, though it was true that he was old. He wore a set of denim overalls with no shirt underneath and the hems bunched around the mouths of brown and blue cowboy boots. His ears were pierced with string and his hair cropped at the shoulder, and his arms laden with chunks of Navajo turquoise set against a crude span of hand-needled tattoos. He was missing two fingers off the right hand. He stepped slowly through the half-mud and knelt and looked the girl over with black eyes that had started to blue a bit around the edges from age and too much sun.

"What does she owe you?"

Smith stood, breathing slow, gun still aimed.

"Forty-six hundred dollars. For killed cattle."

"I can't give it to you. We have a shipment coming in tonight that needs to be paid for. Guillermo, help her."

Guillermo went to his knees and cut through the girl's bandages and wadded them up and pressed the bundle against the bleeding. Smith didn't move the gun.

"We're moving product in two days. Stay the rest of the day and we'll discuss your terms this evening."

Awan bent down beside the girl and then looked up once more at Smith.

"Put the gun down, son."

Smith stared at the old man, deciding, then put it in his back pocket.

"What happened to her?"

"Gang man shot her. Nine millimeter. Just grazed, there's no entry wound, no guts hit. Thirty-six hours ago."

Awan bent closer and turned her chin with his hand.

"Child."

Guillermo left the bandages where they coiled from her stomach like the stuffings of a crude doll and went to loom behind the man, as if there were shade in that room that was all light.

"How did you find us?"

She blinked and focused her eyes at him but did not speak. He appraised her and turned to Smith.

"When did she last eat? Has she had water?"

"Water. Nothin to eat."

"Her blood sugar's probably shot to hell," Guillermo spoke over the old man's shoulder.

"Get a piece of sugar cane from the storeroom."

Guillermo cast a last sideways look and went out.

Awan lifted the handful of bandages and they came away tissuey and damp.

The wound leered in a black open seam across her skin, still running slowly.

"Child, I'm going to have to stitch it."

She shifted and turned her head.

"No. It's been tended to already."

"It's clean but it's still bleeding."

"It's been tended to."

"Closing it all the way would do you no good but I have to put a few stitches in to slow the bleeding."

She turned her face to the wall of shelves and did not look back from it when he went out and Guillermo returned with a chunk of sugar cane and she didn't reach for it so he put it between her teeth and then the old man came back with a bent needle and plastic line and set to work.

Smith watched the closing of the fissure, realizing the bargain he had made.

When the stitching was finished he stayed behind the men until Awan came back for him and they went out together. Was half sure if he went through the door then turned around again that she would be gone and irretrievable, or he would be.

Awan spoke to him when he hesitated again on the threshold.

"I know. For all she does it feels safer to have her in sight than out of it." He went ahead of Smith. "We'll be eating soon. Come outside."

Smith followed him through the main building to a shed attached behind, dark and unlit, and strayed as the man walked through, cast his eyes about the room.

It was an equine run-in shed that had been laid with its original open side to the main building and fitted with a sliding door. It was large enough to fit half a dozen horses had it been put to its intended use. The shed's door to the outside, the building's only opening that had an actual wooden door with a visible lock, had been cut in line with the door to the main building, and this Awan opened and exited through, back into the light, but off to the left and in the further dark sat sacks of pesticides and chemical drums and two metal racks. The racks reached to the low ceiling and carried trays of green powder on baking sheets sheathed neatly onto their shelves. Beside them was a workbench lined with four tabletop mechanisms, things with steel funnels at the top and a handwheel and small output tray at the front. There was a metal cylinder the size of a pen lying next to them, a small tree cut in relief at its base, and Smith walked over and picked it up, turned it over. He set it down. Had suspected as much.

Outside, the land was flat and distance was an odd thing but a few yards off lay an enormous fire and a dozen dried stumps set out around it, the circle punctuated by a few harried plastic chairs. Beyond it lay a corral with four mealy mustang ponies, two gray and two skewbald.

Smith had not realized how many manned the compound. Some of the men dozed in the chairs, others drifted in and out of the fire heat on wasted legs, another hauled a hose between hardy-looking plants in cinderblock pots. All of them had faces awash with the desert, features carved as if of material not made to move, but yet they did move, with a weariness driven through them in the way that they worked without urgency but also without pause, and it was a weariness that appeared not as an affliction of the climate but of their own inexhaustion, wrought by some indomitability at the core.

Some of them spoke intermittently but they were gentle sounds that were washed away in the air.

A solitary blond man stood watching the fire and laid another log on it. His hair was shorn short in the crew cut style and he wore a dirtied T-shirt like most of them and was tanned

dark as any of them, but there was something about his expression that suggested it had not been rendered by years in
the sun. His eyes were darkened brown and his face nervously
lucid. In that environment he did not look afflicted but instead
appeared alien, something grafted. He could not have been
more than thirty.

In the heat of the day the fire was something redundant,
or perhaps something defiant. The men sweated around it but
still did not stray from it, as if to assert that the temperature,
the slow burn of the body out here, was nothing they feared.

An old woman in a woven poncho and dress went about
those at the fire with a half dozen tins of food carried between
the crook of her arm and the uncertain landscape of her chest.
Her hair was white, had the translucence of cobwebs, formed
a fog around her face then continued as a steely braid whose
plaits fit together with the rigid tightness of insect shells.

Awan was seated on a stump directly in front, looking at
the fire, and Smith went and sat on his heels to the man's right.
The old man pushed a dusted milk jug of water over to Smith
with his boot heel.

"I don't know who you are, but it's clear that wherever
you're from is far from here."

Smith took his mouth from the jug.

"I'm not—"

The old man held up a hand, a movement that was courte-
ous but incontestable.

"I have no intention of asking you who you are, and don't
believe it would be fair of me to require it of you."

Smith nodded.

The woman approached them empty-handed and Awan
spoke to her in a language that Smith did not know and she
went away.

A man by the fire was nailing a fresh sole onto his boot
and when he had finished he set the heel, foot inside, on a rock
edging the fire and leaned down and trimmed the outlying
pieces of leather with a bowie knife as they went brittle and
curled off in the heat.

Smith had consumed half of the jug's water and was pouring the remainder over his head when Awan spoke again.

"You're not afraid of her, are you."

Smith said nothing.

"You have my respect for that."

Smith lowered the jug and turned to look at him. The man
was sincere.

"I aint unafraid, I'm just pissed off."

"You don't know what you're dealing with, do you," Awan
said, watching him from under white-patched brows. "The
first time I saw her, she was ten years old, wearing a stolen
mink coat raked with mud. She'd tried to make up her face to
look older but the smears of blush and eyeblack were violent,
and her hair was matted and wild, as she came up through the
fog of that desert dawn carrying a man's scalp."

He stood and pressed his hands into the wrinkles of his
overalls, firmly as if to smooth blue-bleached canyons, then sat
again beside Smith.

The woman brought over two tins of an unidentifiable
food and set them in the sand and the old man ate several fork-
fuls and stared off into the expanse of land as he chewed, the
fire intercepting the view of whatever he saw out there. Smith
did not reach for the other tin. Could not enter into obligation
by taking food from them. He watched the man eat, hands hot
with hunger and throat cold.

"We were working in the south, down near Grand Stair-
case-Escalante. You know it?"

Smith nodded. Heard of it. Wind-ripped spires of sandstone and not a shred of grass nor life.

"We'd had our northern lab for a decade and a half but had just split from the Nation and were working with a group from Albuquerque for distribution. We sent one of our men out to pass a dealer a half kilo, but this time he met with a band of three of them and they were high and were it crack or crystal or both we don't know but they were uncontrolled and angry and when they saw that our man was Navajo they decided to rob and scalp him.

"A group of us were waiting at the top of the canyon road and he'd gone out and walked from there and three hours later we'd sensed something was wrong and took the trucks offroad ten miles out into the desert and then sent two men out further to scout for him and they came back dragging him by the shoulders to keep him upright and he'd been shot in the back and that was leaking too but most of all his head was a bloody hood. You know how head wounds are."

He paused here with a glance to the glass eye then went on.

"The scalping ended at his forehead and there was sand in the wound and he was losing consciousness and the two scouts dropped him there in our circle expecting me to declare him to be left for dead. The scalped man was curled in a ball there in the sand clutching the edges of his skin where it'd been cut but too afraid to touch his own skull, and I believe one man even grabbed a shovel from the back of a truck.

"With the attention on the dying man we did not see the girl approach and now some say that they saw her but I did not remember it. But Guillermo, he was still a teenager then, said that she appeared from nowhere or out of the dust and fog or from behind some mesa and had stood there and looked at the man, and then had said 'right,' and run off. Just one word, 'right,' and was gone. I didn't see or hear it. But twenty minutes later she returned through the gray clouds that were waist-high that morning after the first rain in forty-two days and she was carrying the scalp.

"Now, we thought it was our man's, of course. We got him back to the trailer we lived in then in the sand flats just off the reservation and on the way all our men had given up their shirts to slow the blood from his back now that there was a thought he might live and at the trailer we packed the gunshot wound and then reattached the scalp. Our uncle was still with us then and had been medicine man for the tribe and so he was the one to stitch it and it was as good a job as could be done and the man lived, though the top of his head was slightly skewed from then on. He worked for us another three years and was apt and aggressive at it, having recaptured the soul that his heritage had him believe had been momentarily lost. And then one night, he had a dream."

The blond man came to stand at Awan's shoulder and then Awan waved him off.

"Later, Matthew."

Smith watched him go.

"And he dreamed that the scalp that was sewn to his head was not his own. That the girl had come back with a scalp, but had never said whose scalp it was.

"And it was true that we could never be sure. His attackers were black-haired too, and who can know the back of his own head. But whichever is true, she proved she is a thing not of the earth that we know, and one whose ways no nature-fearing man should venture to interfere with."

He courted the remains on his plate with a tortilla.

"We saw her constantly after that, as we were firming up

ties with the cartel and shortly after they sent her to travel with us. She was with us for nearly a year while we built outposts through new territory. But no one knows even now why she was there on that day when it happened."

Smith said nothing. The sky was fanning with darkness like gangrene spreading and the fire threatened to overtake the sun as the primary light source.

There was the advancing sound of a diesel engine and Guillermo came jogging from the left wing of the conglomerated buildings.

"We got Chanel No. 5 comin in!"

Guillermo supported Awan by the arm and the two limped toward the front.

When they had gone Smith unbuttoned the top of his flannel and reached down the sleeve to check the arm once more. It was as it had been and he knew if the fever did not break soon it'd take his ability to stand. He buttoned the shirt again as voices returned through the doorway.

The wind-reddened truck driver was jawing as the men worked past him rolling steel drums.

"Now I can only give you four, that's as much as they won't notice."

The man was about to go on in his explanations but Awan stopped him and gestured to Guillermo who went back inside then brought an open shipping envelope packed with bills.

"Four barrels is what we agreed upon."

The men spun the barrels on their edges and lined them up against the back of the shed.

The driver finished counting the money and checked the serial numbers on the barrels once more and turned to go back through the building but paused at the doorway.

"Say, how about a sample for the road?"

Awan frowned but then nodded and Guillermo passed the
driver into the back room and came back with a few green
tablets and implanted them into the man's open palm, and
the man nodded and smiled a more ingratiating smile than
was justified and went off. Left Guillermo standing beside the
final barrel, drumming his fingers on its top. He caught Smith
watching him and half-smiled, jerked his head at the line of
containers.

"Safrole. On a perfume shipment an' he cuts a small bit
out for us. Fuckin Chanel No. 5, this shit was gonna become."

Awan came back over.

"Sparin no expense for this one, are you, boss?"

"No. None at all. Keep it moving."

The appearance of the safrole took over the direction of the
evening, unhindered by the arrival of the girl, and every man
rushed to flood the shed with gloved hands and set water baths
of powder and oil in racks above the bonfire two at a time.

The smell was acrid but most of the men did not heed
it though Guillermo tied a gray bandana across his nose and
mouth.

Smith watched them for a while as they funneled equipment between the fire and the shed and the blond man Matthew still charged with managing the fire and Smith saw now
why it'd been kept up at a consistent heat.

A yelp and a swearing half in Spanish came from within
the greenhouse and Awan stood from where he was crouched
giving directions to men beside the fire, with the oldness and
patience with which one would expect a tree to stand.

Smith rose and followed to the humid-sweat room of garish

floral. Guillermo and the blond man were already crouched at her retracted feet. She was lucid-faced, awake.

"How did you find us? Washakie is gone," asked the old man.

Washakie in Box Elder. North of home.

"I know, I went there first." She took a breath and the air entered and exited the motionless body as if by its own will and not hers. "I asked around."

The old man frowned.

"How many still know?"

"None of the ones I found. Cleaned them." She might have shaken her head but it was pinned by pain against the black and white Navajo blanket and so she spoke from a head that was ghostly still. Her hair was splayed in a medusal halo around her and the only thing that contrasted from the monochrome was the paling clay of her face.

Awan nodded. She had done right.

The blond man brushed a coil of hair away from where it had fallen in the girl's mouth.

"You'll rest now?" Awan asked.

She blinked hard, in a slow movement to reset the thoughts, then answered.

"Yes—but are you still making?"

Awan opened his mouth but it failed to conceal a moment's misgiving before his reply.

"Yes. We can do far more here than at Washakie. And when you are recovered you won't want for work, if that's what you came for."

The girl neither nodded nor voiced affirmation and instead let her eyes fold closed and her mouth lay itself out in a line of implacability.

There were five of them now, men left standing while

the force at their feet retracted into sleep, in that place with vaulted ceilings that became a house of worship for the wet that clung in droplets to its walls. With stalks past the height of arm's reach it was a place of obscuring, a forest that held hopes of things slouching in the darkness, because when you were made to fight them at last you would know for sure that they were there, and it would be an act of steady eye and steady earth, away from a desert where sand and light blended in a place with no hiding, only hallucination and a flail, where you are forced to war as much with your own blindness as with the thing clawing your chest.

One by one, they departed for drier grounds. Awan fell into step with Smith on their way out, the old one's careful limp at pace with the other's fever-wrought stagger.

"You know, she will recover," he said.

As much a warning as a prayer.

In the winters they'd made a constant fire in the stove at the heart of the pineboard house. Wouldn't let it go out for weeks. They were children then, and they'd curl like cats in front of it on old braided rugs and read from the family Bible, as the father was a man with small use for words or want for them and when his stories would run thin for the telling there were sparse other books in the house for them to turn to, and none provided so much epic as this one. The father had taught the children to read when the time had been right for him to do so, and now Wyatt would sit and read aloud still with his finger on the lines. There were nights that they ran branches like warhorses across the wood floor as Old Testament kings and there were nights they reversed to earlier pages after reading that those kings had gone to their doom, the sadnesses and failures taped closed with greasy finger stains, and there was one night in which Lucy asked if Cain and Abel were twins and he'd said no, they could not have been, that two halves of the same would not have gone apart like that. A soul don't break that way. And she'd nodded and held his hand tight.

But eventually they came upon Jacob and Esau, and those truly were twins. They'd gone to the father and asked which had the birthright but in their not truly believing in there ever having been a mother and the father never speaking on it they got no answer, and hoped that they were right and they were just one.

And they'd traced the verses with their fingers for hours, sneaking the book into Wyatt's room after both had been sent to bed, and when the last lights in the house went out with the father off to sleep and she knew he was still awake too she put the words to it and asked, "Which of us is Jacob and which of us is Esau?" And he had answered, "We're us and neither of us is either but we're both." And she replied that she would never take a thing from him or let him leave home and he said the same and they'd fallen asleep with their hands on the scripture, fearing that they were wrong, pressing into the paper with some rebellion against fate or with pleading or with complete passivity in their sleep and their legs intertwined to keep them warm.

He awoke before dawn and put the book away under the bed, her blue eyes black in the dark as she sat up to see. The world outside the pitch slick walls dark and frozen and violent with waiting. The book wasn't for them. Because they weren't twins they weren't two, they were fire. And a thing without edges.

Cold had fallen with the dark and they drew up chairs still a good distance from the fire; from ten feet away the heat was enough to singe the knuckles if they outstretched a hand. The old woman came around with plates once more. There were two dust-faced children playing in the dirt against the side of one of the outbuildings, barefooted and in frayed T-shirts and faded athletic shorts in sizes far too large, and they fell back as she passed.

The woman bent to give Smith a plate but he raised his hand against it though he was shaking from hunger-weakness.

"I don't want to be in your debt."

"Please." The old man said it with a host's cold evenness.

"No sir."

"It's not charity. I need more men."

Smith nodded and took the plate.

"I told you we would discuss the terms of her debt to you. In two days we will have our largest deal of the season. Three hundred thousand pills, to wholesale for three million dollars as there are no borders to cross before they're distributed."

Smith said nothing.

"We're selling to a Vegas man, Medina. For security, I used to contract out extra support from the Cordova cartel. I would have gotten at least a dozen more men than I have for a deal this size. The Cordovas have disintegrated. Whoever's left is making a grab at whatever property and operations they can get, suppliers included, and there's not one among them I can trust. Especially not now, with her here. You can never truly be a free agent in this world, can never stay truly neutral, no matter how you began, and now I'm out of men. I'm offering eighty thousand dollars cash, over two and a half percent of the take, for each man that stands beside me with a gun.

"The girl has already signed on. You could wait around and attempt to make your claim with her afterward, with one who has neither honor nor a sense of duty. Or, you could take one of the places yourself."

The old man watched Smith and Smith watched a wooden pallet go up in the flames and the nails go vertically into the dirt as the wood that held them crumbled like paper in the heat.

"You have been hunting this girl for a reason. If it's for the reason that you said, perhaps the money would fulfill the retribution you seek."

Smith shifted.

"I aint never committed a crime in my life."

"From what the girl has told me, you have killed a man."

"We thought he was an elk." He could not have stopped the words.

"I was told it has not been two days since it happened."

Smith's fist was to his mouth and he took it away.

"That was self-defense."

"Self-defense in a situation that is bound to turn violent, when you yourself decided you would be there, is not truly self-defense."

The old man continued.

"It is like going bear hunting, and when the grizzly turns on you and you shoot it dead calling it self-defense, when you were the one who went into the woods in the first place."

"I understand. I've killed, then."

The patricide. The son, the father. His son, daughter. No father. No father's son.

He wished the old man would say something but he did not. They waited in silence for a long time. A brindle-furred pup walked among the men, nosing at their plates, unaware of all of the other things that made the world what it was.

"Eight-zero thousand, sir?"

"Yes. For your standing as intimidation against any robbery attempts, and manning a gun to protect the men and to protect the product if anything should happen. Then you can go back to whatever corner of the country it is that you've run from."

"I didn't run."

Awan was silent.

"I'll need some time to think bout it. Sleep on it at least."

"As you want."

A shadow moved in the doorway of the building. A few of them paused, then Guillermo ran over to it.

"You'll tear your stitches you idiot." He went onto one knee to get one of the girl's arms about his shoulders and they shambled to the fire together.

"I was cold."

The featureless men around the fire looked back and dispersed slightly at the girl's approach, and when Guillermo set her down she folded herself against the ash-flecked dirt, beside the stones that rimmed the fire pit. Put her hand flat to one of them to take its warmth.

Smith watched them, unmoving, feeling outlandish to them but knowing he had just confessed to their leader that he was among them. Killer. Watched the men he feared becoming or perhaps was already. He felt another shot of pain from the arm and shuddered.

Awan nodded to where the bandage underneath deformed the lines of Smith's jacket.

"Is that what your fever is from?"

Smith flinched at his words but put a hand to his sleeve.

"You can tell?"

"It's a bad infection."

"I know."

"We can make a poultice that would cure it—"

"No," Smith shook his head, "I've got antibiotics."

He walked over toward the girl. There was something else in going to her now, less strength in the hands now that she was no longer a dying thing but an awakening thing. The others saw it as he passed. He crouched a few feet from her within the empty space they had left around her.

"What do you want?" She said it without moving.

"The pills."

"No, I mean what do you want?" She rolled over and took a packet from her bag and threw it at him. He took three and pocketed the sheet.

"You already know."

"Maybe not so much now." She opened her eyes. "Killing that man back there—you won't be caught for it, you know."

"I know. That don't hardly make a difference in it."

He sat further back in the sand and took off the jacket and removed his flannel. It was better, but not good. He pulled the messed bandages away and tossed them into the edge of the bonfire, where they curled black and fractured into ash. Washed it with one of the water jugs left out until it burned.

Matthew appeared at his side holding a rag. Smith took it and the man sat down beside him.

"Figured you'd need it if you're gonna do us any good later. Same people shot you as shot the kid?"

He wrapped the arm and the cloth was rough but nearer than the remaining bandages, in a dark unmanned truck a mile of emptiness away, and he put the flannel back on and buttoned it and mounted his jacket upon his shoulders.

"Nah it weren't."

Matthew turned his head, took out a can of chewing tobacco as he watched him. A little ways off from them the girl had turned over and unthreaded the plastic bag from her belt-loop. She untied it and reached out a hand to Guillermo and he handed her the knife from his belt, an antique push-switchblade.

The girl flicked open the knife and Matthew caught the twitch in Smith's face.

"Oh, shit." Matthew opened the dip can and passed it to him.

"You still aint told us your name yet." He spoke out of the side of his mouth, and his lips were chapped as if burned.

"I s'pose it's goin to stay that way," said Smith.

"Where you from, then?"

"Box Elder County."

"Don't know it."

"You heard of the box elder tree?"

"No."

"It's a type of maple, like any other of the maples on the outside. But if you damage it or stress it or expose it to fungus, nobody's sure what does it, when you cut it down the wood will be stained like blood inside."

The horses had clustered at the edge of the corral to see the fire and their eyes alit in the dark, the curves of their irises rippling like the fan-shaped fungi that grow on bark. He saw that the girl was watching him.

"Bloody red stain, just like flesh. So when you're choppin trees for your own fire you never know if you're taking down just regular wood or somethin that will open up like meat on the inside. All you can know is that there's bloody ones in your woods no matter what."

Matthew did not answer, and eyed the palms of his hands under the firelight.

Then the girl spoke.

"It's the opposite with men."

"What?"

"Some don't really bleed."

The girl went back to pulling stones from her bag. She took out forty at least, each small enough to fit in the hand, and laid them out in four straight lines. Most were crudely numbered, in etchings faded or fresh or packed with dirt. Using Guillermo's knife she set upon the ones that were yet unmarked.

They varied from sandstone to basalt, shale, and there was a chunk of turquoise and a trilobite as well, and with them the rabbit's jaw. Its leather cord had been ripped off. He watched it, so far from home, knew it was not yet time to take it back.

The moon had risen and obliterated the swath of stars around it but the rest toed slowly along the horizon as the earth spun with the progression of the night. Men still stirred about the fire, passed unmarked bottles of whiskey around.

The girl continued working on her stones, lying with her back propped against a stump and studying them in turn, a rolling in the hands and bringing to the nose that told not composition but memory, before scraping a number onto its face in slow but precise method with the knife edge.

After a time one of the younger men, a teenager with long hair and one deformed ear, leaned over to the girl.

"What's all this here for?"

She stopped and set down the trilobite.

"The rocks?" As if the boy might have asked her purpose in this place in this country in this world.

"Yeah."

She stuck the knife into the dirt.

"To leave my tracks across the earth."

"How so?"

"For those who weren't born with the arms to move mountains, what other way would you mark your passage on the earth than by at least moving the smallest stones?"

"That don't change anything though."

"By whose standards?"

"Anybody's."

She picked up the trilobite and threw it to him and he caught it against his chest. The men on either side of him bent in to look at it.

"That thing's been traveling three hundred million years so far. And the only thing that managed to move it before I carved it out of a rock were the continental plates."

He held it up to the light, eyed it, and tossed it back. '724' was scrawled into its side.

She caught it with one hand and turned it over in palms so washed over with dust and blood that they had gone lineless and smooth, like gloves of wine-colored kidskin.

"Things that have traveled thousands or millions of years until they get to you and then you throw their fate. That's the greatest hand any man could have on history," she said.

"But you got bones over there too."

She picked up the rabbit's jaw in response. Not yet numbered.

Smith knew Matthew was watching him again.

"You think that counts less?" the girl asked.

"Nah. Not if you're the one that put them there."

"You equate taking a life to bending the path of something a thousand years old."

She considered for a moment then spoke again.

"It's an interesting thought, leaving your stain on the earth as a trail of bones. Ones that wouldn't have fallen in that place if it weren't for you."

The teenager nodded.

She picked up the knife and continued.

"But who would do a thing like that. Would you?"

"I might. If the justifications were there."

"But then there's no point, if it's something you would have done anyway. True violence has no reason behind it, but killing when it's justified is a byproduct of life. Like leaving behind waste or the bones of a chicken you had to eat. No more than any other man did before you and will do after you and so on until they're all gone."

"That one there's a rabbit aint it?"

"It is, but that one means something else."

She pulled the knife back from the dirt and set into another stone. Matthew spoke up.

"So would you say that what a man does counts for nothing unless it's beyond what he has to do to survive?"

"Not entirely. Everything's done for survival to some degree. But there's a difference between killing a bird that you'll starve without or killing a man who's got a knife to your throat and killing a calf that will feed you for a week or killing a man who will probably come back for you with a rifle inside of a month. The man who has a knife to your throat has brought his bones to that place knowing he might leave them there for good. But the man who is gradually readying a bullet for you will not see it coming if you get to him before he thinks to go for you. You always have to survive, but sometimes you have the foresight to survive so much that you move bones."

Most of the men were listening to her by now. The way in which she spoke was foreign to them in both its words and articulation, and its alienness made it as unquestionable as the divide between her appearance and the unfounded otherworldly voice.

The teenager with the deformed ear said shit, the only bones he'd move were these shit horses that kept going down in the desert, and Guillermo nodded to what the girl had said in a way in which the others could see that he did not know but understood. Matthew got up and placed another log on the fire and retreated as silently as one could behind a landslide of sparks and the girl continued on with her numbering. After a time, Guillermo rose and crouched beside her as they talked in a low voice.

The two children had spent the evening pestering the horses and sat at the edges of the fire now toying with a small calico kitten that squirmed in their grasp. The younger one, no more than five, lit a stick in the fire and commenced lighting its whiskers until it struggled away from them.

The girl paused in her speaking and unfolded her legs from where she sat and stuck out a foot to catch the kitten in its path and gently kicked it upward and handed it back to the boys.

The children clutched at the kitten and ran off but when the animal stumbled back into the firelight an hour later all of its whiskers were gone and its tail broken off and cauterized black and bloody at the base.

Awan had gone back into the building, and Guillermo had heard what he needed to hear from the girl or had heard as much as he could stomach and had taken a seat on his haunches by the woodpile. As she rested with open eyes they went black against the reflection of the bluing embers and when she shut her eyes the pupils appeared to continue in their darkening below the lids.

After a while the men drifted one by one from the fire and then collectively in groups or in chunks and Smith did not know where they slept, whether it were dark corners of the store or in absconded areas about them dug into the sheet of sand. The woman came again and ferried the children off into the dark toward the outbuildings and they grudgingly went, with blackened hands stuck with grime and sand and bits of fur, and one of them sucked its thumb.

When the last of the men had gone, Smith took the sheet of antibiotics from his pocket, removed two more, and outstretched the sheet toward the girl, an offering to she who still sat with her legs crossed on top of one another, a dead desert saint. She opened her eyes, and took it from him.

"You said some men don't really bleed."

"Did he bleed?" She said it quietly.

"Not on me."

She watched him for a long time, then turned her face back toward the fire and closed her eyes.

Before morning he awoke by the dying fire smearing its smoke into the sky light of the coming dawn and the girl was gone. He found Awan on his pallet bed behind the counter in the main building and went to touch the man's arm but the man's eyes were already open.

"I'll do it."

———◦◦◦———

She'd gone back to her own room when he left, but last night she had gotten too cold, and so Lucy ran down the steps with bare feet after sleeping in his bed alone for the first time. But there was still no one there in the kitchen, so she went back upstairs and laid back down in the bed. Still kept her head to that isolated corner of the pillow he didn't use.

"What are we gonna do, Wyatt?"

And then to fill the silence of the one that was not there beside her she spoke again.

"We can stay like this forever, caint we, Wyatt?"

And she smiled and nuzzled her face further into the pillow, then smudged her lashes into the cotton at the knowledge that behind her in the bed there was no one there.

An hour later she ran down the steps again, taking the pistol from the bedside table, and skipped breakfast because she didn't want to open the cabinet and remember that there was one less cup now, and she laced on her boots and ran out to the cattle, while behind her upstairs the skins gasped and swallowed the fifth day's salt.

She stood among the cattle in the field, and there was a sound from within the woods and Wyatt was not there and she leveled the pistol at the aimless green and found that she was only used to firing a shotgun, that when her right hand held the pistol with bent elbow the left arm had extended to carry the weight of a barrel that was not there. The swooping veils of an owl's wings unfolded into the air above the pasture, the nightbird chasing sunrise too late. She lowered the pistol, sat down in the grass, and stared out at the green like a prayer or in submission. That there was something of defeat in that firing a shotgun was ingrained perfectly in the muscle memory of her arms.

Part Three

CHAPTER EIGHT

Too Many Demons in the Desert

He was given a can of gasoline from the storeroom and began the hike out to the truck. The sun had not yet breached the mesas that crawled the horizon but the light was enough that the visibility was good. As he passed by the ridge that was shaped like the horse's back, he turned to look at the compound. In the matte air of sunless morning the greenhouse sat as a leaf-colored prism in a wash of ground without color. Like a pocket or a casing, filled with the only thing left alive in the desert. He wondered if the sense of it was something you could survive off of. Whether the men here had sought it dead already, or the drying death had been an act of the landscape upon them. He could see no one. He turned back to the faceless cliffs.

Thirty seconds later he stopped again and turned around. Guillermo was behind him, taking heavy steps with a shovel and an armful of black wires. Smith waited for the man to catch up.

"If I was a coyote I'd a eaten halfway through your leg before you seen me."

Smith took up one of the black boxes that had fallen and started on.

"Woulda heard you a hundred yards away up in the woods. Aint know why it's different out here."

"That's 'cause in the woods, huntin is a matter of hearin a hundred sounds at once and figuring out which it is you're trying to find. Out here it's a matter of quieting your mind enough to hear just one."

The truck was in sight, undisturbed. They walked on unhurriedly, and Guillermo lit a cigarette and talked around it.

"So, you named my gun yet?"

Smith took the pistol from his waistband and popped the cartridge open and passed it back to Guillermo by the handle.

"She's all yours."

They reached the truck and Smith began filling it, looked for the place where the shotgun was buried and marked it in his mind.

Guillermo laid out the wires and untangled a few as he stood there.

"Motion detectors," he explained. "For under the cattle guards on the road. Radios back to the place. Rain took em out two days ago, otherwise yall wouldn't have made it near as close here as you did."

He lit another cigarette and started to rewrap them as Smith closed the gas cap. When Smith turned for the doorhandle the man slammed a palm to the edge of the truck bed.

"I followed you when I seen ya out here to tell you one thing. You aint taking your chance and runnin now, are ya?"

"I'm not runnin."

"Then I gotta tell you one thing. You gotta know it."

"One thing." Smith repeated.

Guillermo switched the dead cigarette for an unlit match between his teeth.

"You're disposable now. Whatever use that girl had for you up until this point, she's done got her worth out of it, she's in a place now where she's safe and can get work. There aint no more reason keepin you alive if any situation arises in which it'd serve her or suit her to kill ya. Those situations always arise. Awan aint safe from it an' I aint safe from it, if she ever stops havin a use for our organization. We seen the method she used in gainin rank with the Cordovas."

Smith's hand tightened on the truck door.

"It's a risk of our industry, but not yours. We need her now, and it's better to have her for you than against you. But yer free for the moment, remember that. If I was you I'd run while I can."

Smith swung up into the truck and Guillermo started on past him toward the cattle guard. He started the engine but after a moment he called out the window.

"Why a greenhouse?"

Guillermo turned around.

"We have to provide a viable surface operation if we're gonna hide the other one. That's what Awan says. That's why we got all this shit to make the place smell nice."

"All the work just for that?"

"Nah." The day was warming and beads of dirtied sweat had striped Guillermo's face in narrow bars lighter than the rest of it.

"Those bitches are all way high maintenance to grow here. All a us say we coulda done with just a few shitty perennials to throw the police off. But Awan wants those. Authenticity is what he calls it. But we all know what he actually does it for an' he knows that we know."

"What does he do it for?"

"Because he can. Because then he can make things that the sand and the desert don't want him to make."

Guillermo shrugged and started walking again.

"Awan's got his flowers but at the end of the day god bless him he's got his ecstasy formula right."

"That so?"

"Yeah. More than anythin else I know."

Smith rested his forehead on the wheel for a long time after Guillermo's silhouette had receded into the white light of the open plain. An equidistant and limitless emptiness on all sides of him, save for where the girl traversed the arterial shadows between the fire and the compound like a clot. He raised his head and lowered his hands and drove back over the road that was not really a road, for the first time with a full belief in blood.

⸺◦◦◦⸺

When they were teenagers they had long been taught to butcher livestock and hunt full-size game, and in the spring in which they turned fourteen there was a bullcalf born with which something was not quite right. They'd watched it for a week, observed its walk and whether the pigeoned back right hock was a severe enough impediment. Whether it lent itself to the crippling of the hip. And at the end of the week the father said that yes it had to be done and asked that they would do it and it was not an unusual task for them and more often one of them would have been asked to do it alone on the hunt or in the hog pen but it was a calf and too heavy for only one.

Lucy had roped it first and led it by the nose into the barn and she'd covered her eyes when he shot it though she'd seen the like and done it herself many times before but still shied from it when she had the chance but she was upon it as fast as he was when it went down with the shot and they'd laced the rope across the rafters above and threaded it through the Achilles tendons and hoisted it up.

The barn was warm at night, the walls of the ground floor cut into the bank of the field's slope, the ceiling bending low under the bales and equipment above, and the corners packed high with timothy hay so that it seemed more a nest than a place with edges, and he'd set the lantern on the top beam of a stall and they'd set to work.

She made the first incision since she was quicker and more precise than his blundering teenage hand and she went around its back to work on the hide with Wyatt at the underbelly.

He leaned around the upside-down calf to speak to her.

"Don't it ever freak you out, doin this stuff? When it's just the right size to be a man?"

She didn't take her hands from the hide but looked back at him, her eyes algaed with green from the flame of the lamplight.

"It don't freak you out more when it's a rabbit? Somethin so small it never had a chance."

"I was just sayin."

He turned back to his work and their voices vaulted to one another over the splayed bare hips of the calf.

"It's always worse when they're small."

He didn't answer as he worked his knife down from the pelvis and she went on.

"It aint real anyway. There's always more of them to do and as long as we live there's gonna be more. Couldn't handle the cutting up if I thought of it as real, thought of em havin blood and guts instead of just colors and smells."

"Aint real?"

She yanked down the hide below the shoulders with two hands but was expert in her movements and it did not tear.

"You done guttin that thing yet?"

"Gettin there. Hold up."

He looked around the carcass at her again and a piece of hair fell into her face and without a thought she wiped it back and her hand left a four-inch smear of calf's blood across her cheek. He pushed the knife downward further with one hand underneath the skin and the other gripped overhand on the handle but did not keep his fingers well enough away.

"Shit!"

He stepped back as the bag of entrails went out and then split on the concrete and he jerked his cut finger to his face, the knife still in his right hand.

She was against him before he looked up and he could smell the hay on her hair like on a barn cat's fur and smelled the vague maple of her skin and felt the heat of her above any of that and her face close beside his, and it was all him, it was all him at the same time and he realized he was at once two people, and how antithetic to loneliness was it to occupy two bodies at the same time. She drew the cut finger into her mouth and took the blood but it was already hers and so she was merely preventing them from spilling it and her hair was in his face and as it dragged across his forehead it made it feel raw and her hands were cautious now. After a moment she took his finger away and pressed her thumb against the cut on the seam of his fingerprint. It had slowed in its bleeding and a last bit ran around the edges of her thumb.

"I thought you said it aint real."

"That there is real."

———✦———

He watched the greenhouse closely as he drove up, and its green seemed to mount higher at his approach before the sun crystallized it and it all turned white.

Out back the men had busied around the fire again and the smell of cooking fat blended with the nasal burn of the chemicals. Matthew was manning the fire once more, and Awan was giving directions crouched in the shade of the woodpile. The girl was walking.

She moved slowly, with a crane's gait of placing a foot and then the weight after it, but still she was up and circling the yard, as if the wounds of the day before had been no more than a surrealist's take on the landscape. She had on a new shirt, another T-shirt of black, not bullet or travel-wracked but still a worn brother of the first.

The teenager with the deformed ear emerged from the set of buildings, carrying a bottle of whiskey and a boxcutter, and went directly to the girl.

The rest of the men were working in the yard now, back at the synthesis that had begun the day before and now there were plastic crates brought out and filled with the powder and laid out along the wall to dry for the simple reason that there was no other place to put them and even outside there was no attempt to hide them.

Matthew came and sat next to Smith, passed him a pan of breakfast.

"I offered to do it, but she wouldn't let me."

The tattooed boy took the lid from the whiskey bottle and sat down beside the girl. She leaned back and he reached the boxcutter into the flames then ejected its razor blade and only in his motions did Smith see the seriousness of it.

"She's gotta cut out the necrotic stuff; a surface shot like that one makes a mess of it. You're not the only one rotting out here."

Smith watched her from above his plate.

"What is she?" Felt for the first time it was a question that could be asked.

"Her father was a leader in the Cordova cartel. Wanted a son of course but when she wasn't he didn't care and raised her like a boy anyway, and so she learned all that their boys did. Before she was eight years old he began taking her on drug runs, either to protect her from what would happen to her if she were left alone at the compound or to capitalize on the security she could bring to his dealings, we don't know. Even cartel men are less inclined to cheat or kill when there's a small child present.

"But naturally things still went to shit in some of their dealings, and the girl saw a lot and saw it early, even though he always protected her. She grew a knowledge of fighting and of guns and of how men act under the influence of desperation and fear. And when she had occasion to put that knowledge to the test, she proved she was a prodigy. After that it was encouraged, and the kid-daughter that normally would have been doomed to become a drug mule instead became a paid killer, and the maker of the kind of destruction I'm sure you've seen firsthand by now."

Matthew laughed when he finished telling.

"Of course, that's just what I've been told. Any man out here who's seen her with his own eyes believes every story about what she's done and not a word about where she's come from. There are too many demons in the desert not to count this one among them."

The girl had pulled up her shirt and was undoing the band-ages. The crude stitching was caked with blood, and the lines of it made darkened track-marks strung almost arbitrarily over the wound. The dead tissue at its borders had gone black or near-black green, and the odor engendered a physical recoil from the boy but Smith sat too far off to smell it.

The girl pulled the shirt up a bit more so that she could see it well. She ran a finger over the frayed skin at the edges of the tear, then started at the left edge. Working the razor blade in parallel to the flat of her stomach, excising anything that had gone necrotic from the heat or the force of the shot.

Smith put down his plate and pushed it to the side with the sole of his boot.

"Where are they now?"

"Who?"

"Her cartel."

"They're gone."

The boy crouched watching her there with reverent black-rimmed eyes.

"The Cordovas had most of the territory here—hands in Phoenix, Albuquerque. A quarter of Vegas. Within two years she'd worked her way to be one of their main runners and went out for special hits. Her reputation alone made them more than a few deals that would have otherwise been shot out. But they had too much power, or territory maybe. All of those in the top ranks came to believe they were gods be-cause they could break society's rules, and break them more smoothly than any of the other fugitives out there. It was too large of a network dependent on a few whose egos had come to manhandle their decisions.

"She wasn't one of those of course. She doesn't have an ego, only action. But the result was a culture of control, a nearly feudal power structure. She wasn't a decision maker but someone they sent out whenever they needed things to happen. When she saw that her superiors were replaced only when violence took them out—because no one is fired or quits in this business, they're only 'dispatched'—she saw her means of climbing the ranks.

"Her abilities aren't backed by reason, and she took it too far. Six weeks ago she killed four of the Cordova bosses at their compound along with everyone else present, and razed their supply route for methamphetamine. The very cartel she had meant to run was brought to its knees. In the weeks after, while the mid-ranks fell into a mad rush for power, she went through and extricated every desert and suburban Cordova stronghold she knew of. They weren't all on her side, and it didn't always work. Rival cartels smelled the blood and poached the small-scale city dealers and left those still loyal to the Cordovas either for dead or for the police to pick up, which is worse. The entire cartel dissolved."

The boy jumped back as the girl swore halfway through the cutting; she had not made a sound beyond a hiss until then. He stepped back toward her after a moment and poured a swig of whiskey into her mouth.

"So she's a free agent now?"

"She's running."

Smith nodded.

"A few of the old bosses didn't die. They were radioed from the compound while out at a meeting. Her father's one of them. He's leading the manhunt for her now."

The boy leaned in again with the whiskey and she waved him off.

"It's not that she fears them or had any unbreakable ties to the Cordovas in the first place, besides her own blood and she hardly seems to believe in that. I'd guess she tracked us down not for protection but for work. She wants to survive by her own ways, but in these parts and by what her ways happen to be, it would mean working for another cartel, by any definition an enemy of the Cordovas. Which she would do if they would have her, but whether they would is still to be said. Her skill is valuable, absurdly so, but cartel men are as vengeful as they are violent, and they've seen her kill as many of their men in a desert battlefield as they've seen her lure into a bedroom and leave with snapped necks."

"She can do that?"

"She can do anything."

"She couldn't kill me."

"And how do you figure that?" Matthew smiled without anything of kindness in it.

"'Cause she tried and she aint done it."

"Then she aint tried." He nudged the heel of his boot toward the firepit until the rubber smoked gently. "She believes in an immortality gained by taking away others' when they play their lives against hers. She's already gotten it—she's already immortal at this age, untraumatized and unabused, given the fate of any other skinny brown girl born in whatever floorless shack or wilderness she came from."

When the girl was done the edges bled but only softly, and what were left were neat pink lines framing the black ends of the stitches. She went to replace the old bandages but the boy went inside for new ones. Leaning forward she threw the amputated skin into the flames, three jagged lines of grayed bloody tan.

The boy came back with fresh cloth and she tossed her old bandaging into the fire as she had the pieces of her flesh and she rewrapped herself and sat for a while, with no intention of standing.

He watched the exhalations of breath that she performed with patience, not pain. Smith's own body something of rotting and of something undoubtedly missing and this girl so much more bullet-wracked and still alive and alive hard enough that she might heal. Watching the body that was wrought as if by strength of will over chemical reaction, reawakening in antithesis to the desert's calcifications. The body with which his war would be over come this time tomorrow, vanished in a flourish of dust to the south and to the north, behind his truck, toward home. He crawled to a space of shade behind the woodpile and at last felt safe enough or cared little enough about his own mortality to sleep.

When he awoke the day was nearly past and he awoke to the sounds of the teenage boys arguing as they mucked the corral.

"Why does anyone have horses out here anyway? There's only one direction to go besides nowhere and it's going away from something. The only reason there's horses in the West is for you to find em when you're on the run."

"It's 'cause you caint ride for shit."

"Just 'cause you can ride aint mean you got anyplace to go."

Smith stumbled up and the boys ignored him. He went back to the fire.

Guillermo was laughing at something the girl said and the fire smelled of spilled gasoline and liquor. The hardware and grates had been cleared from it. The perpetual fire, a light that gave nothing in a place where men were not sure whether it was the combustion or the heat of the day that made them sweat, yet they fed the fire nonetheless. The old woman was going around with plates again and Smith took one as he passed and went to sit beside Awan.

Guillermo and the girl were across the fire and it was with scant words of Spanish but mostly the language of the Navajo men there in which they talked, and the girl's words held weight even when muted and made Guillermo nod solemnly, expressions flashing iterations of the broken animal teeth.

Smith spoke to Awan first.

"What is she telling?"

"Stories of her childhood."

The other men had crowded around the heat, crouching in the shadow like a leaderless pack of wolves. Their eyes shone out of dulled sockets as if disembodied from the melting exhaustion of their faces, with a sense of something like excitement or hope.

"There's something that caught you when I asked her how she found us. What was it?"

Smith drew back from his food, watched the fire reflected in the whites of the old man's eyes.

"I know Washakie."

"So you're from the North. Tell me, is the desert something of discovery for you?"

"No. It's somethin I've always known. Even in the North you feel it there." Had known it and felt it and watched it wash up over the edges of his land even when he was young enough that he hadn't yet inherited it or understood its weight on his fate.

"Men think they know the desert like they think they know violence. But they're always wrong, on both counts."

It was dark, and in the cliffs far beyond something growled, a sound grating against back teeth that were already cold, the voice strained and mineral as if it had come from the stones that lined all of the stomachs out there that had thirsted for too long. The two teenage boys sat with the whiskey bottle and tried to imitate it, to get it to call out again.

Awan and Smith watched the girl by the fire, the sparks expiring in the air above her hair and her breathing so still that it would suggest she was more of earth than of man. Her face bare under that light looked like something yet unborn and Smith realized it was more familiar when painted. And he thought of the rough-stitched slash riding below the black T-shirt at each breath but half-believed were he to lift the shirt it would be gone.

After a while Awan got up and the girl moved to sit in close confidence with him and they spoke in whispers as she listened like a student and gradually the hollowed men at the fire retreated to the buildings and to sleep.

All went quiet. The stars' light collided at the edges of their auras, veining the sky like a sheet of shattered glass as the fist of the earth recoiled from it and turned, pausing until it would bash up against the atmosphere to create the constellations once more after the coming day. These places that were beats between violence, that foretold it and had the mark of past violence upon them, where the enactors of it sat and told stories of the things they had seen but never of what they had done and would soon go and do more that they would also not tell.

The girl had curled into her place of dirt by the fire and Smith went to his truck. He rolled down the windows and lay down in the cab, put his jacket underneath his neck. Lucy was so far. So far from the nights when, sensing her gone from the room beside him, he'd dress and go downstairs to find her on the floor of the sitting room, where the moon ran through the window and colored the carpet in violet and navy and she'd sit hugging her knees behind the splotch of light with her bleeding fingers in front of her, and would look up at him and say, "It was like he was here, Wyatt. He came right in here and I tried to show him my hands so he'd know—" and he would kneel opposite her and she'd thrust her arms into the space below the window and the light would drape them in the colors of flowers that kill when eaten. And he'd reach out a hand to hers, and she'd crawl back sometimes and sometimes not, and they'd go to sit against the wall below the windowsill, washed in watercolor.

He woke up a half dozen times in the night, in a fevered half-consciousness that the girl had slipped away and left, not knowing why it was that he cared whether she had gone or not. Twice, he knew she was there. Three times, he got up and went to find her curled by the fire and could not tell if the exposed eye not pressed against the sand was open or merely painted black with the side of her face. Each time he had stayed too long, looking. And once, before dawn and between these times when she feigned sleep or really slept, he could not find her. And then, in a shift of clouds, he caught her outline seated atop one of the skewbalds– a black figure of tiger's glowing eyes, steering a behemoth's shadow below the moon.

Inside the toolshed, dark-faced men worked tirelessly at great vats of green powder while others tore open brown-paper sacks of chemicals and emptied them like bladders into the oil barrels used for mixing. The ones with smaller hands turned the rungs of the pill pressers until the calluses were bored through on their fingers but it was dark and they did not see the blood when they wiped their damp hands upon their shirts.

CHAPTER NINE

Time to Run

They were to leave at first light, and noise ran among all of the buildings in a roar as they worked and at last they had left the fire to go out. The shed was cleared out and only half a safrole barrel remained. The men had placed a sheet of plywood to close the front doorway of the store to fend off the sand-saturated wind and they were talkative now for the first time, rambling and shouting out orders as four worked with scales and gloves counting out pills and weighing them to verify the count and ferrying them down the line of tables that they'd pulled from the greenhouse, to more men who packed them into bags.

They took four trucks in total, two pickup trucks and two jeeps, leaving Smith's since his was without a false plate. There were sixteen men including Smith and the girl, the old woman and two children the only ones who remained on the property.

When the sun rose they set off, and the old woman did not stand in front of the compound to see them go. As they trailed their vehicles onto the dirt road the brindle hound was beating a line in the dust of the lean-to as it paced back and forth.

Smith rode in the back of a jeep with Guillermo, with the oiled TEC-9 that had been shoved into his hands and an extra magazine stuffed behind his belt.

They were headed down to the top of the land that encompassed Monument Valley, south enough for there to be mesas to mark their path by but not so far south that a stray hiker would ever stumble across. Awan and his followers had left the Navajo Nation but not abandoned it, Matthew had said, and for whatever protection from the cartels Awan could give them, he was repaid with use of the lands from which tourists and law enforcement would be deterred on the days he required. They would have a place of goliath sandstone shrines to obscure their dealings, where the rock was great enough to intimidate men, though both teams would arrive fully equipped to slaughter the other.

The line slowed as they went over the cattle guard that marked the mouth of the greenhouse's dirt road.

"I guess you done noticed Awan aint got any cattle." Guillermo dropped his cigarette on the floor as the jeep bounced over the panels and picked it up, then gave up and threw it off the side of the jeep and into the dirt.

"Yeah."

"He was paranoid after the last place went belly up, wanted to cover all his bases. Bought a whole goddamn herd because he thought it would look more right if he had one."

He pulled up the collar of his shirt and wiped his mouth on it and then let it down again.

"Awan bought this herd, or at least what he thought would make up one, ten longhorn heifers and a yearling bull. But after a few months we seen that this greenhouse business were gonna work and them cattle were just a pain in the ass so he set em loose."

The man in the passenger seat started passing around a sack of sunflower seeds, and they all took handfuls and let the folded shells fall into the wind like crumpled paper or wings.

"So now somewhere out in this country there's a pack of wild longhorns roamin about with no brand and overgrown hooves and left to fend for themselves. We all say someday that herd is gonna come back around and it's either gonna be superevolved from havin to fight off coyotes on their own all this time and they might even be predatory by then, or it's gonna be inbred to all hell after havin only one bull and are gonna have eyes in places they shouldn't be or somethin the like."

After they had driven for two hours they slowed the trucks to a stop on the side of the road and some had only half-bothered to get off of the road because they knew no other vehicles would pass in the time that they were stopped.

Most of the men went off separately and stopped at the barbed wire fence that followed the road some five or ten yards off and pissed into the sand, and Smith sat down upon his heels and watched the air bend in the heat off the road. A lone lizard crouched at the opposite edge, had apparently run off from heating itself there as they approached but now toed its way out again; a yellow-spiked fan about its neck was the face of one of Awan's orchids exposed to the desert for too long.

The girl came and sat beside him with her heels out on the pavement and he sat back and did the same. Realized that even his boots were not of this country. Were of something wet and northern and were rounded with none of the bite of the skull-jaw toes that Guillermo dragged through sand.

She'd repainted her face in ash again, blackened from her eyebrows up, and had tied back her hair with a string of the same plastic line that had been used to sew her stitches.

They sat there for a moment, heels against the pavement as they felt the desert pull the moisture off their exposed skin, and then the girl took the package of antibiotics from her pocket.

"You missed me on purpose when you shot under the truck, didn't you?" She popped a few of them into her mouth like chewing gum and held out the packet to Smith.

He nodded.

"How can you shoot that well with just one eye?"

He took a few of the tablets and handed the sheet back.

"I was re-taught depth perception after it happened. Used paper targets, memorized the buckshot patterns down to the inch for every distance within the range of the gun. I went on practice hunts with him until I was sure again."

She nodded and the air was still and the footsteps of the men behind them resounded with weight against the mesas beyond like greater ghosts.

After a while Awan called out for them to move on, and the girl climbed into the back of a pickup truck in front.

They were counting cattle guards again for direction, and another hundred or so miles out they reached their mark. A man from the first truck in their caravan jumped out to open the fence gate and waited until all had turned through from the road then closed it again. They went on, now in dirt that was also sand. It was soundless under their tires, even as they pounded closed the escape routes of tarantulas and lizards and other mites that had dug underground there.

The way was uneven off of the road, and the truck in front had to brake many times to skim the edges of a flood-scarred

arroyo with its tires or to reverse and take the long way around
an archway that could not be forded. Several miles in, one of
the jeeps clipped a cliff-side and lost its side mirror and a man
jumped out from it and threw the mirror in back and ran to
catch up as the caravan had not slowed.

They were just above the lines of the national park's territory and they passed a lone shack as they sped across sheets of
sand marred by the odd piece of crippled-looking brush.

Half an hour later they drove below the butte that Awan and
the buyers had marked out as looking like a barfight-broken
hand, fingers cracked and vertical with a disjointed thumb.

It was five hours from their first setting out and Awan
called out that this was the place. They passed through a wide
archway to the other side of the butte and encircled the trucks
in an arc, end to end, and now the wheels sat half in sand and
half in the footings of stone extending from the bases of the
formations behind them.

The men got out of the trucks and held their guns readied in both hands against their waists and Smith did the same,
the group carrying a mixture of salvaged TEC-9s and AK-47s
and the odd Texas-looking pistol that had likely been passed
down through a family. There was no sound from the south,
where the monuments blurred in the midday heat, and some
of the men turned to the north to check that the others were
not going to come through the same archway as they had but
at last they saw clouds of dust to the south and behind it the
grayed grills of the trucks of the buyers.

The others came within twenty feet of them and as the
dust stilled they shifted their six vehicles into the same Cones-
toga arc formation.

The first man to get out came from a middle truck, and
he wore all black and a leather jacket with a skull and a red

scorpion wound through the eye sockets painted upon it. He was Mexican, his head shaved and his hands empty. A whitened scar riveted from the bridge of his nose and divided into three through the right eyebrow. The others spilled from the vehicles and flanked him in black denim and kneepads. It was a uniform, a mixture of black button-downs and T-shirts, and a half dozen of them wore canvas jackets even in the heat and looked untouched by it. Two of those in black cowboy shirts went to the man's side, carrying semi-autos.

Awan stepped forward with two men at his side as well. The engines cracked and went silent, and seemed the signal to speak.

"Three hundred thousand pills, for the agreed-upon price of three million US dollars."

The man with the painted leather jacket nodded to either side and men went into the trucks and brought out five cardboard boxes and set them in the sand. There were near twenty men with him.

"Six hundred thousand cash in each box."

Awan nodded at his men and they brought out the fifteen bags of pills and laid them in a line of black plastic behind him.

"We'll count the cash and then leave you the pills."

Awan nodded again to one of the men flanking him and the man went forward to one of the boxes and opened it then went to his knees to count. They all watched as he began to pile stacks of bills on the ground beside him.

"Tell Medina, as usual, it's been a pleasure doing business with him," said Awan.

The man in the leather jacket laughed and turned to the man at his right, though the rest of the crew kept straight faces held forward.

"I'd rather not."

The man beside Smith opened his mouth.

"Oh, *shit*, that's—"

But the shot had already been taken and the man who had been counting the money rolled back with a bullet to the head.

Awan's men opened fire immediately as they dove behind their trucks and another ten men emerged from the buyer's vehicles and started to shoot.

Smith got behind the cab of the pickup truck and the windows were not down so he shot through them then continued to fire. One of the opposing men had been thrown backward against the truck with a shot to the chest but got back up laughing and stumbled on his way forward and his jacket fell off the shoulder and exposed a bulletproof vest underneath. Another shot came from Awan's crew and hit the man in the head and the window of the truck went marbled in reds behind him.

Three-quarters of Awan's group had made it behind the trucks when the firing had started and the three remaining lay bleeding in the sheet of sand between the lines and soon every truck whose driver had not thought to leave the windows rolled down had them shot out and men laid their guns across the lines of pickup truck beds and riddled holes waist-height through the entire line of metal before them. They soon hunkered down and crouched with arms reached up to fire their guns and wouldn't raise their heads to that level and fired blind at the opposing trucks.

The man beside Smith began to stand to aim his shots and ducked down when a bullet came close but was roused by it and leaned forward as he cursed and "these fucking Cordovas I'm gonna fucking kill em all and have their bowels for breakfast," and in a noise that sounded like a punch he went down with a hit in the forehead and Smith sprang back from the split skull and flung himself into the line of fire in the process and then the girl was there and outstretched a hand and pushed him down.

She crouched behind a wheel with an AK-47 and he crawled to the rear wheel to do the same as she bent around the engine to fire and he lifted his gun up over the edge of the truck bed. A bottle with a lit rag hurtled over and ignited one of their jeeps ahead but their men behind it already lay with entrails stringing from exit wounds.

Smith hazarded a look over the top of the truck bed and the Cordova men were crouched around the cardboard boxes hauling them back to their vehicles and Smith took a shot and knocked one of them onto their back and probably killed him too and then he fired again at a man that was walking aimlessly toward them, stumbling with a head wound but gun raised, and the man went down.

One of Awan's men was going for a box of money and he squatted to lift it and when he was hit in the shoulder he slumped across it, hips coupled to the cardboard box of cash. He was still breathing and shuddered a bit and a Cordova braved the gunfire and came close enough to pull him up by the hair and shoot him. The Cordova pushed the body backward, leaving a pan of red that would filter through layers upon layers of bills before whatever the cash hadn't winnowed from it reached the sand and dissolved.

Smith had forgotten that the truck at the front was still burning and the flames spreading then a man lurched screaming past them on fire in an uneven gait until he fell and it had been Matthew's shot that brought him down and then Matthew had done an about-face and started shooting at the others again with no pause in the trigger-finger.

Those on the other line had fallen in large numbers but still the vehicular absorption of bullets slowed the bloodshed and Awan ran behind his nine men remaining, giving orders to shoot and to conceal themselves behind axles and engine blocks and not to make a run for the money as the cash was likely in false-bottomed boxes.

There was only a small alleyway between their blockade and the wall of rock behind them and the space was littered with bullets and glass and the rock face soon became a canvas for blood and organs shot out against it and one man, mostly whole, lay reclined against it.

Smith ducked up and saw that there were a dozen Cordovas left at least and he dropped down and reloaded and when he came up again a shot snapped the metal bracket from the roof of the pickup and it landed square on his sternum and pitched him back.

For a second he lay panting against the mesa where the side of his face had been thrown against it and he tongued the blood in his mouth like syrup. Without moving he turned his eyes to look at a trilobite fossil in the sandstone that was cleaved in half by a bullet hole an inch from his face. Thing had traveled three hundred million years and countless miles into the dirt and under seas and back up again only to be split by the stolen bullet of a cartel man. Goddamn shit way to go, even for a prehistoric bug. For a moment his hearing blurred and then went concrete as a voice came out of the murk.

"Get the fuck up."

Guillermo grabbed his shirtfront and swung him back into cover behind the cab.

Another man had ventured out for the money and he stood between two Cordovas who had their hands upon him and only one with a gun still and he threw his elbow and broke one of their noses and knocked a punch to throw the gun but still the two men took him to the ground and in a roil of dust it was over.

Their line was spread thin and they had men behind each of the trucks but the burning one and that made seven spread behind three vehicles. The girl ran from her place behind the wheel well and across the open space between two bumpers to get to Awan.

"What's your plan!" She screamed it and all of them could hear but there was no other volume that would have surmounted the gunfire.

"Fight them off!" It was a harrowing sound from a man who had not yet raised his voice before a single one of them.

The rear tires of the truck they crouched behind were hit and the truck dropped six inches lower with an addled sigh. She was on one knee with her gun propped on the other, reloading.

"We're outgunned! You can't!"

"We have to! There's no other choice!"

Smith watched them from where he crouched and she turned her head to survey the vehicles and there were still the three not burning but not a single engine that hadn't taken a shot to it.

"Awan you can't do it! You need to run—"

Her words were cut off by a bullet that flew between their heads and both ducked and then came up again.

"I will not run."

The old man panted it but all the others heard and with it Matthew yelled and stood above the pickup truck bed and fired against the men that were stepping forward to take the bags of pills and he took down three and then he dropped again as bullets perforated the truck's cab. Their numbers were close now, despite Awan's being outgunned at the start.

A man let his leg stray from cover and screamed as his ankle was hit. A Cordova was on his stomach now, firing beneath the wheels.

The girl saw it and turned back and did what none of them would have dared do, and grabbed Awan's shoulders.

"You cannot beat them! You need to run!"

Whether it was a gesture meant to coerce him or to beg him they did not know. But he spun his hand out and struck her in the face.

Guillermo and Matthew had frozen at their posts and watched the girl instead of the gunfire.

She stared, and would not raise a hand to the cheek where he'd burned it, and they saw it sear red in the clouded air. Awan spoke before she could.

"I . . . will . . . not . . . run."

She dropped her hands back onto her rifle and leaned up over him to fire at the Cordova that had centered in on their spot then crouched back down to meet his eyes.

Smith watched the girl's face fold into one of absolute fury, a madness in defiance of reason and of nothing but hate, and then she was running along their lines and ducking under the gunfire and she ran out through the archway whence they'd come and was gone in the din of bullets entering rock and the crackling of burning engines.

"Do you love me?"

The threads of blonde hair crossed over her eyes in the field and he handed her an ax.

"Well, do you love me?" he answered.

She laughed.

"I aint never told another living person that. But you're me and I'm you, aint it the same?"

It was spring then but she wore no coat and he still had two eyes. She went on.

"Why are we doin this anyway? A bonfire in the middle of the day for no reason."

"It's a Sunday."

The logs lay in a crusted gray pile by the table-sized stump of the dead oak that had sourced them. Wyatt rolled one down from the top and split it with his ax until it was in shards.

"Aint no Sabbath for farmers," she said as she stood.

He kicked the grass from the skin of the earth in a circle with his heel and picked up the shattered pieces of wood. Made a teepee with the kindling and stuffed in the grass he'd uprooted and lit it and she knelt on the other side of it and blew on it until the flame took hold.

"I had some extra wood to burn," he said.

He rolled another pair of logs off the top of the pile and kicked one toward her.

"Some extra wood and so we gotta burn it. I like that."

The light was upon her brow and it seemed the wind had painted it there.

They swung their axes in tandem. Hit, split, kick to the side. He rolled more logs from the pile.

"Why?" he asked.

Hit, split, kick to the side.

"You caint ask me that, Wyatt. It implies we don't share the same head and you don't already know."

Hit, and her ax stuck. She yanked it out of the bark and took another hit and it went through, but she was lagging behind. Wyatt took a moment to set a few pieces into the growing flames.

"You don't ask yourself 'why' bout anythin?" he asked.

Kept chopping. She was lagging behind him, never had before. The second time he stopped to feed the flames he looked
over at her.

She held the ax with a loose wrist and was staring up at the
surface of the cloud-washed sky with her hair pooled around
her face as if she were underwater. She bent again and swung
again.

There was no pit for the bonfire but he dug a narrow
trench around it with the toe of his boot as it grew. The breeze
was cold and snapped against the edges of the flames.

"Nah I do. Do you ever think that—"

She'd swung again and the log hadn't split.

"I can't—I don't know why I can't." They were fifteen and
still wearing the same clothes and she looked at her arms and
then looked at Wyatt's and his were tight against the fabric
and it was visible in her eyes that she was seeing now that hers
would never grow that way.

"Stop," he said.

She shook her head.

"Tell me what you want," he said.

He reached for her and she swung again and the log did
not break and with an exhale that expanded into a grunt she
kicked it whole toward the fire, where it rocked on top of the
kindling and smothered the flames.

"A bonfire for no reason in broad daylight on a cold day,"
she said.

She turned toward the smoke and sat down on the log,
black streaking through the air in front of her face. The smell
of smoke brutishly masking the scent of her so that it was as
if you weren't there anymore at all. He pulled up a log and
sat down in the scentlessness, disappearing beside her, the fire
dead and their feet kicking at the exhalant embers.

Smith looked once more at Guillermo and Matthew beside
him and they were still firing and he could not, no longer, and
he turned and sprinted along to the archway and one of them
shouted something at him but he didn't hear it. Through the
archway he met with the girl's leveled gun and when he put
his hands up and she saw it was him she pulled him against the
side of the mesa that flanked the arch.

She had most of a magazine left and hefted the gun against
her hip and checked his and he had four shots to go and she
shoved it back into his hands and said "goddamn useless thing."

They had flattened themselves against the mesa wall and
a Cordova came through the arch and from where they stood
she opened fire on him and he went down with six shots to the
torso.

Another man followed him and cut out into the archway
from the side and the girl had not seen him but Smith lunged
forward and with two shots to the head took him down and
marveled at his hand for a moment at how steadied it had
been. They were closer to the archway and to the gunfire now
with that affront and she was still shouting and hadn't taken a
breath as all the words spilled.

"Idiots are going to get themselves all killed they've got
no space with that wall behind them and if they close them in
from either side they'll just fire into that nest and take them all
out and they're fucking done for goddamn useless idiots I tried
to tell him I tried to tell him!"

And she started at a run from the fight and Smith followed
and the horizon lay heavily yellow to the north before them
and she was leaping over brush and dodging rocks with one
hand balled against her stomach and the other holding the rifle

and did not stop when she skimmed a cactus and kept moving with spines in her bare calf.

Several minutes and half a mile out she stopped and dropped her gun in front of her and bent and put her hands on her thighs and yelled "Shit!"

Smith thought it was for the cactus spines and she ripped these out but then she turned and grabbed her gun and was running back toward the fight.

He followed and overtook her and when they were almost to the archway he stopped dead.

It was Awan. He staggered through the arch and raised his arms, a shot to his thigh bleeding and pistol in one hand and mouth open about to shout something. An arm came from behind the arch-side and drove an ax into his head lengthwise. He sank to his knees then slumped facedown as the blood spread translucent over the steel.

The girl passed Smith and ran toward him, passed her rifle over her back by its strap and leapt over a boulder and crouched to lift his face and put it upon her knee and for the thread of a second it seemed a sentimental gesture and then she leveraged an elbow on his temple and wrenched the ax from his skull before grabbing the pistol from his hand. She lunged backward against the opposite side of the arch and fired at the man behind. He slumped in the archway on top of Awan, shot through the cheek and teeth cracked symmetrically around the wound in white like the patterns on butterfly wings.

She threw the pistol into the dirt and kicked it toward Smith and he grabbed it, still holding the TEC-9 in the other hand. A stream of blood was emptying from Awan's boot as he passed.

The fire had died in the first jeep but another truck was burning and another one steadily leaking gasoline like putrid urine. About fifteen men left still firing at one another through trucks that were perforated hulls of steel now. A Cordova man with a rifle dove onto his stomach from the other side and took out a man cowering under the truck closest to the girl.

Their men were still pinned between their trucks and the mesa face and one scaled twelve feet up the rock like a sand-bloodied monkey. He took a handhold and turned with a TEC-9 and emptied a clip one-handed overtop those that lay behind the opposing trucks before he was shot down and curled into a ball as he fell and lay there.

Two Cordovas had tried to drive away in two trucks in a row and had been caught in their escape and the windshields matched with great hibiscus-colored blooms, textured by cracked glass and iridescent violet in the cooking sun.

The girl ran behind an engine and hunkered down there and two shots passed Smith untouched at the shoulder and he ran half-bent behind the cab too.

Matthew was at the hood, AK-47 steadied in the divot in front of the windshield and him ducking down between shots, eyes wild and face bloodied with muck and black dirt like a mask over the burned skin around his eyes. Mouth open in a fixed and boundless void, screaming in the face of everything and nothing at all with a voice that could have belonged to the fossils below their feet.

Guillermo squatted behind him feeding him magazines from a toolbox. He looked over when Smith and the girl crowded in and yelled over the blare.

"Where's Awan!"

"Dead!" the girl answered.

"Fuck!"

The cartel men were circling around in front of the

archway and closing in the space between the two lines of trucks. There were just a half dozen of Awan's men remaining and at that angle the two teenagers were sprayed with bullets. The one with the deformed ear grabbed at the girl's ankles from the ground, crying, "You did this, you knew the whole time they'd come for you—"

A Cordova came around toward them and Smith leveled the TEC-9 and hit him twice in the chest and without ammo threw it away and aimed the one he'd taken from Awan. The girl kicked the now-dead boy from her feet and ran forward after the shot and sank the tomahawk into the forehead of another and hammered her fist on top to drive it in further as the man went down before ripping it out again to a myriad floral spray of pink filth across her knees and over the sand.

The girl flung herself back against the open door of that second truck and exhaled in a shudder like a dog's to throw the blood off of her and ducked in. Came out with a trash bag under her arm. Matthew still screaming.

She threw the bag at Smith and he hugged it to his chest.

"Take it and go!"

Guillermo lay in the dirt with one eye rolled back to stare at them through the open cracks in his skull.

Smith stood huddled against the cab and she shouted at him again.

"Time to run!"

"What!"

"Time to run! Time to go!"

She ducked and bolted toward the incoming line of men, flung the ax into the neck of one as she passed and left it there and ran through the arch and Smith tight at her heels. Leapt over dead Awan and dead Cordova and continued running for he didn't know how long, for half an hour or an hour or two hours until she collapsed into the crevice behind a boulder, heaving. They could no longer hear gunfire and the desert silence was prickling again and their heaving enough to tear at the ears.

———◦◦◦———

Five miles back, the last of the blood drained from Awan's boot, mercury-slick and cast in shadow by the torso of the man who had landed on top of its owner.

The red that was now black-violet after passing through the filter of the wool sock and mixing with leather-sweat ran and darkened a final thread flower on the lip of the cowboy boot's embroidery. A drop clung there and the rest ran past it, down and down, into a pool forming in the desert like unscrawled ink tossed into the sand. As it leached in and spread, it softened sand that had not seen water in six months and excited the larvae of microscopic creatures that had remained frozen in wait for it. And so the liquid that was hot but no hotter than the desert seeped in the shapes of petals or scars into the depths of the sand and touched the nurseries of mites or talitridae below and collectively they all hatched and breathed in water and then as quickly as it had come the water had dried again, and the mites died and were all gone as well, an instant after having been created by the blood and sweat in the boot of an old man.

A turkey vulture groaned from above, an utterance of want from a throat without voice. The darkness stained the sand like a burn, and was a burn, in that this layer upon time would be marked by firefight and gunpowder and when these bodies were overlaid with sandstone as the trilobites had been that was all they would smell of when unearthed. The buzzard circled. It would feed soon.

———

Smith and the girl leaned to either side of the boulder, still low on breath, Smith still watching to the south where the battle had been. He had never seen men fall like that. As if the animation was gone from them in an instant. When running deer were shot their momentum carried them another few feet before they fell but the men had just gone straight down; you felt yourself taking them when you pulled the trigger. And perhaps had he not been there they still would have died anyway this fight still would have gone on and there had been so many bullets in the air and perhaps they hadn't been— but he knew they had been his. His stomach overturned and he dropped the bag and bent at the waist with his hands to his mouth and the girl was on him within a second, pushing his shoulders back against the rock.

"Don't vomit. Whatever you have to do don't do it."

He nodded and swallowed and gasped and sank to the ground, leaned back on the boulder.

"You lose that much water out here you die. Tell yourself whatever lies you have to to stop yourself."

Lies. You're not a killer and they didn't die. You're not a killer. You're not black in the soul and you haven't blacked Lucy's soul by association.

"Why'd you go back?" There was sand in his throat.

"Had to kill more of them first. Or else they would've come after us easy."

"That it?"

She coughed.

"Take out all the trucks too."

She turned suddenly. It was a lone figure running over the horizon from the south that she saw, and she threw herself back against the mesa and aimed the rifle and Smith crouched behind the boulder with bag in one arm and pistol readied in the other until they saw that it was Matthew.

He shied when he saw them and froze for a moment with eyes wide and hands up, and took longer than he should have to realize who it was but when he did he let himself fall into the sand. Wherever he'd been cut before was still bleeding and coated the entire sheet of his forehead in red and his blond hair was glazed intermittently in crimson and gun-oil black like the fur of some putrid mechanical animal.

She went to his side and rolled him on his back.

"Matthew. Matthew get out of the sun. You're too heavy for me to pull you."

She moved aside and Smith dragged Matthew by the shoulders until his face was in the shadow of the boulder and Smith and the girl trembled there in the shade like frozen soldiers at a fire.

Matthew did not move and finally she spit in his face and he raised his head and opened his eyes and wiped a hand on his cheek and it came off a mixture of blood and saliva and he licked it off, thirst already setting in. He closed his eyes again.

"Were you the last man standing?"

He groaned and turned onto his side.

"What the hell do you think."

"And?" she asked.

"I'm the last one of our men standing. There's at least three of the others left."

She sat back on her feet; it was too hot to go out of the shade to stand.

"Alright. What do we have. There's three shots left in the AK and I have a knife and a box of antibiotics."

"Four shots left in the pistol and a knife."

"Keep that jacket on, it'll help when the heat surpasses body temperature. It doesn't look like Matthew has anything."

Matthew slurred in the heat.

"I got a lighter an' a pack a cig'rettes."

The girl exhaled.

"Fire then."

They were silent for a few moments.

Matthew turned to speak but kept his eyes closed.

"They got the pills."

"Of course they did," she said.

"There's water in em trucks."

"We're not going back," the girl said.

"Nah I'm not sayin that. I was jus' sayin there is."

"Shit," said Smith.

"Yeah, shit." Matthew said it with eyes still shut and coughed and ground the toe of his boot against the rocks.

"What about the police?"

"Aint no police ou' here." Matthew answered him.

A mourning dove called out from among the rocks above and the sound seemed to inflict more heat on the air.

Matthew turned against the boulder face and felt that it was cool and with his hands against it lifted himself up and when he'd made it into a crouch he opened his eyes and looked the girl square in the face.

"You! You *ran!*" He lunged at her and, overpowered, she slammed hard into the cliff face beside and the rifle went off against their ears and when they both recoiled at the sound she threw up a knee and hit him fast in the gut and he went to the ground and she had her gun to his head in a second.

"I ran. And we're the only ones still alive. Now how do you figure that."

Matthew spat out blood to the side and curled his lip.

"If you'd stayed and fought . . ."

"Dead! They're all dead! Either accept your luck or join them."

He put his fists to the ground and coughed out blood again on all fours and gave her a look that showed he'd consider the second option. The girl saw it too and squatted in front of him, gun across her knees.

"Let them rest. We have other things to deal with now."

To the north ahead of them loomed the Utah desert, two hundred miles of implacable sand and a sun that sent down drying spires of light like the invertebrate ticks of the scorpions that burrowed below the surface of its skin.

CHAPTER TEN

No Wolves in Utah

The three of them sat in the shade of the rock, Smith with his skinned cheek that had spilled down to mat in his beard and Matthew painted red down to the eyebrow and the bruise on the face of the girl darkening through a myriad span of colors as if to perpetually adjust its meaning.

Another vulture did a single circle above them and then smelled something else and moved on.

The three stared to the insurmountable north and the sun tilted as they sat and their space of shade shrank. The girl was the first to lean forward and she took out her knife and cut off one of her sleeves and tied the fabric so that it rode across her nose and mouth. "To conserve the moisture." She handed the knife to Smith and he did the same with the right arm's flannel sleeve then passed the knife to Matthew.

"I guess you know what we have to do." She said it with eyes still to the north.

Matthew nodded before he slit the bottom of his white T-shirt and tied the fabric across his face.

Smith pulled away the black plastic from the bag. Underneath it was a layer of cellophane with a smeared handprint of blood across its top. But within it, tens of thousands of light green pills.

"That's two hundred thousand dollars if we can get out of here alive," said the girl.

Smith stared at it for a while, the iterations of green cylinders like fragmented pieces of what was once the greenhouse, a ragged, shuddering breath in the desert, then covered it up in black plastic again.

The cliff beside them gave no more shade with the position of the sun. It extended north for another mile, no way to get to shade before then. The girl swallowed and it was guttural in a dried throat and Matthew had already begun to sweat through the cloth on his face so that it was visible on the stained cotton.

She stood and they followed and the three began their staggering passage in the midday sun, their adrenaline from the firefight no longer an aid and now a dead weight.

She had the rifle hung about her shoulders and Smith carried the bag, the pistol in hand against it. Pistol taken from dead Awan who had hired him for protection, that he had used to kill more men, but you are no killer but yes now you are and is the reason you cannot see the blood upon your hands the fact that it bleeds out of Lucy's instead? She standing there in the field of cattle and her blonde hair upon her shoulders that your shoulders looked like once and her standing there staring at her hands wondering why and wondering how and you're not, you're not—

The girl walked ahead of them and Matthew fell into step beside Smith.

"You know where the fuck we are?"
"Nah. You know where the fuck we are?"
"Nah."

———◦◦◦———

There were things even greater than elk in those woods, and it took two men to catch them. At seventeen the father believed Wyatt counted as enough of a man to go. For the week leading up to it, he practiced on targets backed with bales of hay, emptying the shotgun then switching to the knife for close range. And when the day came that they were to go, they tacked up four horses, two for riding and two for gear.

That morning the trees were blue and heavy below clouds shaded with implied snow, and they would reach the base of the mountains by sunset. Lucy rode alongside to the edge of the field, and Wyatt was sure she'd say "to hell with the livestock" and ride out with them, but instead she turned at the edge of the treeline, the toes of her horse's hooves just barely sinking into the fallen leaves with the shattered-china sound of breaking frost, and murmured some reassurance to the father about tending the cattle before turning her animal's head back around the way it came. She reined it there, a few yards back from the woods, as they walked their mounts and pack animals into the trees. Wyatt watched until she was gone from sight, the exhalations of her horse in the cold raising a column of smoke that obscured her face in its efforts toward the sky.

They could hope for no more than ten miles that day through the bogging snarls of undergrowth, and even less when the snow began to fall. At some invisible place in the woods lay the legal border of the ranch. It was unmarked, and it did not matter because there was nothing but wilderness beyond, miles upon miles that no man had ever seen. Yet for Wyatt there was still a sense of crossing, of moving between the land that was theirs and this other, this new, the awareness of being the first to lay eyes on it making it seem as if they were gone from the surface and now walked the underside of the world, affixed to it by some trick of gravity. He assessed as they rode whether this part of the woods was still familiar and at times felt that it was and then at other turns and when certain branches slid snow-covered and wet across his face he wasn't sure anymore. But after they had gone an hour they would have covered three miles and that would be farther than the property reached and he could be sure, sure that they had passed into the unknown.

The mountains were a shadowed hood above them when late in the afternoon they decided to stop and make camp.

The snow was falling harder now, and the fire protested and spat and wept ash as the flakes landed in it. They'd brought no hay for the horses but the heat of the flames warmed dormant leaves around their clearing, ran the frost from them in rivulets and for a moment the leaves were green and alive and spring again before their consumption by the foursome of rope-foamed mouths.

They'd strung a tarp to cover the bedding and the saddles but the fire would melt it so they sat cross-legged on either side of the flames under open air. The father was dividing blocks of brown sugar with his knife, because that's what you use for bait when you're hunting bear.

"You understand why this is different, Wyatt," said the father, when he had laid out the sugar into palm-sized patties and far enough from the fire that they would not melt but not so far away that they would freeze.

"This is a killing we don't have to do. We'll eat the meat

but it won't taste as good as if we'd just killed a steer. There's sport in what we're doin.

"Some men make excuses—like the vague threat that it might come down from the mountain and kill your horses. But a man ought to have more faith in his horses than that."

The father wiped the sugar from the knife blade on his pants then went on.

"It's alright to do it like this, sometimes. We won't waste it. Just have to take responsibility for it, is all."

There was jerky in their packs and they took it out and held it in their gloved hands in front of the fire to warm it. The snow had not slowed and the men packed it underneath their blankets to form a cushion and the horses ducked their heads below the height of the smoke, and in unison man and animal slept.

The father was up before sunrise, had taken a single horse. Wyatt was smothering the fire when he rode back up and flung a bundle at his son. Wyatt caught it and looked into his hands: a squirrel, killed with a knife. The father wouldn't fire a gun this close to the target of the hunt and was among few men in this world who could get breakfast without needing to.

Wyatt re-stoked the fire and they ate and broke camp enough to protect it from the weather but left it there, and rode further up the mountain. The father had laid the sugar blocks that morning.

There are three ways to hunt bear: baiting, calling, and dogging. And the father wouldn't risk the dogs.

The father had been scouting all morning, and had found the signs and trails. They would take the four horses up and when they neared the bait would leave them. They would then call the bear on foot.

They were riding among boulders here, and the ground leaned toward the mountaintops at a visible pitch. At a point they paused and could see out over the ranch, crop fields stitched to the earth in discolored bandages. The hairs of smoke from the house's chimney were what struck Wyatt— he had not yet thought of Lucy. He had felt no separation because she may as well have been right there. That the ground here was as much her as the body, even as the interlacing of feeling that connected them below the dirt stretched and expanded, amoeba-like, with the places they walked upon and walked upon anew, coating everything in between them with themselves.

"You see it from up here it makes you wonder that you could've ever had any control over all it," said the father as they turned back to face the mountain and continued the ascent.

"There's a thin balance between the things you're given and the way you can make things be," said the man that had raised his children alone.

"This place takes somethin from you. As you take from it, each time it takes a bit back. Only a bit at a time. Don't let it sneak up on you." "You" meaning both Wyatt and Lucy, as the father had no reason to differentiate between them, so rarely used their individual names.

The horses were slipping along the rocks and the men stood up in their saddles to lean their weight between the animals' shoulders.

"If you take good care of it then a lot of the time you won't want, and not wanting, not havin to want, is the best thing in the world."

A quarter mile from where they'd set the bait they tied the horses with slipknots so that they could easily break away and the father took out a wooden mouthpiece, the bear call. They stalked low through the undergrowth, guns still slung on their backs, Wyatt at his father's heels.

"You've called turkeys. This isn't it—be more frantic, constant. It's a dying rabbit's voice."

"It's always a rabbit."

"That's the role they've gotta play."

The father stopped behind a bluff and they hunkered down and he blew the call. It was a shriek, one of broken backs and of legs caught in traps and of birdshot in the ribs. Again and again and the father continued and they heard the bear far off and the father continued the shrieking and quickly it had gone on for longer than Wyatt had ever heard the real thing; it was a sound reserved for last moments. The bear was responding, fumbling in the brush a hundred yards off.

"Take it—"

The movement in the trees ahead had stopped. Wyatt palmed the mouthpiece.

"There's a gully back there, he must've gone down—draw him out, go."

Wyatt blew on the call once and shrank at the squealing sound it made.

"Go!"

He watched the undergrowth for the bear and blew the call and shrank with it again. Took a few steps and again, shrank again. And then the bear began to crash ahead of him and his shrinking from the false rabbit's cries became something like running, and as the snow nicked his face and the bare branches whipped the emptiness of his clothes, through the faunal warmth of the ground and the anesthetizing cold of the air, the wind fetching minuscule storms after him without direction or source or end or fate or mandate to bring them to the ground, the rabbit dying again and again, with a goliath roaring in the shadows ahead of him, the running became something like flying.

The bear died with no more drama than its size warranted and with no more complaint than the event justified. They dressed it there and made camp for the night and in the morning divided the weight among the horses and had to sit forward on their saddles to make room.

Lucy was in the chair in the living room when they returned and she'd taken down the needlework that the father normally did and she'd pierced her fingers on it in lack of skill and there was blood. They got the salt from the pantry together and the bear's hide took up the entire kitchen floor and they had to step over it for three months, each of them scattering a palmful of salt over it each time they passed, making an hourglass of grizzly fur to mark how a family spent its days. And when on one spring night it was ready, and the weather was already much too hot for it, Wyatt and Lucy sat on the edge of the porch with the hide over their heads so that the sweat streamed down their faces like the rain falling from the porch roof ahead of them, and he told her how it all had happened.

⚬

"Shade. We need some shade," Matthew slurred almost incoherently but the girl responded.

"No shit. Close your mouth before your spit evaporates."

In the August sun it was already far above ninety degrees. There was no sound save their steps and in the silence these grew to a crashing noise as their boots plunged through the wheat-colored grains of sand. They watched for the break in the mesa and after a half hour of slogging forward they saw the northern edge of it and the girl made two steps that were the start of a run and stopped herself and returned to a

slow, crestfallen walk to conserve energy. The sweat dripped
through the black upon her brow and smeared the rest of her
face in gray.

The sun was overhead still and excised most shadows from
the land but there was a small outcropping on the north end of
the plateau and the three gathered in the tight circle of shade
it made.

"We wait here until night," the girl had said.

They lay there together, not shrinking at one another's
touch as they would have if fully conscious, and the plateau
rose above them flat and foreboding and as if providing shade
only against its will.

Smith pulled his knees to his chest but it was too hot so
he outstretched his legs and the light hit them like a burn and
he pulled them back in again. Pinned under this beating sky, it
felt like something that must abate but he knew would not because you never stop to think how lost you are without water
in the desert. Then in his mind her hands were upon his shoulders and the twin was there as he was, and as he breathed in
hard under the torn segment of his shirt he breathed all of her
lightness in.

Night fell long hours later and he thought he had slept and
then the memories of waking with eyes washed white in the
sun and turning in the sand without rest came back and he no
longer knew if he had.

They had shifted their cluster of three by inches as the sun
progressed and they waited until dusk had passed to rise, either to shy from even that bit of the light or because it took
that long to rouse themselves from their paralysis below the
sun.

When the stars were visible they started to walk.

"Where's the road?" Matthew asked.

"Straight to the west but it turned to dirt twenty miles before we got here. We might not be able to find it and if we end up overshooting it there's another five hundred miles of wilderness after that."

"And the greenhouse?"

"Dead north. We head there."

They were three shadowed figures in a line, black in the dark but underneath still going pink in the exposed spots where the sun had scalded them. Through a valley they pushed their boots through brush and cacti and Matthew had taken the pistol since Smith held the bag and he carried it readied against his chest out of habit or with wishing he'd be given the chance to prove his survival against another man instead of in a winnerless fight against nature.

They had been going for an hour at least when the girl spoke to Smith.

"You're counting, aren't you?"

"What?"

"You're counting the men you killed."

They moved automatically, as if riding something separate from them. War-torn cowboys on shuffling mounts that consisted only of their own quadriceps.

"Yeah. Seein how the number feels."

"How many?"

"Three for certain, and maybe four. I'm not sure."

"Three is enough for one day. Let the fourth man lie."

He did not answer.

"You know, the first one is the only one that never leaves. Like the first animal you kill. But the others go. I'd bet the faces of those you killed today are already gone."

The first animal the blackbird he'd taken with the Ruger with Lucy there and the hole in its chest reflected in the man's

eyes when he was pinned beneath the motorcycle and pulling the trigger then and the father, when had the father been
shot and which of them had shot him, he didn't remember
anymore, and the faces of the men today: the one who cast
his arm up to cover his face as he buckled to his knees and
when he lowered it down again he'd smeared blood across it,
and another who cried out at the sky with his mouth wide like
a smile. Someday you forget them. He didn't know whether
he'd forgotten the father's face or whether he saw something
of the father's face in every man he'd killed.

He tightened the bag of drugs against his chest and walked
on.

"What're the odds of them comin out here after us? They
woulda heard the shot."

The girl answered him.

"Not a chance. They know it's nearly certain that we'll be
dead by sunset tomorrow."

Matthew broke and shouted "fuck!" into his hands but it
went out into the wind and there was no echo.

They watched the sky deepen and the stars alit across the
air as if a hand had struck waters of glowing algae, pulling
waves of light in an ocean that none of the three had ever
seen.

It was nearing midnight but still they had not stopped to
rest and their way was straight, their tracks diverting only when
mesas blocked their way, but one direction ingrained in their
brains, and it read not as *north* but as *away*. The girl's walk was
still her strange movement of feet first and then bodyweight
to follow and while the men's shadows moved forward at a
constant pace hers was lurching, that of a beast whose mouth
leered from its stomach.

Soon a herd of clouds hunted in and the ground was strewn

with patches of deeper darkness, some the size of mountains. Another hour north and Matthew stopped.

"I heard somethin."

"It weren't nothin, your ears are hallucinating."

"No, I heard somethin."

The girl had stopped and cocked her head and the black on her face obscured it so that only her eyes were visible, two gold-backed insects traversing a wreck of charcoal and burnished slate, soiled wet tarp.

They heard a trotting sound to the west and then it too stopped.

"Shit—"

And the girl turned around and threw her back against the men and they faltered then understood and stood shoulder to shoulder in a triangle.

"Wolves," said Matthew.

"Aint no wolves in Utah," said Smith.

"Coyotes," said the girl.

"They hunt in the day."

"Not when the prey is as easy as this."

No need to stay quiet when the things already knew exactly where they were. The clouds were heavy here and they could not see.

The trotting resumed and seemed to gain double time and it was only then that they understood there were three.

"Save your bullets," she said.

"But—"

"Save your bullets."

They waited for a long time like that, breathing as their shoulders joined with each collective inhale. And there was nothing. Without a word the girl turned from their circle and they moved on.

They were making good time and walked in a line through one another's footprints, and they passed in and out from below the clouds, with a train of shadows that sometimes absconded into the dark and other times reappeared to follow them under the pin-marked desert sky.

Smith walked in the middle and a lizard crossed in front of his foot and followed for a few paces, leaving a line in the sand from its tail and little footprints on either side of it like the scar of a stitched wound where once the world had been sewn back together. They crossed into another dark space and it ran off into the night to weave its tracks over the width of the plain. And then, in front of them, the girl screamed.

It was a sound not of fear or surprise but of anger, and they reached her in seconds but there was a snarl that followed and the sounds echoed together and whether it were hers or the beast's Smith did not know but she had fallen forward with it then rolled up onto her knees by the time they got to her. She had one knee on the animal's throat and one knee behind it and was hammering the butt of her gun onto its skull until it lay still, and she lay back in the sand with her legs still wrapped around the coyote's head, holding her arm to her chest and shaking. They looked at her and she shook her head.

"There's probably more. Just give me a minute and stand watch."

She kept the arm against her and shuddered twice more before she stopped and looked up at the sky and let the dim light sink into her eyes until their color was visible again. Her forearm had an arc of distinct punctures and two darker than the others where the canines had gone in and doubtless the wound was mirrored on the other side that she held to her chest. At last she sat up and sucked the blood off the outside of the forearm and did the same to the underside and then rolled it in the sand. She rose using the uninjured hand for balance and swung the rifle over her back then squatted once more and put the coyote over her neck.

It was a starving thing, fur the color of the landscape tight on the outcrop of ribs, and the jut of its hips was a mirror of the desert and its stone. It could not have weighed more than thirty pounds. Swung easily about her shoulders, and the blood of its skull ran down across her waist and then down her clothes and the only bit of it Smith could see was the trail's ending down her right calf.

"Move on. There's more of them."

And the noise of their trotting resounded like the scrawling of their sins into a paper forged of sand.

———◦◦◦———

"Move on until what." Matthew spoke, knowing that he'd lost the most blood and had the most blood upon him, guilt below his voice for having brought them on with the smell. They'd been going for half an hour.

"Until they smell their own blood and move off. Then we'll drink."

"Yeah, if it don't all go out through his head."

She said nothing and lifted up the coyote's skull with her hand. They all knew it had gone for her because she was the smallest.

A quarter of an hour later and the iterations of four-legged footsteps had slowed but were still there, with a tone of aimless curiosity or of something pitiful and hunger-based knowing that there was nothing more efficacious for them to do. When the men and the girl came up over a sand ridge at the base of a mesa they could see the two coyotes in the moonlight, ten yards off, shying and circling one another as they kept their distance from the party that had stopped.

"They want the dead one," said the girl.

"To eat," she said.

As they made their way down the hill the girl let out a cry to scare them off. The sound emanated harsh into the desert and rebounded with despair but still with aggression, the sense as much an addition from the mesa faces as in her voice to begin with. One of the coyotes barked in response and the pair strayed a bit but continued on behind their progress, jostling their shoulders against each other as they jogged through the sand.

At last they came upon another red-rock archway and the girl said they'd stop there.

She bent down and unbridled the canine from around her neck and held the right forearm to her chest as she sat down in front of one of the rock sides and Smith and Matthew took the other. There was nothing to make a fire with. The girl took out her knife and cut a length from along the bottom hem of her shirt and tied this over her bleeding arm, then turned the dead coyote onto its back and worked down from the chest to gut it. She let the gut-sack fall to the side and picked up the body and bent it at the middle on her lap, then rolled up the tied sleeve from over her mouth and it rode upon the midsection of her face like a half-consummated noose. She waited for a minute and then propped the coyote's head against her knees and she dipped her face into it and came up bloody from the tip of her nose downward.

She passed the bunched animal to Matthew and he drank and came up bloodied in the same manner and then reached in with a hand to pull at the meat.

"Stop."

He looked up at the girl with a swath of muscle in his fist. "Digestion dehydrates you. We're not eating."

He shrugged and let the meat drop back into the cavity and passed it to Smith.

Smith sat with the coyote in his lap and looked at the two bloodied faces in the dark beside him. Creatures gone half animal or half infernal in the sloughs of visceral muck on their jaws. He looked down into the cavity that was still wet in the crevices of it and then at the crushed head of the animal. The blow that had done it in was visible in the ellipsoid outline of the butt of the gun and the brain leaking out around it and he put a hand to it and snapped off a piece of the skull along one of the seams and used this to scoop out the remaining mouthfuls of blood. His face stayed unstained excepting a single line that ran down from the right corner of his mouth, and he sat back from the drink in a trance with the red lining his teeth like velvet coating ceramic.

He stood and laid the emptied carcass at the feet of the girl and she crouched over it and began to skin it. Still the coyote's unfallen peers skittered at the invisible border they'd drawn between the humans and themselves. One of them was a good bit larger than the other and had a broken tail, and the smaller one circled it back and forth with rolling shoulders above a sunken back.

They had left a space between them for a fire though there was none to be had. Matthew sat back and swallowed, then another look of directionless panic gathered into his face and he spoke.

"I'm the only one here who's given a name."

"Does that plague you?" The girl said it flippantly as she ran the knife along the left foreleg.

"Yeah it does. I don't wanna die so anonymous in the desert."

He turned to Smith.

"You still aint told us your name."

"Aint no need for you to know it."

"You know mine."

"You aint know hers."

"She doesn't have one. You do."

The girl was taking a rest from skinning and sat with her eyes closed, blowing her breath upwards from under the cloth tied about her mouth, the reverberations in the cotton the only thing about her that moved.

"Ten miles we did tonight?" asked Matthew.

"About that much. We'll try for twenty tomorrow," the girl answered.

"You think that out? We aren't gonna make it through a week."

"You got another way you'd suggest?"

Matthew was silent for a moment to fake considering when he knew there was no other way.

"Nah. It's just that—fuck it. I didn't get into this business to die like this."

"Yeah, but you got into this business to see if it were possible for you to die."

Matthew didn't answer. He smeared some of the blood off of his chin and looked at it on his hand.

"And are you starting to think it possible?"

Matthew glared and then burst out laughing.

"Damn you," he said.

The ends of her eyes curled against the black paint and under the cloth over her mouth she must have smiled.

"I died in a desert once already, some hellhole far south of this. Five days without water before I fell against a saguaro and then got myself up by my own will the next time it rained."

She sat back and pulled her plastic bag around and took out a few of the rocks to roll in her hands and then went on.

"I won't do it again."

"That aint up for you to decide," said Matthew.

"Yes it is."

Matthew inhaled. His hair had hardened with blood and muck like a helmet and was traversed with cracks now.

"No. This aint right. We don't deserve to be here. After Awan and all the others who fell. This isn't right."

She dropped the rocks.

"In the wilderness there's no such thing as right."

"Fuck your principles."

"You've had water, and blood's thick enough that we might as well call you fed. You won't die in the next few hours. Awan already did."

Matthew chewed on his chapped lower lip, his token from years in that climate. It split and sent a coil of his own blood to join that of the animal on his jaw.

The girl had started skinning again and when she was finished and the fur laid out in a headless four-legged outline in the sand she stood and lifted the skeleton of meat and gathered the guts into her arms and walked out to where the two coyotes still shivered against one another in the starlight.

Smith watched her, the impish figure carrying a bundle half the size of herself in the feeble blue shadow. They shied as she approached them and then at the lure of the smell they shied less and when she tossed them the gut-sack and it burst upon the ground in front of her they ran to it immediately. Smith watched her like that for a while, tossing pieces of the thing she'd killed as charity to the species that had tried to kill her, so that they would survive by her doing the thing that they could not have brought themselves to do.

After a while she tossed the rest of the carcass to them and came back to sit under the archway. Her forearms were lined in muck besides where the one was bandaged and Smith knew she would not clean it because it would keep the sun off her skin, and he regretted for a moment that he had not covered himself in it as well. But it still meant something, and stalking through the desert covered in blood was a thing that he still did not want to do. Not yet.

She came back and did not fully sit down but bent on her haunches and stared at Smith from across the archway.

"Whose ghost is following you?"

Matthew was war-torn and tired as well but it was clear to whom the question was directed.

"What ghost."

"The one that rides your shoulders and speaks from the eye you've got left. We can see it."

Smith swallowed.

"A man's."

My father's.

No, it is my sister's. My sister who got a ghost without having died and they must be wandering the house now, together or apart or leaning back to back across that dust-flaked bed in the emptied room, platinum hair rolling over each other's shoulders. And one of them or both of them make that pilgrimage to his grave each night as if they would bid him rise, and if he ever did rise one of them would have to go and he did not know if it would be the ghost or the sister. Just as he did not know which of them wandered the hall outside his bedroom door with feet cottony blue in the moonlit dark when she could not sleep.

"Shouldn't be the one you shot by the juniper trees."

"It's not."

"Is it the rabbit jaw man?"

Smith shook his head and looked away from her. She watched him for a long time; he felt it.

After a few minutes the girl crawled back to the hide. She'd discarded the pulverized skull but left the intact lower jaw attached to the skin and pulled the torn mouth over her head like a necklace, the empty eyeholes bordering her throat and the teeth riding her sternum. She cut the rest of the hide into strips and rolled their wet sides to the sand to dry them as much as could be done and left them for now. The strips of hide made a segmented blur in the sheet of sand that ran out from the archway, as if a step upon them would break through to the mesh of channels underground, where perhaps there was light, because the desert held too tightly to its memories of daily burning for the grasp of the heat and sun to be punctuated by turns of the planet, and that the walls of the tunnels along which the tarantulas walked were lined in a blue glow, and that there was something of life or of beauty out there after all. There was a cracking sound and it came from the mouths of the coyotes, gnawing the sinew along the vertebrae of their brother.

The girl took out another sheet of ampicillin and swallowed some and passed it to Smith and he took two and they made for powdered stones in his drying mouth but at last he got them down and passed the packet back. Matthew took none; a cut to the head required nothing in the face of gunshot wounds.

"Tell us something," Matthew said.

"Something of what?" she replied.

"A thought, or a story."

The girl nodded and took off a boot to re-stuff the newspaper lining of it, a thing for the hands to do while the mouth spoke.

"I have a story. It's one I heard years ago down in Texas."

"Tell it."

"I will."

She turned the cloth on her wrist and gripped it then went on.

"In El Paso there was a girl who bore twins, and was nei-ther scared nor sorry about it, but gave them up because she was deep in work with the cartel and found that to be her call-ing and did not have the time. And so the twins, they were boys, were sent to live with families that either were connected to the cartel or paid it protection money, and one was raised with balance and level-headedness and he became a doctor and the other was raised with fury and retribution and he returned to the cartel and became a killer of men.

"After they had passed their thirtieth year the mother still had not searched them out. In her uncommonly long lifespan for a cartel woman she had learned that men build the illu-sions about their ill-begun destinies early in life, and she had no wish to take their illusions now. And so within the same tract of country they continued on, one saving lives and the other one taking, though it was never the other brother's victims who the brother revived on the hospital bed because the other brother was swift and always effective in his jobs. And neither knew a thing about the other's existence.

"Then one day the doctor got a man in the hospital bed that looked exactly like him. The man had been shot through the gut and he was critical but savable and on the second day he awoke and the doctor was sitting in a chair by his bed and the man said, 'you look just like me.' And the doctor also said, 'you look just like me.' And they joined hands and cried and when the man in the hospital bed fell back to sleep the doctor doubled his dosage of morphine and killed him."

"He killed him knowing it was his brother?" asked Matthew.

"No. It was the father," said the girl.

Smith looked at the girl and then regretted it. She could not have known. She was testing it. Matthew had called her fluent in reading fear.

"No man's ever killed another just for lookin like him," said Matthew.

The girl looked back to her boot and restuffed it then moved on to the other one.

"Don't say 'ever.' At this point in history every reason man could use for killing he's used. But you're wrong—there are men who fear their image in others. It's something to do with sharing their fate."

"And so? If you believe that one is part of your fate then you oughta protect them," Matthew said.

"No. That's not true. The only way to influence another's fate is by destroying them. It's the only thing that can be done permanently and by an action within your control. To try to protect someone is to try to intervene in the actions of the world against them but that's something you can't face alone or entirely because if fate has bullets for them you can only take one.

"You wouldn't even know what you were trying to protect, what is it in someone else you can really know, when all you can be sure of is your own existence and be wary of it if that. Regardless of whether the other shared your existence from the start or was the source of your existence in the first place. You can lash out blindly against not knowing but it will always stay the same. Fratricide may have been the original killing, but all it does is wipe a side of your face from this earth. Patricide avenges yourself against the one who made you and damned you to walk a land in which deserts exist. That's what the doctor-brother was trying to do."

There was a narrow line of light coming from their right. The girl got up and laid the strips of hide across the shoulder strap of her gun then slung it across her back.

"We should make more distance before the sun is up."

They went on. Behind them, the pair of coyotes chewed slowly on the cartilage of their fallen comrade, lolling on their stomachs at the gluttony.

<hr>

The depth of that night was so deep that the glow at the horizon did nothing to crack the sky's sheet of black. As he walked he could feel the blondeness washing over her shoulders as she ascended the hill in the fog and blowing backward as she delved into the woods like a hand into water. Under the branches the air would go from lack of light to true darkness that was not a lack but a thing in itself, a thing seeping from the earth that turned blades of grass up and made the webbing between the veins of dead leaves run frail. The darkness would meet her like a charcoal wall but if anyone could coax a wall into bending it was she, and she would slip through untouched with a bare foot put first and the tossed hem of a white dress to follow.

The bare feet would sink into the mantle of the forest floor, damp moss for carpeting and dead leaves to arch in a cradle beneath each footfall and coat the heel as it left the ground. Toward a shallow hole that was really below the hill but no, now it had to be in the center of the woods, and the saplings with their bark ripped by wind all pointed that way, that way, and the cedars aged like stone lent their shadows to that direction as well, in rejection of the moonlight's angle. She would follow, the twigs snatching at her hair as if to keep a piece, just a piece, she won't feel it, but the velvet steps would turn to a run and the chattering of trees rise out of a whisper and the noise building and then, and on, until she landed upon a clearing in which all was silent. And then, she would spin. Spin and spin again, not looking at the ground as the out-flung dress obscured it like a flower and the moon mottling through the canopy to paint her dancing legs and her eyes closed against its acrid light and her arms weightless in the air and then when at last she slowed, and when the skirt went limp and when the flower fell, she would look upon the unmarked grave. "Ah, father, there you are."

They kept in close beside mesas whose shadows they could walk beneath, but there were still stretches of ground without any walls to hide beside and they felt the ground growing warmer. The blood on their faces had started to smell and it was something muscular and almost cold and after a while it dried and stopped smelling at all.

The horizon to the east was churning in crimson as the sun rose dead to the side and created a pool of color more violent than the drippings he'd seen on their mouths in the navy dark of the night, but exposed to the daylight the red of their faces gained a new violence as well. That their feeding on the land should leave a mark altogether more putrid and leering than their slaughtering of men had.

Smith walked behind the girl and watched for so long that he saw the strips of coyote skin wrapped around her gun strap start to curl in the heat. The sweat was making his hands start to slip and he gripped the trashbag of pills hard enough that the plastic ran beneath his fingernails. When the sun was fully up they found themselves in the center of a plain, and no shade to be given.

The girl pointed to the north where another mesa lay a half-mile ahead. So far that if Smith raised a hand to cover it it was gone from his sight.

"We have to go."

Matthew groaned and sank to the ground and the girl gave him a strip of hide to put his teeth into.

"We have to go."

He rose to his feet again.

When they came to the mesa they fell below it. The girl went to her knees and started upturning sand with her hands, trying to bury herself in it, and found the sand was already hotter than the air. They spread out the skin strips that were dry enough now and passed them among themselves. They tied them along their wrists and covered their necks and bound them to foreheads that were blistering with sunburn and the hides clasped to their skin like remoras when wetted by the sweat. Hung with the skin of the desert and bloodied with its children, they laid down to sleep.

And he thought of her, Lucy running through the shadows of the woods, that she would be in search of something to warm her, a source of heat real or felt. Go somewhere cold, Lucy, take in the shadow and damp. Because if you can reach water then maybe I won't die.

⸺✦⸺

"No, it's the heatstroke."

"No, I'm so cold, I'm so cold."

"Matthew, it's the heatstroke. Stop talking and close your eyes."

Smith turned to see and the girl was kneeling in front of Matthew, his head lolling back against the cliff in full daylight. She was close to him, like something like a healer or a mother but she heard Smith and her lurid painted face looked his way.

Matthew was no longer sweating and they knew the moisture had broiled into a heat on the inside.

The sun went on in its passage of burning and Smith lay with his head against a rock with his eyes closed and once the girl shouted and sprang up to fight coyotes that had not followed and were not there.

Like an antithesis to waking at morning they all began to stir when the light waned toward sunset. When Smith awoke it was if he had awakened from something like dying and was unsure that he hadn't, and if you died would you take the violence you've committed with you or would it remain as a scar upon the earth. And if the physical manifestation of it meant a thing, he knew that if he survived and made it back home and lived a long life that his body would rot into moss and dissolve centuries before the dried out bones of those he'd felled in the desert started to decay.

He raised himself onto his knees and then stood. The girl and Matthew already walked before him, blackening figures against the dying arsenic red of the sun.

Their footsteps forged forward in the bluing sand and tarantulas emerged from their tunneled holes then plunged back into the earth as they passed. They had been exhausted even before they had begun walking and their feet moved forward like dragging metal, their shadows giving the girl an extra limb with the rifle strapped to her back and Matthew's a torso missing limbs as he held the pistol tight to his heart and Smith's shadow something poorly winged and top-heavy as he carried the bag of pills against a sweat-dampened chest with his elbows out.

In the clear starlight they could see their way, and see it well, better than when the daylight had swept blindness over their brows and bleached it all out. The light ricocheted off the stone borders of their world in blue. They went on, leaving tracks behind them that shone navy in the ground, grouped in a set of six but of four different boot tracks in a wandering herd.

They soon reached an empty plain that stretched for miles, and they traversed it like the grotesque deep-sea carnivores that charade with the bodies of their prey as they hunt over the lightless sand. They each fell a few times in turn in their exhaustion, but the others were too slow to notice or to react and each had raised themselves quickly and continued behind the others.

The stars were thick as a net above their heads, and then there was a star that was touching the land. The girl dove to ground.

"Down, get down!"

They crouched down beside her and she settled onto her stomach and squinted.

"Someone's there."

They knew it at once: it was the shack they had passed on the way south.

Smith pulled the shirtsleeve from over his nose and mouth. Inhaled. He could smell them.

"Horses."

The girl started laughing like she had when she'd cornered him in the bed of his truck and he knew how close to death they'd been.

"There's no cover. We'll go quietly until the house comes into view and then we're going to have to run."

They stalked forward, rolling their footsteps to avoid making a sound. The girl readied the AK-47.

The shack was made of plywood, no more material than would have fit in a single load from a pickup truck. The light came from within it; there was a window cut out at the side. The box of a home was flanked by piles of metal trash and scrap, old fencing, and a pool-sized basin to collect rain. The corral was beside it, to the east. Made of barbed wire strung up between hammered rebar. There were five horses standing motionless as trees within it.

At two hundred feet away they were as close as they thought they could go, counting that whoever was in the house would lose a degree of night vision from the lamp. The girl was readying herself to run.

A few of the horses shuffled to the side, and an enormous black mule raised its head between them. Swiveled its hare-like ears and looked directly at the three, and snorted high into the night air. The light brightened double as the curtain was shoved from the window.

"Go go go!"

The girl was lighter and faster in the sand and she was around the front of the shack first, then backed from it as the man within advanced with a gun held out. She had her rifle to him as well, and she glanced into the open window as she walked backward toward Smith and Matthew.

The shack-dweller was old but muscular, the tendons of his arms eroded by malnutrition. He wore no shirt and a graying beard hung to his chest with his hair in knotted locks. His eyes bleary and sun-ruined.

"Who's er? Who's er?" It was the voice of someone whose

first language was not English or for whom language was a thing long forgotten.

"He's the only one," said the girl.

"He's blind," said Matthew.

"He can see plenty," said the girl.

"Then the man's gone in the head."

The horses were all gathered at the edge of the corral, watching. The fence was only the height of their chests. They were narrow-boned, desert-fed. Scars roping their chests from leaning across the wire for the water trough.

The man was breathing hard and each breath combed his vocal cords and made a sighing sound.

"Who are ye?!"

The girl jerked the AK-47 at the hermit in response and he stepped back but kept his gun raised at her. It was a rot-handled Colt, Vietnam-era antique. The whole of his hands were callused as if encased in brown shells.

The girl shifted the gun to lean on her hip with her left hand over the trigger and wrapped her other arm over her stomach.

"What are ye things?"

"Start saddling them up." The girl spoke over her shoulder to Matthew and Smith.

"The horses?" the hermit cried.

The girl did not answer him. She called over her shoulder.

"There water in there?"

Smith and Matthew had already set upon the trough, soaking themselves with handfuls over the tops of their heads and the girl looked their way hungrily. The dust upon them ran down as mud and their bloodied wet bodies shone in the light of the lamp.

The hermit looked back and forth from them to the girl, training his eyes upon either spectacle with equal wonder.

After a few minutes the men relented from the trough and Smith checked the bag against one of the piles of scrap metal and started hunting among the junk. There was old tack piled by the loose gate of the corral, all of the leather heat-cracked. Matthew laced an arm through a bridle and started untying the gate.

The hermit flinched and looked away from the girl and toward where the sound had come from.

"Not them horses!"

Matthew opened the gate.

"I catched thems out of the desert I'll be damned if I's give em up now!" The hermit turned his gun and shot the horse nearest to him clean between the eyes and there was a scream but it was the girl's and she had cracked the barrel of her rifle down on the hermit's wrist and the pistol skidded into the sand and she kicked it toward the men. The horse oscillated in place for a moment, then sank into the corral fence, the wire reverberating with a singing sound.

Smith was on the gun first and opened it up.

"It's empty. There was just the one shot."

That last shot that you always hold onto in the desert.

The hermit was on his knees in the sand now, clutching his head and rocking back and forth.

"Keep saddling them up. Leave me the mule," said the girl.

"No I's be damned them horses no." The hermit had lowered his hands and was screeching now and watching them as Smith took the thickest piebald mare and Matthew a roan with a docked tail.

He would not stop screeching and the girl barked, "Shut up!" and pushed her gun in closer to his face.

Smith walked the piebald over and took the gun and the hostage from her and the girl sprinted to the trough, climbed directly into it and did not surface for a few seconds. When she breached the water the two remaining horses skittered but did not break the lines of their already-broken corral. She left Matthew holding the mule as well as his gelding and took the gun back from Smith.

The hermit was rocking back and forth again, weeping.

"He got food in there?" asked Smith.

The two loose horses were toeing around the dead one, curiously. Looking with turned heads at where the fence angled down from the weight of its back.

Matthew tied his horse and the mule and came over and put a hand on the gun.

"Ah leave the man be already. We got what we need."

Smith eyed the girl.

"Was there food in there?"

The girl nodded.

"Just cans, we wouldn't be able to carry much but it's another day of water."

"He's harmless, let the old man go already," said Matthew.

The girl's back teeth showed when she answered.

"He's not harmless. His shot hit exactly where he wanted it to. And he'd rather have his own horses dead than us riding them."

"Please, please please." The hermit with his face to the sand now and tears and snot blacking the ground beneath.

Matthew let go of the gun and ran a hand through his hair.

"There's no truck, he aint got no way out of here. We can bust up his radio so he can't call anyone. Come on, most human contact the man prolly gets is someone bringing in supplies every couple a months."

The girl shook her head.

Matthew turned to Smith.

"You—you, say something! We don't have to do this, this isn't right."

Smith looked at the girl and she would not take her eyes from the man on the ground. So many dead so far and some by his hand and some not, but he was thinking of Lucy. He inhaled again and looked at the legs of the horse that could take him back and then looked at the man curled, beaten, on the ground.

He nodded at the girl and walked away.

The hermit sensed the shift and took his hands from his eyes and sat back and then stood and stumbled backward and the girl shifted the gun to touch the side of his temple. Propped the butt of the gun against her hip once more with her finger on the trigger and the other hand free.

"Please, please damn yous . . ."

And at the last minute she lowered the gun and yanked her knife from her pocket and slit his throat. Save your bullets.

<hr />

Fresh hides had to be salted daily for twelve days and they would be finished soon and ready for hanging, but Lucy was not strong enough to string them up herself.

She lit the lamp then stood in the center of them to give them their day's worth of salt, still barefooted and in a dress that skimmed her ankles. And as she turned this time in the firelight she saw them as humanoid outlines, faceless shadows, and the unjointedness of their limbs made it seem as if they moved and they circled her and hummed and reached and the three, three silhouettes too familiar to what she once had had, once had been, and she flew from the door and down the stairs and thrust her hands into the sink.

Above and behind her the skins on the floor tightened further with a collective grating breath and it looked to be snow that had tracked across the hides and along the floor and on her hands, but snow that sucked the wet out of everything and desiccated the living as much as the dead as it pulled the veins tight and cracked the skin over her knuckles. It was not snow, and would show no more sympathy than anything else in this house, than anything in Box Elder had.

There was a sound against the kitchen window and she jolted at the noise and wrapped her burning hands in her skirts and took the pistol from the sideboard and went out to see.

It was a blackbird, out too late. The little thing lay splay-winged on its back on the porch floor, and could not move. Needed to be put out of its misery.

She leveled the gun at the bird but her hands were weak.

"Wyatt, I caint kill it."

And again, and a piece of blonde fell into her face as she leaned down toward the flailing thing.

"I caint kill it, Wyatt."

And she pulled the pistol away and bent her arms and held it there to her chest and at last bit her lip and with her eyes to the wing-prints on the window slid a boot forward and stepped on it.

Part Four

CHAPTER ELEVEN

Heatstroke

The hermit managed to get a hand to the wound on his gullet before he died, then was quiet thirty seconds later. The girl was already in the shack, digging through mothwing stacks of old newspapers and rags and pulling whatever was of use, which was only an armful of canned vegetables. She took two of these and sat down in the sand and opened her plastic bag and Smith reached for the other five but she said "wait" and took out her knife again. Punctured the lid of the first can and the smell came out rotten and then she did the same with the next then grabbed the others from Smith and did the same again, then threw them at the shack with a cry so anguished that the voice could have come from the sum of those who had fallen on that ground that day.

Matthew was standing by the dead man when she passed on her way from the shack to the water trough.

"Goddamn you."

Smith was close behind her and Matthew turned and grabbed his arm.

"There are some people in this world, that killing them when you get the chance means sparing the lives of a hundred men." The light in the shack was a solar-charged lantern and it started to fade. It went from white to a toasted gold as it lessened, alone among the marauders while legions of stars flickered along the mesa-tops like enemy fires. "What you did was no act of mercy. Everything she does is on your hands."

Smith turned his working eye away and shook him off and went to hunt for anything useful among the piles of metal trash that bristled like rust-skinned cacti in the growing dark. He half-expected the rogue herd of cattle to break from among them, that the shells of car doors and kinked unusable piping formed some steel-and-aluminum woods from which strange metallic vermin would crawl. His hands itching to bleed to know that they had just fought. Matthew walked the perimeter of the place, futilely searching for tire marks from the caravan that they could follow back north, but they had all been washed by wind.

They each took turns drinking as much as their stomachs could carry and then drenching their clothes and then they were laughing, watching the dust run from them back into the sand. Matthew shouted a blissful curse to the desert while facing the east where the sun would later rise and poured a handful of water over his still-bloodied head. The stain turned to pink upon his sideburns as it diluted and left him a half-lucid carnival clown with a forehead wound and solitary burned eyebrow the only things to manifest that there was not merely hysteria but also violence within him.

They all took a final drink and rose one by one. The girl left the gate open for the remaining horses.

The mule's eyes widened at her approach, and its shoulders were above her head but she spoke to it and roped its mane around her hand then gripped and got up onto it.

The loose horses were stumbling among the wreckage of the place, nosing it. The night had made the place cold and they shivered from their shoulders as they walked. The men were mounting their horses when the loose ones bolted. Smith's mare bucked but he kept it down.

"Coyotes," the girl said, and she kicked the black mule into the dark.

The horses pulsed forward in the cold and expelled steam through their nostrils and their eyes that would have rolled with white instead stayed liquid black in the lack of light.

After half an hour they slowed. The girl circled the mule back around so they could speak. The animal had venomous-looking eyes and was foaming around the bit as it gnawed it.

"Matthew, you're the horseman. What's your call?"

Matthew looked down from the saddle at the face of the roan. Its pattern dissipated on the face and left two clear white circles around the eyes like goggles.

"They're okay. Used to distance and low water." His voice cracked on a dry throat and he had to pause to catch his breath.

"Push em as far as we can tonight while it's cool then let them take their own pace come daylight."

They kneed the horses and walked on, side by side. The girl leaned forward and laid flat on the mule, so dwarfed by its size that she looked like a spider's young clinging to its back.

After a while Matthew spoke against the sleeve that covered his mouth.

"Are you still counting, man?"

"It's not wise to talk more in your state," said the girl.

"Not wise to stay silent and let your brains go to the desert either. There's two things will kill you in the desert, and half of it's the thirst and the other half's letting your mind go to it."

"I aint counting them. Only tryna count how many more days this done bought us," said Smith.

The girl murmured from where her face was half-buried in the mule's fur.

"We had a man come through one of our supply chains once who could've mathed that out, how much time we got from drinking that amount of coyote blood plus that amount of water. Down to the minute. A photographic memory, but for numbers. Some religious understanding of them. He was in accounting, laundering money or whatever way you want to put it. To know how much money would be coming in he'd memorize figures and delivery schedules and could calculate market prices on any given combination of goods in a second. A genius."

"Where'd he end up?" asked Matthew.

"At one time after a spat with some locals we were low on security, and so he went out with them on a run. He ended up with his gun to a man's head when they were accused of ripping us off and the boss made him recite the current figures and wholesale prices right then for everything from E to marijuana at every grade so they could adjust how much was owed. He was so traumatized that his memory must have snapped, because after that he couldn't remember figures unless he had his gun aimed. In the rest of his meetings from then on out he'd have to go stand in the corner and prop a gun to the wall and recite the numbers so no one would think he was pointing it at them." She said it with no nostalgia but with the detachment of something that was no more hers than any other fact or history merely because she had been witness to it.

The mule started to toss its head and the girl laid out her arms along its neck to cover its nose.

Matthew turned to Smith.

"Was that your first gunfight?"

"Depends on what you'd call a gunfight." He could see the girl ahead lower her chin to ride upon the canines of the coyote jaw. The arm still burned quietly.

"Well, a havin to kill men indiscriminately."

"Yeah."

"You thinking on it lots?"

"Nah. There's a good deal more to be thinkin on out here."

"Got that right."

Matthew eyed him and Smith knew Matthew now thought him merciless.

"And you? Were that yer first?"

He wanted noise to kill the silence.

"Nah. It's not the reason I got into the trade but it's part of the trade."

"You aint from here. How'd you do it?"

"I'm an import, fresh from the suburbs. Got mixed up with the wrong crowd or the right one, depending on how you put it. But I realized quick there's no other life than this one, this's the only one that's real."

"What makes it real?"

"The nature of men."

"What nature is that?"

"Survival. Fighting to live. The concept of 'living' is a construct. It's the only state any of us have experienced and so we have nothing to compare it to, nothin else we've ever been. In itself, it doesn't mean anything. But if you bring in the threat of death, suddenly it's got a definition by opposites. You can see living and not-living right there in front of you. It's only in those minutes that you're actively aware that you're living."

Matthew wiped his nose under the scrap of his shirt as the animals walked on.

Lucy would be spreading hay among the cattle now. Feed for bovine guts that carried planks of meat over bones and made rumbled grunts in the dusk, as if it were the mountains beyond that moved. She could never spread anything whether it were salt for hides or hay for the living or grain for chickens without spinning, and he saw her there, out in the fields where it was black save for the opalescent shine of cattle eyes as they watched her with the dull expressions of animals that trust you. If the moon was bright enough there her skirts would show white, and the hay would fall to the ground before they did. That maybe, out of something of innocence or good she took longer to fall back to earth than anything else.

They used to lie on the backs of the cattle out there, when the cattle had bedded down in the pasture for the night. Stretched on a sheet of fur that was warm and lifted with a breath every few moments, and they'd watch the sky and say all of the typical things about the stars that were so pleasurable to say. The mosquitoes would always go for the cattle instead of them and the air tasted amber with the smell of timothy cud. Lucy settled down onto one of them now, and looked at it all as she used to. Behind her in the house, the hides were softening like the skin of her palms across the whole bedroom floor, white and a week old.

In the south, the three moved along on their mounts, charred and dried with viscera, the horsemen of the apocalypse as the water steamed from them in cold, their fourth member following them as a series of limbs dragged across the desert by coyotes' teeth.

The girl held out an arm at the first glimpse of sunrise and they stumbled to a stop to watch it and Matthew's horse trotted forward then sank to its knees to roll in the dust but he yanked it back up.

"We'll ride them out until dark. We need to get as far as we can, there's no point in conserving them past that."

They kicked the animals back into motion and the horses snorted objections and tossed their heads and the girl's mule let out a full bellow. In the stagger north, their riders were shadowed effigies of ruin, clothes stiffening in wrinkles and cracks as the water departed them.

The sun completely dried them within the hour and they all placed strands of coyote hide between their teeth to try and suck from them whatever water was left. They got little moisture from it and it tasted like bone. Once they stopped to piss into the sand and in the same pause took up stones to roll against their sapless molars.

When dark finally fell, their eyes were too sun-ruined to notice it. They'd gone fifty miles at least and they went down into the yellow wash below an archway and as they stopped and dismounted they pulled the bridles from their horses and used them to hobble their legs.

They went to take off the saddles but Matthew was too weak and Smith had to lift it from the gelding for him. They sat in a circle with no fire and nothing to drink and nothing to eat. The horses mumbled their mouths along the brush in the foreground and it was dried brambles and nothing much but still something and the girl put a few strands of it between her teeth as well and then followed it with more antibiotics. The air started to cool once more and the three lay back and let it take the heat from them.

"The horses are flagging," said the girl.

"No more than their due. Should get another day or two out of them," said Smith.

They both turned to Matthew, whose face was collapsing and then contorting as he moved in and out of consciousness. When he furrowed his brows it cracked the dried blood on his forehead, and a bit of foam was wetting the cloth over his mouth. He did not speak and they watched him with something of concern, something of futility, and also something of the knowledge that they themselves were not far off. For the latter reason, they eventually looked away.

"You hungry?" Smith asked.

"No."

He sat silently and toed at the sand, felt its heat fold over the top of his boot.

She looked at him.

"You're expecting me to kill something."

"It's your most consistent habit so far."

She laughed and crossed her legs, but it was a thing not like laughing, with the child's sound in her mouth.

"It's not a habit, it's a method."

"There a difference?"

"Yeah. Killing's not an end but a transfer of power. Like how protein is never wasted in death, just redirected to another use, power's the same. It's transferred to control over life, or one more day alive. If you kill sincerely, it's impersonal, done without hesitation, and with the intent to use it to its fullest purpose."

She rocked back and forth a bit. He looked out into the gray washed night and then took out his knife and began to dig at the muck caking the seams of his boots. Matthew spluttered once at the sky and then lay still. She stared hard at him then looked back and continued.

"Only killing done without a purpose would be gratuitous, but there's no gratuitous violence among men. A fox goes into a killing frenzy and destroys more than it needed but it doesn't know why. Each man is born with an amount of power, and some amass more power by violence, and others test it in violence and by gambling either gain more or give all theirs up to others. Power not as brute strength but as the number of days a man has. Every man has metal waiting for him whether it's a bullet or knife or gurney, and an act that extends your days beyond what you were born with can never be gratuitous. That's the truth behind all killing. A truth Matthew doesn't know."

Matthew rolled over and then pulled himself up against the rock and closed his eyes again.

Smith put the bag of pills behind himself and laid his head upon it.

He had carried it for so many miles. Carrying two hundred thousand dollars like a chunk of a ranch against your chest, the last bit of green in the desert as if it would generate life again, your life, grow a forest if you planted it.

His gums no longer felt epithelial, as dry as the skin of his cheeks, and the arm was nothing now in the face of how much the rest of his body ached. And Father, did it feel like this when you died, even though I carry the fate with me and you went as if fate were the thing that commanded it. But Father did it feel like this, when your wetness went out in blood instead of in sweat and by the time you hit the ground were you as dried as the steer carcass I passed by out here and if or when I fall out here will I feel the same, feel as if I've been shot.

He took a ragged breath against the cloth and put his hands behind his head and dug his fingers in close to feel the pills.

Will I feel as if she'd shot me too.

<hr />

He was at the kitchen table, memorizing the patterns on the pieces of paper the father had given him, fingers rooting along the perforations like reading braille. When the father realized that the loss of the eye made it so that Wyatt could no longer shoot, he had taken paper targets and pinned them against the edge of the woods. Shot one from twenty-five yards, twenty-three, twenty-one, all the way down to one.

Wyatt was getting good enough now that his father could show him a pheasant in the woods then shoot it and bring it over and ask him how far and Wyatt would turn the animal in his hands and look at the shot pattern and say "twelve to fifteen yards," or "between twenty and twenty-five," and then he would turn and look again at where the pheasant had been and commit to memory that the distance that looked that far away was that many yards.

He had the sheets spread out on the bare table in front of him and the paper flakes hanging from the shotgun holes were like bleached leaves. It was January now.

She came in from outside before the father did, and her nose was snowburnt red and she left her boots at the door and the ice stuck in two rings of white around her calves that dulled to gray against her socks as it melted. She sat in the chair next to his and rocked for a moment where she sat then smirked and fell sideways onto his lap, ripping the target out of his hands.

"Lucy get up, you smell like horse manure."

He slid halfway out of his chair and she was laughing now and laid her head on the part of the seat he'd vacated.

"Better to smell like it than look like it."

"Keep messing with that yearling he's gonna run your face into a fence so hard you're gonna wish you done looked like it."

She stood back up and wiped her knuckles in her dress; the snow had gone to water on them.

"Nah. I got a saddle on him today."

"Not a chance."

"Swear to God, Wyatt."

"Hell, well done."

She broke a smile and flicked a patch of snow from her sock.

"Pulled a rabbit this morning an' it's there if you want it."

She nodded and went over to the woodburner and nudged at the meat then took a loin from the pan and he pushed aside the papers and laid his gun on the table to clean it.

Lucy went to stand by the window and he watched her for a long while. Her dress had been pulled over the legs of dirty jeans and she lifted the mud-caked hem to wipe her hands, flashing cotton-patched denim knees that were translucent with wear. Her hair was unbrushed; now that she would let it grow she would not tell it how to do so, and it tangled as a golden fur collar around her neck. The wind was making a sound against the glass like something prying, and she had her fingers to the pane, letting the moisture fan out from them in ovals that turned clear. The ice melted through the glass in the places she touched, and she was laughing at once in spite of the weather that could do nothing to her and out of pleasure that for the two of them there were horses to tame and rabbits to eat off the stove. And he understood then that she was the sort of thing that made houses warm.

Smith kicked out a boot but it only met with sand and he threw an arm forward and it met with sand as well.

He was still on the desert floor, staring up at a black sky bleeding aquamarine in the presence of a coming dawn that was not yet there and so he lay like something sunken with his head against the bag of pills. And after a while he rose and went to the piebald and started to undo its hobbles and the girl heard him and rose and did the same and it was when she turned that she saw that Matthew still lay prostrate in the sand.

She pulled the mule by the mane over to where Smith stood with his arm looped through the reins of the mare and said, "Hold him," and Smith took the animal's muzzle in both his hands and it was enough to make the creature stay.

The girl went down into a crouch beside Matthew and laid her fingers without pressure on either side of his throat and then with a cautious hand raised his eyelids. After a moment she lowered them again.

"Matthew's dead."

She stepped back and there was no sound but then both felt the hammering of their thirst returning and that Matthew's blood had slowed in his veins. Smith looked to her and then to the body, wide-eyed.

"I won't do it."

"I wasn't going to ask you to."

The girl went to Matthew's horse and removed its hobbles. It stood there not moving and the girl finished tacking the mule.

There was not the time nor the spare energy to bury him there in the sand and so the girl folded the cloth on his mouth up to cover his eyes and took Awan's pistol from him and put it in her pocket and after a moment's thought went back into his pockets and took the lighter and pack of cigarettes.

The roan that had been Matthew's still lingered there.

They mounted their animals in silence and looked once more at the figure slowly turning gray then turned their animals to the north and went on, until they would not have been able to see the ghoulish red still painted on his face if they had looked back.

Dawn was full across them within the hour and as they hunched on their horses their eyes were on the ground, and they passed without seeing below mesas and spires of red rock grander than anything manmade they'd served witness to before. It was too hot and Smith pushed his jacket down around his waist and unbuttoned his shirt and tied it over his head and looked down at his arm. Still a dug-out gash on the bicep but the spider legs of infection retreating into it now, a week out from the shot.

He and the girl rode parallel, alternating which was against the sun and which rode in the other's shadow, and after a while there were no shadows to ride in. The horses made no more objections, were too weary to do so or had settled into their fate. Matthew's gelding would linger behind aimlessly for a time, then jog to catch up and keep pace for a while, only to repeat the lingering and jogging again.

When it was full daylight the girl untied the coyote skin from around her forehead and pushed her hair down to cover her neck from the sun and retied the skin to keep it there. She stood up in the saddle to get at her bag and took out a cigarette and passed one over to Smith.

She lit hers and raised it.

"A toast to our dead Matthew. Since he died in the desert and soon we probably will too, might as well have a smoke and waste our breath in talking."

He nodded and took the lighter from her when she held it out. Her eyes were nervy and he had not seen them like this before.

"So, Wyatt, tell us about yourself."

He flinched at his name's being unearthed here. The only one who had said it in front of her was Lucy.

"You seen enough over the past few days that there can't be much more to say."

She exhaled through her nose and it seemed a gesture that matched the animal she rode.

"But that's the thing. There has to be something behind it all. For starters—is Lucy your sister or your wife or both?"

"Good god."

"Just asking."

"It were never anythin like that. It's that she's the only person I've ever really known. She was me, I was her."

The girl eyed him.

"How long were you two out there alone?"

"Technically, five years. Figuratively, longer'n that."

The girl lay back on the mule and shielded her eyes with a hand. He felt suddenly at ease or suddenly hopeless and did the same, even though it exposed more for the sun to beat down upon.

"Tell me about them. All the ones from before."

"The ancestors?"

"Yeah. The ones that put you there."

"They came there decades before, but in a country in which there aint no town and nowhere to center people's stories there aint much more history than that. Great-grandfather came west in the 1860s, civil war and whether it were being farsighted that the South was gonna end or just cowardice and abandoning a homeland we aint know."

He paused.

"It's a long story."

The girl nodded, her cigarette between her teeth. A bit of ash landed on her chin but she did not brush it off.

"Fill the quiet."

Because if you didn't say it now it may never have the chance to be said again.

"That man was Wyatt Sinclair and he went to Utah, land that for some reason he had to get to farther than Texas and why Texas hadn't been good enough there weren't no reason, save ambition or again bein a coward, with Utah just as dry but farther, so many more miles toward a gold rush that had already done ended but not toward it enough, and away from Texas where all the cattle of them days were run, Utah a desert and no Apache to fight in it but so cold in the dark months and no water to freeze and so the waterings of your eyes freeze to your face, and still not far enough for coastline or gold.

"Old man Sinclair marked out this property, two thousand acres of old pine and maple that stood against the cold and the dry and lined the ribcages of cattle. Sinclair a man that done insisted on refrainin from history, not fit for the warrin over a split nation or the growing Western coast or the frontier against Mexico and cutthroat natives that scalped. Just went to Utah, to fight no man but fight nature, but that's a battle that can't be won by fight or strength of the arm and done took the fight outta him and the fight outta his generations after. Out of his bein a coward of men or out of ambition toward fighting something bigger, but against nature he couldn't win. Would not. Did not."

The mule stumbled and the girl jerked her hands out to catch herself and lost her cigarette. Took another and passed a second to Smith.

"And then it was one thousand seven hundred acres, three hundred sold off in pieces in years after to failed men from Vegas and Salt Lake with just enough cash for a half-size trailer but more cash than them Sinclair-Smiths had on hand. And it was fittin that Sinclair lost his name by a line of females; two daughters and one of them wifed by a man from California and the other run off god-knows-where and all that determination or cowardice buried in the tractor ruts on that land they done tilled with artificial irrigation into ground that aint want it but when forced still gave up wheat.

"And then that land left to the only son of the woman that hadn't run off and the man Smith that done came from the West."

Smith went quiet. Took his hands from above his eyes and let the sun eat away at his retina.

"Then what happened to him? That one was your father?"

"He died. Aint nothin more to it."

Had died young and unsuccessful against the land like the ones before had died old and unsuccessful, but shot in the chest, gone from that house by the road that was there before the road was, built small for the times as if failure was imminent but too large for now, with empty rooms for the self-orphaned daughter to wander in the shadows that too many windows made. And this seventeen hundred acres, without a name as any estate should have been given and without a purpose, so that Sinclair's descendants forever after were chained to it, to absolve it of its namelessness and give it some purpose, to give the three generations before some purpose for whatever it was they had left undone, before the desert fractured it all to dust.

"You think it was fate?" the girl asked.

"How so?"

"Fate that they ended up on land where no one has a business to ever be let alone try to man and so led you here, to where you are now."

He sat up from the horse's back.

"Of course."

She tossed her finished cigarette to the side, knowing that, in the desert, it would feed something.

"Fate is only a number, a count of how much time you have left."

But what of fate not as number but with hands, that had folded the leaves in that way and bent the daughter's sight so that she believed the father was an elk, she who had hunted and navigated those woods a thousand times before.

"Damn this place." He shouted it and the mare spooked and then settled to a walk again.

The girl kicked the mule to catch up the few paces. She looked forward as they rode on and was quiet for a long time before she spoke again.

"Who did you lose?"

"Don't matter. Why so much asking? Tell your own history since we've got air to fill."

"No point. It's my aim in life to defy my past. It's your aim in life to resolve yours."

<hr />

In the midafternoon, the roan broke from its jog and barreled past them, and did not stop until it was another quarter mile out, where it shied and spun in its tracks.

The girl was up in the saddle immediately.

"Coyotes. It has to be."

Smith looked at her and she shaded her eyes and looked

backward to where the horse had come from. There was a faint string of dust-colored dots on the horizon that separated and grew then shrank again as the animals moved.

"Shit. They must have gathered at Matthew."

Smith had turned around his horse to look. "At least eight. That's enough for a horse. If we run them we might end up without horses anyway."

"We have to catch the roan."

"It's spooked out of its mind, you aint gonna catch that thing."

"Shit!"

From her face, she knew as well as he did that there was no outrunning them. Coyotes could cover twenty miles in a day.

They had perhaps an hour until the distance was closed, and in the heat they could not give the time to waiting. They nudged their animals on.

The mesas here were low, and their bases swept down to the flat of the earth and expunged the sand from it, the ground a sheet of red rock jagged where opposing mesa feet met and parted again. The girl rode standing in the saddle, a fixed figure bent to run without the ability to do so, a frozen and impotent posture under the wasting hot air. The horses were uneasy but exhausted or too without faith to run, and so expressed their fear in stumblings and lurchings that resounded in their hooves against the stone as they marched without heart or passion from the coming tide of teeth.

The roan was a red silhouette standing in the distance. It was waiting for them, staring, as only grasslands creatures can do, at once at the open expanse to the north and at the pair of horses and riders with their low train of pursuers stippling the white-air southern horizon. Smith did not turn around to see. He would hear their nails on the stone when they advanced onto that ground, and until then, looking would give him nothing. The fate does not change for the watching. And if time was a flat plain then there was no escaping it nor beginning or ending of it; there were always coyotes, there was always a gun in your hand. Lucy was always four hundred miles away.

Within half an hour the clicking sound began as the pack passed from the sand to the rock, their nails skidding over it as they tripped in their hunger. He could not say that he did not think it would have happened like this, with blood under an August sun, but he could not have foreseen that death would have the audacity to arrive at a lope. He knew the girl spoke because she could no longer stand the sound of their footsteps.

"Navajo legend says the mesas are the bodies of giants that a pair of twins fought and killed," she said from the back of the mule.

"You believe it?"

The roan was minutes from them; it had not moved. Its head was lowered to graze on plants that were not there.

"I don't think those are what giants would look like. Giants go among regular men."

"Cartels."

"We've already fought one," she said.

"Didn't win."

Day was hot and white where it flowed over the cracks between the tops of the mesas, a molten river above them.

"Not cartels. They're too large to feed on men so they're not a danger to them; they feed on civilization instead. What they did in the desert was self-preservation. A bull's an herbivore but it'll kill you if you cross it."

They met with the roan; it pitched its head back and forth and fell in to walk between them, the sclera of its eyes settled within the sand-patched face, placated in the grain-and-sweat air between its brothers.

"How many ticks does it take to kill a bull?" she asked.

"Ten per pound of body mass til they start losing weight. Then it's just a matter a time."

The sound was no longer a clicking only, in the multitude of steps, but a rumbling and a snapping of teeth as the dogs bit at one another's heels.

"You see? It takes a tick to kill a giant," she called out.

The roan reared once between their faces, the calico of its dinnerplate cheek a blurred impression of the landscape, before it shouldered its weight against the mule and the pair stumbled in their tracks. The horses were making sounds like murmuring.

"A tick on the back of the world, with a gun," said Smith, as he kicked the mare.

"Yes."

The roan went to move past them but the girl swung her mule to the right to cut it off. Smith's heart was thrashing in his chest; the coyotes were too close.

"No. You're not. There aint a word for what you are."

"And you have a word for what you are?"

"Too many." He drew Awan's pistol.

The sound was growing so loud that it shook the rest of his addled senses and the crags of the mesa walls on either side of them seemed to shudder like either side of a titan jaw. The girl reined her mule to fall in behind the others.

There was a cry as a coyote fell from the blow of the mule's hoof and at last they turned. The pack filtering from among the mesas like a mud tide across the stone, floating febrile eyes. The girl kicked the mule hard and it reared, and when it came down she planted the AK-47 between its ears and shot the roan horse in the back of the head.

The mule broke into a wild run at the shot and Matthew's horse went tumbling down, washed over in the wave of desert fur with the blood of its last rider still on its consumers' muzzles.

The crowd of mesas broke into an open plain, and the girl hacked at the mule with her heels and circled it until she got it under control. A few of the coyotes had sprinted after them but turned around at the mounting smell of blood.

They rode until they reached a plateau. The girl slid from the mule and turned away.

"We'll stop here for the night."

Four shots left between their guns.

The horses were burned out and shaking, and they stayed close beside one another and huddled against the cliff-side as they listened to the devouring in the distance.

Smith and the girl fell against the rock alongside the animals. She lifted her shirt to look at her stomach. The bandages were dung-colored with sweat and she closed her eyes and leaned back.

Dark was coming and he could feel the coolness starting in the way salt pulls at the mouth.

A hawk cried from the top of the plateau. The elevated column held trees gone alien from whatever evolving besets seeds that are blown upward to the sky, and what life forms and gardens lay on that island in the mid-atmosphere no man would ever see or know. The girl noticed it too and got up and stepped back, strained to get a look.

"It's green up there." She wandered around the base, looking for a way up, but found none.

"But it's not for us." She sat back down. Not for them, confined to the lifeless ground with scavengers peeling apart a horse a quarter of a mile from them and they no better, having scavenged the horse in the first place by the blood of fellow man.

The cold was growing and Smith took the tied shirt from his head, clasped the arm once more, then put it back on.

"It's your father."

He looked at her.

"The rabbit's jaw man."

He nodded, said nothing. Looked back into the darkening air.

"You can always tell a patricide. Always. But the thing is, you're a patricide, but I don't think you're really the one that did it. Are you?"

He shook his head.

"Have you told it?"

He rested the back of his head against the rock.

"No."

"Ever?"

"It's not somethin you tell."

"You never told her?"

"You know it was her?"

"It couldn't have been anyone else. You never told her?"

"But she's the one that done it."

"That's a reason as good as any. Few of us in this world really know what we've done."

He lowered his eyes and the girl adjusted the fabric on her wounded forearm and was staring at him again when he looked up.

"There aint but one way to tell it and I'll aim to tell it right. There was an accident. She thought it was an elk. In the woods she shot my father and that's where he went down and it took her ninety minutes and a mile to drag him out from where he fell to the edge of the woods. And I'd let go of the black steercalf I was breaking and let it run and went to her to help and just stared from her to the man and back again and when I looked back another time she was gone.

"She left him there and walked up to the house, and I followed after her. In the kitchen she set the shotgun on the table never to pick it up again. Didn't say nothin, just put the gun on the table like that. She didn't cry and if she'd cried the tears were on the father and there weren't no lines in the dirt across her cheeks anymore.

"I went to hold onto her but she shied from me like a dog and so we went back for him and laid him out in his own bed and changed his shirt to cover the hole and we left him like that for two days and passed in and out of the room as if it would change somethin or mean somethin and at the end of two days when we knew there'd be a smell soon we wrapped him in a sheet and I drug him to the base of the hill and buried him. There were no playact of a funeral though she was there when I spilled the final shovelful of dirt, her standin in the shadows at the mouth of the woods, and when I was done she came up and put her rabbit's jaw necklace on the beam of the wooden cross above his head."

And after he was breathless from the telling of it and no weight had been lifted from his chest but the girl seemed to have inhaled it and fed upon it.

"You wouldn't let her be the patricide."

"It weren't her fault. It were an accident. Call it somethin outta the land that got him, fate or somethin like revenge. But she didn't deserve to be broken that way. I'd kill the man who killed him and broke her, but there aint no man. And what can you do when it's the way things are you want justice against?"

"You test it."

He had forgotten his thirst and remembered it now, wanted water but there was none. He knew how he looked, face burned and ragged with the moisture having long ago evacuated the skin and the animal parts wrapped around his head and the arm no longer rotting but something that used to rot. The appropriate face for a patricide. And he knew now, he was Jacob, bound to wander the earth.

A pair of nightbirds called out, floated down from the top of the mesa.

"Do you think up there it's paradise?" he asked.

"If it's got mud or water I'd call it that." She closed her eyes sitting up. "But paradise isn't real, no tree of knowledge would have fruit. It would have to have been a box elder. A tree of knowledge wouldn't feed you, it would just show you that the blood had always been there."

He laid the bag of pills behind his head but could not sleep. Her face leveled at the desert as if challenging it or watching from another eye. She wore the paint of the land, of all of the animal blood and disassembling of life that he and Lucy had grown up fearing as they trudged along carrying that out-of-Eden pain of having to kill to survive. And he knew that the girl was the closest thing to something hell-sent he would ever know, but in a place like this it would take that sort of god to get you out of here. He shut his eyes to the sounds of fevered yips as the coyotes urged their young toward the feed, and the girl crawled nearer. He made a space for her and she rested her head on the opposite end of the bag of the pills, and they slept.

<hr />

He dreamed of Lucy that night. She was in the darkened leather chair that was still darker than her in the moonlit

black with her fingers that should have been practiced enough
to be stitching embroidery but instead had stayed clumsy in
grief. They were bleeding out against a gratingly rough flannel shirt repaired three times over that might as well have
been burlap and at last when a nightbird cried out in the
emptiness she would come awake and raise her eyes and
then the man's ghost was there and skeletal thin but still
there in the room.

And she would stand to go to him, and as she did the shadows from the trees outside and from the angles of the porch
would wash over her and color her face in indigo and purple,
as if the old bruises from rolling around on the farm as a kid
in the years and years before were resurrected from beneath
the skin. And as she moved farther into the moonlight from
the window the shadow bruises would open in violet slits and
empty themselves in dark over her cheek, and then across her
collarbone where the light pooled, and then overflow across
the chest and the arms and the legs draped in the colors of
the sunsets that come before thunderstorms. She would kneel
in the puddle of blue and look up at the man and raise her
supplicant's hands and the needle and thread still in them,
flannel shirt dropped, and lavender-indigo-swirl-stained and
white-faced would whisper, "Father I'm so sorry, Father I'm
so sorry." And the wound in the man's chest would run to mix
with the shadows of her own.

"You think we're gonna die?" he asked.

"Nah. Only if you say it."

Her voice was hoarse.

"Plus, it's always the horse that dies before the man does."

The sky began to stream in cracks of pink above them and it was still cold and such a strange sensation to try to wrap the cold around you while huddling like trying to grab up warmth. Their eyes shone where still it was dark and the cracked stains on their skin made them shine all the more in their dried casings, though Smith's false eye had grown dull with the dust.

Hungry and without a thing to grasp his teeth on, Smith jawed and it caught the side of his cheek that had been cut and split the wound again, and he lapped up the iron taste on the inside of his mouth in an act of violence so insular and private.

The day was hot when they rode out and he started to see the silhouettes of the men he'd killed in the shrinking shadows of the mesas.

They were only a mile from where they'd slept when he snapped.

"You knew, didn't you!"

His horse stumbled at his shout and the girl looked up from dozing in the saddle.

He wanted a fight. And then he had thrown down the bag of pills and was off his horse, heat-mad, walking toward her.

"You know, don't you. You've seen it all so you know."

He grabbed her leg and when she leaned down with amazement in her face he swung and clipped her chin.

"You knew how it all happened! You knew why!"

She was off the mule in a second and latched onto his torso. He rolled and she hit the ground hard on her back and he took another swing at her and he missed. She dragged a claw across his cheek as she scrambled to dodge the punch and his next punch hit her square in the nose. The girl rolled overtop of him and his back hit a rock and he kicked up at her and she dislodged herself and stood, staggered backward.

"Stop it!"

"You know why she did it!"

"Stop! You're gonna get us both killed."

He laid against the rock, coughing hard to regain his breath, and she felt the wet and ripped the cloth from her face. Her nose was spurting blood down her mouth and chin and she put up her hands and soaked them and looked at her palms. She was silent for a second and her eyes went red, fogged from the blow to the face. She put her hands up to her nose again and got them bloodier and then flung the contents of her hands onto Smith.

"This . . ."

She mashed the blood down the sides of her face, down her shirt and held her hands out to him again.

"This! Is this what I have to be for all of you? This is why you didn't run from the greenhouse and why Awan and his men didn't throw me back into the desert. Because this is what you want the killer to look like, so that you don't have to believe the ones you love would ever do the same. So that because she never got blood on her maybe she didn't really do it and none of it ever happened. Because the killer looks like something you've never seen before and probably never will see again, so you never have to look at your fathers your mothers your brothers your goddamn sisters and say, 'This is what we are all like. This is what we all have inside of us.' That even as you do it yourself and haven't washed it off your face yet, you're different and you can see better with just the one eye. She's more like me than you could bear. And so are you."

He watched her as the droplets of her blood started to run on his face. She had recaught the mule and was mounting it, but stopped. She turned back and outstretched a hand to him.

"If you're trying to resurrect your ghost of a sister that's not the way. Let's go."

He took it and rose and grabbed the piebald and the pills, and the girl dragged herself slowly back into the saddle.

The day was nearly gone before he spoke again.

"I don't know why I didn't kill you at Walmart."

She nodded.

"I don't know why I haven't killed you out here."

And she broke two ampicillins from their package and passed them his way.

When they stopped the animals were dehydrated enough that exertion no longer left foam on their mouths and the piebald tongued its bit dry.

Before the girl untacked the mule she leaned against it for support and checked the stitches along her stomach. Her skin was smooth but graying like shark leather in that dying light. He thought of the glass that had lodged in her fingers in the gunfight as she fired through broken windows, wondered if it still shivered there, the manifestation of the reflections of light on Lucy's arms that years-gone night. The girl turned her wrist and removed the cloth. The teeth marks were a black constellation. He watched her examine it, stared at the circular cut now scabbing on her forehead. *Change and scars are the only things that're gonna make us different.* He looked at her child's knees then checked the quieting hole of his arm.

She came over and sat down opposite him.

They were quiet for a moment and Smith could feel where the sun had burned his scalp through his hair and put a hand to it and felt that it was beginning to blister.

There were dried brambles here and Smith collected a few

from where he sat and lit them with Matthew's lighter and in a
few minutes they were out again.

"Why did you take the gamble?" she asked.

"Of usin you instead of killin you?"

She nodded.

"Is it because the sister's as good as gone?"

He didn't move.

"The guilt took her. Never mattered that it were an accident. Took her all the same."

The girl thought about this for a long while.

He took out his eye to wipe the dust from it, but found it
was useless, not a single clean surface among his clothes or his
skin to wipe it with.

"Can I see it?" the girl asked.

He handed it to her and she turned it in her palm. White
glass in a valley of dried rust red. There was too much dirt out
here; he would not be able to put it back in.

"Can we make a trade?"

The girl turned and dug into her bag and held her other fist
out to Smith. Opened it with the rabbit's jaw within. It had the
number 792 carved into it.

He took it from her and she closed her hand around the
eye, which with the motionlessness of staring up from a palm
seemed to have gained something of resolve in being inde-
pendent from his head. Had traveled far enough.

He awoke many times during the night and at one point
the girl was gone from her divot in the sand and he looked
backward and she had scaled the rock face and was sitting on
an outcropping thirty feet up, with her knees to her chest and
her eyes black and reflective, staring out into the night as the
stars came unpinned from their places and shot across the cess-
pool of the sky to collide with the supplicant hands of dead

plateaus reaching from the desert below. He awoke once more and she was there still, and when he awoke next she lay curled in the sand once more, as if she had never left it.

CHAPTER TWELVE

Yours

In the morning the piebald mare was down. Smith tried to rouse it but its eyes did not follow his hand as he snapped his fingers in front of its face and when he shoved its side with his knees it grunted but did not move. The girl looked over.

"I said the horse always dies before the men do." She shrugged. "This isn't good."

She passed him the AK-47 and he shot it point blank. Had earned its bullet.

The girl took the gun back and slung it across her shoulders and started toward the mule but he said, "Wait" and knelt down beside the horse with his hunting knife out.

He stared at it for a while before he did anything, turning over the thought in his mind. That maybe you were always like this. He nicked a hole in one of the neck arteries and put his mouth to the hide.

It wasn't water and it was warm but he was so thirsty.

The taste of livestock and iron so much like the smell in his nose from the morning in the field. The blood spilled in aftermath of gunfire had been different because it smelled of burning, but this was the same as a steer with a leg gone. On that land at home where the bones of that steer still were and had been burned and sparrow-picked clean and the bones of the father still there too but he did not know how exposed, how decayed, nor from how far in the field Lucy watched them do so—

He stayed coupled to the horse's neck, drinking. Coming alive again. Lucy, who now at dawn would still be in bed in white. And she'd char and grow old alone on that solitary pillow but only on the edge because even there she did not belong and even in rest her soul did not have a home. And he knew as she slept her soul or her ghost was wandering among the trees, in the bark-clad dark where she had taken one life and shackled her own.

He rolled away and slumped against the horse's stomach and the girl crawled over and took her fill as well. He exhaled hard, satisfied both in thirst and in having thought to do it.

They took half an hour there, drinking as much as their stomachs could carry. The girl vomited once down her shirt then swallowed what was in her mouth before drinking again. Then they saddled the mule and the girl got up first and Smith tossed her the bag of pills and swung up behind her.

They rode out, the one-eyed man reining the pawing black animal with the child perched on the saddle in front of him, the shadow of the gun across her back drawing lines in the sand behind.

"How far do you think we've got?" he asked.

"Fifty miles maybe. A few more days if we get that far." She shook her head. "But we don't know what we'll find when we get there. They might've made the wounded give up the greenhouse."

"You said you got the directions off one of their men."

"Not their man. When the cartel fell, all were split across different factions. The Cordovas kept each supplier location among only the few men that needed to know, so that the suppliers would be safe from subordinates trying to go and hijack them. These didn't know where the greenhouse is, otherwise they would have met us there."

She was quiet for a while before she spoke again.

"You still alive?"

"Still breathin. You?"

"Still breathing."

A lone coyote came from the west and trotted beside them for a few miles on leathery legs. Half bored and half delirious, the girl had taken the pistol and aimed it at the animal's notched spine and imitated the recoil and the sound of the shot. The mule padded on, unbothered, its hooves each the size of the coyote's head. After an hour the coyote looked once more at them with yellow eyes, staring as if to remember these miscreations of reddening hairless skin and black metal and the fur of its kind, and then it moved on, back into the blinding white air.

Smith outstretched a hand for antibiotics to roll against his teeth.

"Were the men that ambushed Awan there for you?"

She nodded.

"Did you know they'd come?"

She didn't answer, stared out into the plain.

"Are you scared they'll find you?"

"You don't understand. They saw me run out here; they're sure I'm dead."

She lowered her voice before she went on.

"I've never been assumed dead before. If I make it out of here I'm sure I'll enjoy it."

They slowed only when the sun was high enough to beat straight down upon them and it was for the sake of extending the use of the mule but the two assumed various postures while trapped there under the sun, covering their heads with their hands against the heat, or lying face up on the haunches of the mule as if broken-backed, or flat out with their noses in the animal's fur, like an assortment of victims of Pompeii.

With its rigid ears the mule made for an enormous black Doberman with filed teeth, and as the light passed the meridian of the day the shadows of its legs extended into ghostly trees. Smith watched them for what felt like hours, coal-colored lines gliding over the ground.

The girl tired and leaned back against Smith and might have slept. He watched the shadows still and they were still like trees, the trees that had blood inside and rose straight up like burned poles, some wide enough and with enough girth that it was as if they really did have a man inside each of them. A forest of dead men encased in wood and forced to stand, and without seeing their eyes, blinded in woodstuff, you would never know whether they would be looking up in search of some light or staring straight ahead. And in the spaces between them the man that had fallen flat on his back with a shotgun blow, with his face up to the sky like the silhouette printed onto a target, in the woods in some distant corner of Utah.

<hr/>

There were to be no stars this night, the sky blackening with clouds like gunpowdered cotton. At last it was so dark that they cast no shadow at all, that their passage across the earth should leave no mark even in a flickered obstruction of shallow light.

No stars to direct them north but that was still the direction in which they headed; they felt it. A few hours out there was a crash and a storm splintered, a needling of light driven into the ground a hundred miles to the west but with nothing between here and there they still could see it. Soon the clouds coagulated into a woolen sheet and it became too dark for them to see their hands in front of their faces.

They pushed the mule on, and it sloughed through the sand for another mile, stumbling and shying. Then it stopped completely, balking at the faceless dark, fearing the emergence of creatures larger and more nightmarish than he.

They dismounted and Smith tied his jacket around the mule's face to blindfold it. On either side of its head they crossed the plain together, in such blackness that at one point the girl's outstretched hand met with the side of a mesa. The thunder continued to the west and occasionally lit the air with electric bones but when the light would go they would start seeing things in the dark. Shapeless things, conglomerates of the violence in synesthetic sounds and the faces they had seen and maybe killed and maybe lost. And you wondered what the mule had seen to halt it, if the visions were unique to each of them. At last they decided to stop. Smith took the jacket from the mule's eyes and hobbled it.

They lay down and he could hear her covering herself with the sand that was cooler than the air. He thought of the creatures she'd overturn, figured that if she unearthed scorpions or tarantulas that those things would find a home on her and burrow somewhere there against coyote-laced collarbone or mud-covered hip and stay with her for good.

"Why is it always the horse that dies first, and never you?" the girl asked.

"Because of strength of will."

She stopped with the sand.

"Does that still matter out here?"

"It always does."

"That sounds like fate."

The mule shifted and he put a hand on one of its legs.

"Well, maybe it's fate."

"Then what is fate?" she asked, the voice seeming amputated and roving in the sightless black.

"It's somethin you're born with. Somethin that's passed down from the fathers before and shows itself in triggers that weren't meant to be pulled and triggers that were. You caint control it and can only look back on it as explanation for why you did the things you did even if they've ruined you because it couldn't have been any other way."

"Can you fight against it?"

"Yeah, like you can fight against the land."

"But how do you know?"

"How do you know what?"

"How do you know what's meant to have been, and what you've managed to change?"

"I don't know."

"Doesn't she?"

"Lucy."

"Doesn't she know? What she's changed and what she could not change." The girl had not moved but the voice seemed to circle, stalking.

"I aint know what you mean."

"That once there was only one of you."

"Yes."

"That there was only one of you, you saw it and she saw it too. And she saw, thought, that maybe she could make the whole world like that. Change the way the land was and time was and make it all exist for the two of you."

"Stop."

"That so few in this world ever defeat solitude, but by magic or fate you two did and because she had that gift, had that power of existing in another, thought she could make it all be so, could stop the blood and the killing that you did every day and the one that taught you to do it and had become synonymous with the land and the nature itself."

"Quit it, you aint got a right to talk about it."

"And maybe you knew it would happen, because you knew her and she was you, and maybe you didn't stop it because some part of you wanted it too, wanted to see if the world was something you could make your own because 'your own' was singular when you two were the same."

"Dammit, stop!"

"And why should she have thought it wouldn't work, wouldn't change things, when she had the godliness of living in another body than her own. And why should she ever obey the rules of the living when all your life you'd grown up standing on the dead. Did you see the diameter of the buckshot pattern?"

"Stop."

The clouds had not moved and they were still blind, in the cold and the bite of sand beneath his hands and the smell of cooling sweat.

"She broke from it—that's not guilt. It's not possible to torture yourself like I saw. It's solitude. It's that she saw you saw and wouldn't say it and by not saying it you made you two and not one. Did you see the buckshot pattern! Say it!"

"Stop it, goddamn you."

"Did you see it!"

He was shaking.

"Yes. Yes. Goddammit, I saw it. She shot him dead in the chest at less than a yard."

Without emotion the girl put an arm in front of his chest to keep him from falling forward, the warmth of the arm a line in the blackness.

A lone coyote padded across the plain, leaving crab-tracks in the sand as it carried its shallow ribcage through the dark. It paused at a squat of bramble then slipped behind it and emerged carrying a hare by the neck. Trotted on, as the blood ran along its gums, toward the west where the sun had set and tomorrow would set again.

———◦◦◦◦———

The steer had felt the line on its mouth go taut and was just beginning to test it when Wyatt saw her at the edge of the woods and she was not hauling an elk but a man. He stepped off of the steer rope and opened the corral gate and the steer stormed past him into the field as he walked silently toward the barbed wire fence that would let him out to the woods.

She had dragged him for a mile, and the leaves and thorns that had attached themselves to his clothes and hair had snarled into a bed or a pyre. She was stooped above him, had not dropped him to the ground because she had never had the strength to lift him off of it. The shotgun was laid across his torso with his arms set to hold it there as she'd hauled him by his armpits, and at the center of his chest the shotgun's mechanism, from the trigger to the sights, was steeped in liquid rust.

The son looked to the father's face. The man had lost all expression and there was nothing to guide, nothing to speak to there. The brother turned to the sister and the face she gave him was blank and her hands open and clean and he grabbed her into his arms and he shook as he spoke into her hair.

"It aint your fault."

And she pulled back from his hands and looked up into his face, for he was taller than her now. And it was the first time he ever saw fear in her eyes.

———

Smith was down for no longer than a quarter of an hour, then he was undoing the hobbles of the mule below the separating clouds. The girl reached to stop him and he shook her away.

"We're goin on now."

"You'll kill it."

"Now."

She looked at him, saw what she needed to see either to believe something or not to protest, and swung her gun over her back and they rode out.

They were silent from then on and once he thought he felt Lucy's hands and shook them off and rode on in abandonment, of all of it.

And as he rode he learned as she had, must have on that day when he wouldn't say it, that breaking with the other was not a loss but an invalidation, of whatever you had until now thought you were.

The sun rose and lit the fields of sand, and they crossed through the land that stretched for hellish hours, sheets of blond that wiped away his perception of his past like grinding across the folds of the brain.

And if it had not been fate that bent her hand along the trigger then it was not for him either. The slaughter since he set out from home—it had not been some mandate of fate laid out by the ancestors before you nor some selfless duty to a sister and a ranch that meant more than just that. No, the things you did, you did alone.

He rode on merely because it did not require moving.

After the fifth hour they passed the scars of a deep arroyo, where floodwaters had once run in a river thirty feet wide. They crossed slow along the base of it, the mule stumbling into the trough as though it wished for a reason to fall. A mockery to the life that used to be there, and beyond that they were in empty sand again.

At last the air began to waver, and Smith almost welcoming it slid in the saddle and went down, landing with a foot still in a stirrup and the bag hit the ground, the little green things hopping across the sand like larvae.

The girl was upon him a moment later and she'd rolled him over on his back and then was crawling over the ground to grab the pills, pulling them from the sand as if uprooting plants. She gathered the pills back into the bag and retied it where it'd burst.

Then she stood above him, holding the bag in one hand and the reins in the other.

"Get up."

He lifted a hand to his brow to see the by now hardly anthropomorphic creature bristling in front of him, covered in the sand and bones and skins of the desert, the impious carrier of the knowledge that destroyed his world.

"So once you thought you had a sister and then by even further mistake once you thought you weren't alone. You'll live. Get up."

Whether the voice held some mark of promise or some lie of past Lucy he did not know, but he stood and wiped the grit from his mouth with the back of his hand and lifted himself into the saddle. They rode on for four more hours, with no reason to stop and nothing to stop for, and no longer any care for the mule. So they went on, his scraped cheek bleeding again.

It was the girl who spotted the highway.

It had started as a roar and each had considered the hallucinatory effects of the desert before letting the other see that they had heard. But the girl pointed first and there it was, manifested in the curved plumes of dust beyond the lizard face of a Peterbilt barreling from the north.

They were a half-mile out from it and the girl was off the mule and scrambling toward it in the sand, falling twice on her way. He kicked the animal into a trot and met the girl coming back from the road. She was breathless, her knotted hair flung about her face like scattered rock and her shirt newly streaked with sweat.

Milepost 48. Another six miles before they would reach the dirt road and they would have to make it by dark in order to see it.

She got up in front of the saddle and turned the mule with a hand on its cheek and they angled toward the highway but kept a quarter mile away and the upsets of dust from the sporadic passage of trucks rose up to the left as they crossed the expanse of the horizon and then faded, and the mule did not stray from the track they had set it upon with their dual set of heels.

The sun had lowered to a pool of congealed orange sky by the time they reached their mark and the girl cut the mule straight to the west. They found the cattle grid in short order and the mule would not cross it nor jump it, and it staggered back and spun where it stood. They took it down ten yards and backward another twenty and kicked the animal into a canter to vault over the three-foot barbed wire fence. It caught the mule at the quarter and its flank dripped scarlet onto the stippled pelt as they ferried their mount against the dying sun.

———

Wyatt had the sheets spread out on the bare table in front of him and she came in from outside before the father did and when she fell sideways onto his lap she ripped the target out of his hands.

"Lucy get up you smell like horse manure."

She had taken a piece of rabbit from the stove and gone to the window while he cleaned his gun, but then she came back to the table. He had forgotten the dropped target on the floor and she picked it up.

"He shouldn't have let you hitch that baler on your own, Wyatt. Or kill that rabbit. You shouldn't have to do any of those awful things."

She overturned the target in her hands. It held the inexorable hole of buckshot fired at one yard.

———

They slowed then dismounted at last beside Smith's truck. There were no tracks coming in; the Cordovas had not found it.

Still fully tacked the mule looked at them and then started to walk away and when neither the girl nor Smith reacted it turned back toward the desert and ran, heat-stroked and exhausted and not just a little mad. They could see it run far as the old corral, fading piece of charcoal rocketing over hoof-patterned ground to brave the cold and heave out hot breaths into it as it wove back west, contraband animal sent back into the desert to die there or to return home to a master who was already one with the dust.

They turned back around and stared at the place for a moment in the quiet, only half sure that they indeed had made it there and almost checked their arms to see that they were alive, then were at a run to the storeroom.

Smith was at the sink first and drank below the faucet frantically and the girl followed and they began clawing down the smoked meat that hung on hooks from the ceiling and tearing chunks from it with their hands and ripped packages of bread from the shelves in a place that had been fully stocked to feed ten men.

The old woman who had been somewhere upon the place came in and when she saw it was only them she began yelling in that old language and covered her face with her hands. The children shied behind her skirts.

They walked past her and carried bags of the remaining food and a few jugs of water and flung them into the back of the truck, then went around the back of the place and ripped the hoses from the piping in the greenhouse. The girl went to drag them out front to empty the water into the ground.

Smith stayed behind for a moment, took a last look at the place that had been color in the desert. One last bloom of the colors of birds, and he felt he could nearly see it breathing. He picked up a shovel and drove it into the glass wall. The shards lavished down into the mouths of the flowers like rain.

Out front the girl was taking an ax to the beam that supported the lean-to in front of the door. The old woman walked out and had stopped yelling and just stared and Smith turned to her and said, "You better go on and gather your stuff then, anything you're wantin to save," and she looked at him not comprehending and the girl turned over her shoulder and shouted in that foreign tongue, still chopping, and the woman commenced yelling again, a screeching of sun-dried bellows, and ran into the storefront once more.

Smith went around to the back, opened the corral for the four mustangs, and they were gone in a squall of dust. The fire had long since gone out. He went into the shed and the girl took up a shovel and used its side to dismantle the pill presses, and without a tool Smith took to one of them on the table and started loosening bolts and pins and scattering the pieces in a mass on the floor. When that was finished they dumped the vats of powder and unfinished paste and used a crowbar to open the tops of barrels of acid and acetone but did not mix them, knew that much. Knew it would all go up sufficiently. She clasped the barrel of the AK-47 one last time and dropped it into one of the vats. They walked out of the place with their shirts held up to cover their mouths and noses, though the fabric had already been caked with others' blood and their own sweat and coyote drippings and offered little air to filter through now.

The girl had taken down most of the plastic siding from the place and it buckled into the storefront in a single point of impact per panel, yellow sheeting shattered in percussive waves. The woman came to stand beside them with a blanket tied up with her belongings across her back and each of the children holding one of her hands. She had only cracked leather sandals for her feet and a shawl across her sun-whitened head and watched the building splinter apart with dim silt-colored eyes.

The girl had wanted to ascertain that there was nothing they had left that was valuable or could be traced and ran

YOURS   271

through once more, ripping open filing cabinets. There were four hundred dollars in the cash register, and the girl gave fifty to the old woman without apology.

Smith brought two cans of gasoline from the shed and the girl sliced open the fronts with her knife and toed backward through the shop like the dog that had laid its iterations of tracks just days before. Was nowhere to be seen now.

When they returned to the storefront the old woman had started south. The girl called to her, but she did not turn around, and the jutting unevenness of her limping form and the soft-footed children faded within moments like shrapnel spun into the dark.

The girl went back to pouring and when she'd wetted the bottoms of the wall she sloshed the liquid up along the structure, and let it drizzle down and did not wipe her mouth as it splashed.

When the cans were empty she threw them through the doorway and Smith bent to the base of the structure and lit it in several places and stood back and watched the fire take root and the girl shivered once and then stopped.

The gas-lit front went up first and then the flames bled backward over the scalp of the store. There was an explosion as the back room ignited and Smith grabbed the bumper of his truck as a six-inch hook of metal barrel was lofted over his left shoulder. He looked at the girl and she remained unmoved.

The fire mounted the roof and became enormous, and while it flared there among the jutting tears of iron sheeting it mirrored the desert opposite it, as the mesas were cast in black shadow in front of the roiling sunset. For a moment Smith and the girl were caught between the two behemoth walls of flame, and then the sun fell below the horizon and went out.

The girl took the keys from where they'd shelved them beneath the rear wheel well of his truck and she threw them to Smith and went for the passenger side but then jumped back. Smith opened the driver's side and looked in. The pool of remnants of skin and blood on the passenger seat was now rife with bugs, small crawling beetles and maggots.

The girl cast an arm across it to scrape them off and then picked up the bag of pills and got in.

He pulled a mile out from the greenhouse then stopped and got out when he saw the pair of rocks leaned against one another. Knelt in the sand he dug up the shotgun slowly, unearthing it like a body or a fossil from some world else. Shook it off when he lifted it and looked one last time at the compound bending low now as if under the weight of the flames. Knew that to others, this was what home burning looked like.

The girl leaned out the window.

"We have to go before the police get here."

And he got behind the wheel and hammered the accelerator north at last.

⁂

They rode as silently as they had on the mule an hour earlier, the girl in the caked slough of the passenger seat with the bag on her lap and her hands roaming occasionally to pick off another bug and cast it out the window.

"Let's get clear of Salt Lake City then find a place to stop. By then we'll be far enough up the state." They both knew it was for their own sense of escape as much as it was for eluding any that would follow.

He nodded and she turned Awan's pistol in her hands and released the magazine.

"We need more ammo. For this and your shotgun."

"Shotgun ammo's in the back seat."

"Then just ammo for this."

They kept on north, and passed the exit signs for the city until the lights along the highway faded and they were back in the part of the country where trees run black with moss and chill.

At the next motel they saw he pulled the truck into the spot furthest from the proprietor's office.

The girl passed him more cash than he'd need and when he got out she'd ducked out from her seat and was leaned against the cab out of sight in the dark. He took the shotgun with him, still would not leave it with the girl.

The proprietor was a malnourished man of over seventy, in a trucking hat with a toothpick in the corner of his mouth and he got out of his chair when he saw Smith come in. It was a few hours past midnight and the air of the office smelled like tobacco and ammonia.

"How much for a night?"

The man's eyes went among Smith's face and his clothing and his gun and the man was stepping back until he hit the wall taped with past years' national park calendars and ads for horses.

"Forty dollars."

"I'll pay you upfront."

"You're supposed to pay when you check out."

"No, I'll pay you upfront."

"Why would you do that?"

"Why would you ask?"

Smith slid a dirty cracked hand onto the counter with two hundred-dollar bills. The proprietor looked down at them and then at Smith.

"Two nights," Smith said.

"That all?"

"That's all."

The man eyed Smith once more and made his choice or decided there was none to make, then turned and brought over the key.

"Thirty-seven, down by the end. Checkout's at noon."

Smith went out without a word.

He walked back to the truck and the girl got the bag of pills and he got the food and water from the truckbed and they went in. Neither bothered to turn on the light, and they collapsed on opposite sides of the bed with their boots still on and a jug of water each next to their heads.

He didn't know how long it had been when the sun rose but when it did it ran across the floor in amber stripes like plow lines. He kept his head beneath the pillow except for some interval of the blurred sense of time, every few moments or every few hours, when he'd wake up gasping and clutch at the water jug once more. Clawing at the sheets to feel for the sand below his nails, looking for the smell of the mule to assure himself it had not gone while he slept. And after a while, whether it was the afternoon's fading light, or passing a certain threshold of how much water he'd restored to his blood, his thoughts moved north.

⸻◦⊙◦⸻

He was waking up but it was not a thing entirely like waking, might have taken days or minutes and no sense in preferring either way as none was the easier. The pressure was still inside his head, and you still open the lids expecting to see the dark of a bandage over your eye but there's not even that. He knew the eye was gone and he remembered the trip to the hospital that was not an attempt to save it but to take out what remained. He instinctively covered the place where it had been and opened the right eye. Lucy sat balanced on the edge of the bed, watching him.

"How long has it been?"

"Eight days. They knocked you out good for the surgery and then two days after you got a fever and the doctor said it was infected and you been fightin it since. You aint remember?"

"Nah."

She leaned across him and put the back of her hand to his forehead. She no longer smelled of hay.

"Fever broke yesterday. It's almost gone," she said.

He struggled to sit up and she pushed the other pillow behind him.

"What about the ranch? Can you two manage? Is it okay?"

She made a semblance of a smile.

"We're fine. You got six more days of this before you're allowed to lift anything. Relax."

He looked at her and things were still hard to look at but something in her face was falling.

"Does it hurt, Wyatt?"

"A bit."

She took his hands and when she turned them over they were strange to him, too clean, the memory of work too far away.

"Are you angry?" she asked.

"Nah."

She went over to the window and pulled up the sash then crawled across the bed and sat beside him, their backs propped against the wall.

"Are you okay?"

He turned to her, found he had to turn further in order for the right eye to meet her stare.

"Are *you* okay?"

"Wyatt, I found you on the floor of the barn then."

"Tell me."

She moved to sit in the center of the bed so that he would not have to turn so far to see her.

"You were on your back like how you'd lie in the field when you'd managed to swipe one of Pa's cigarettes and the weather was good. There was something floral blooming out of your face. I thought it was somethin beautiful, that flowers so red are rare in the mountains. It weren't until I saw the way it ran over your teeth that I realized it was blood and turned and saw the other part of it on the baler wire.

"You lookin at me like that, no more a part of you but had been part of you our whole lives. Had been lookin at me for years. Watched me grow up. You layin there and I didn't know what part of you was watchin me then.

"An' I was holdin two buckets of feed when I'd walked in an' I turned away and still fed those damn horses and hid in the stall for a moment more then came back to you and cried and cried with your head to my chest until night fell and he came lookin for us and we carried you together like you two used to carry me when I got too tired in the woods. Had to wash the blood off my hands, off my dress, from holdin onto you."

She put her head in her hands and he looked at the wrinkles and sweat-stains of her clothes, the darkening grease of her hair, and knew that she hadn't left him since it happened.

"We still don't change, right? Us, we're still gonna be the same, right?"

"Yeah. It's still the same. You gotta hold to what's yours."

Smith woke up choking and knocked the water from the bed-side table. The girl was sitting on the windowsill across the room, two fingers splaying the blinds so that the moonlight pooled on the carpet.

"Thought maybe you were going to die for a second."

"Nah," he said.

"You going to be good to go tomorrow?"

He sat up and nodded, reached for the water.

"I have to make a call," she said.

The room shook with light as she opened the door and when it closed again he turned on the lamp on the table.

The floor was strewn with knifed-open cans of food and wet towels and the pieces of coyote hide torn from their faces and arms as they'd twisted in a hungering sleep. He kicked off his boots and chose not to examine the condition of his feet.

He went into the bathroom and stripped himself of the remaining bits of coyote and left them on the floor and threw a handful of water onto his face and wiped it with the towel, and the towel came away burgundy and brown and a bit green. More water and wiped it again and again until the towel was soaked through and fell to the floor like a rock. His empty eye sulked with the lid nearly closed, a slash of red beneath. He rinsed the cut sleeve he'd had around his mouth and tied it diagonal over the socket.

When he came back into the room the girl was crouched on the end of the bed. She turned around when she heard him.

"Noon tomorrow. There's an abandoned metals reduction mill fifty miles north of here."

He came over and sat next to her, opened a can of chicken.

"Got ammo too?" He nodded at the box in her lap.

"We're in the North, there's not a man out here that doesn't have a pistol in their glove compartment."

"Tomorrow then."

He pushed himself back into the body outline of dirt he'd left on the sheets. Worked the last of the chicken from the can with his lower jaw and simultaneously tried to sleep. Perhaps now would always be among those for whom day and night have no difference.

Two hours before noon, the girl got up and dragged the bag of pills from beneath the bed, leaving it in the pillowcase she'd wrapped it in. Cracked open the box of pistol ammo and started lining her socks and pockets with it and he got a box from his truck and started doing the same.

The two sat there like that for a while on the green bedspread, the girl with her face repainted in dual stripes with motor grease from a car that'd been parked out front.

"We should go soon," said Smith.

"One more hour," she said.

When the time had passed Smith left the key in front of the room and they drove out. When they hit the old wooden signs for the reduction mill, still two miles away, they chose a spot obscured by leaves and left the truck just off the road, out of sight. They walked on from there, the girl with the pillowcase bundled against her chest.

They went along the scrub brush path that diverted from the main road for the last mile, trees that had been broken to make way for it a hundred years old now, regrown and deformed around the places the quarry trucks had clipped them. At the end of it the plain opened before them. Northern Utah. From the top of the hill they could see the green-gray of bluestem and Indian grass stretch for miles before it hit the sinister indigo of mountains beyond.

At the top of the mill was a rectangular steel-sided build-ing, the size of a forty-stall barn and its walls pinto-marked with rust and the sliding door crumpled beside its tracks like a discarded note.

The air was dry and Smith upturned his collar instinc-tively against the dehydration. They stood beside the crippled doors for a moment and looked out at the silent plain. The girl hugged the pillowcase of pills tight like a child dragged from a nightmarish sleepover, pistol in the front of her pants and her ankles braceleted with spare bullets.

The rest of the facility ran down the hillside below, a syn-copated line of emptied vats, for holding water or for roast-ing, thirty feet wide, cast in sandstone-colored concrete and splintered by rebar where parts had collapsed. Every surface of it was splashed in an explosive sprawl of graffiti, quivering in color against the monotone plain. A maze of shattered con-crete down the side of the hill, like a nest of mammoth insects destroyed and unearthed.

Neither said a word but both had been listening. Satis-fied it was clear, they walked through the gutted building and stopped near the other side and waited there in the shadows, the lines of light from where the rain had broken open the cor-rugated roof like warpaint on their somber faces.

A truck pulled up ten minutes later. A man entered and stopped just inside the doorway. He wore a white T-shirt and bleached hair that was tied in a ponytail behind a face with dark eyebrows. There were others behind him, all armed with handguns.

"Jackson," the girl said.

"You made it." The man's voice was angular as he spoke, matched the severe tilt of his brows. He widened his stance and crossed his arms, eyed both of them.

"I said we would."

She then nodded toward the men flanking him.

"Five men. Do I make you nervous?"

"No, no. Call it prepared."

She set down the bag beside her boots and held it by the corner of the pillowcase.

"Two hundred thousand dollars for the lot of twenty thousand," said Jackson.

"I told you. No wholesale price on these. Three hundred thousand dollars." Her voice was cold, cast across the empty floor.

He laughed and shook his head.

"I was afraid you'd say that, and I came ready for it."

One of the men behind him brought forth a navy duffel bag and started walking forward and the girl went to meet him there in the center of the floor. Smith gripped his shotgun tight against his right arm. The man opened the bag and held it for her and when she put both hands in it to count the cash Jackson spoke.

"I'm so sorry, dear."

He yanked the pistol from his hip and fired and the girl pushed off of the man holding the bag of cash and the man was hit in the back instead. She rolled and kicked out her heels against the base of the rotting metal wall and the metal gave and she tumbled outside.

Smith dropped the shotgun into position and fired and one of the men fell and he was running backward through the end of the building and turned and at once he was running beside the girl as they skidded in the broken concrete around the base of the first vat.

The shots came fast and in quick succession; the men had automatics with them. Smith and the girl crouched behind the side of the vat as the slugs shattered through the structure above and rained concrete onto them in colored dust. They stayed tight against the wall, red concrete-bugs crossing their fingers like walking miniatures of the bursts of paint on the stone, and listened to the men gathering around the front of the building and the frequency of gunfire mounting.

The side of the vat started to shake and Smith and the girl made a run for it again, slid down the hillside through the gravel and ducked behind the second vat unscathed. The third vat had long since collapsed, and the broken concrete was buckled against the intact second vat to create an alleyway that ran horizontal on the hillside, scored across by rebar that spiked and coiled from the broken places.

The gunmen were clambering down through the rock toward where the pair was crouched under cover and Smith and the girl leaned around and clipped one in the side but he didn't drop, and one ducked to dodge a bullet as the gravel caved under his feet and impaled his hip on a piece of rebar that protruded from the ground in a hook, and he was yelling while aiming his gun once more and the girl shot him where he lay. The sounds were coarse against the concrete, rang out over the open plain where somewhere far ahead a flock of upland birds took off and blackened the sky.

Smith still firing and loading shells from his socks with the bullets rocketing against his ears and the concrete behind his head singing in a delinquent's history in layer upon layer of illicit paint. A shot winged in close and the girl cried out as she was hit in the shoulder but she reloaded even as it started to bleed.

They had the vantage point in taking down the men from behind cover, and the barrage of shots slowed as the men regrouped on the slope above.

Jackson's voice came metallic and heavy from over their heads.

"They're letting me keep the E if I bring you in, you know."

The girl looked once at Smith then turned in among the rebar and sunken concrete and began to run down the alleyway between the vats. Smith followed and they moved as if underground, below the skin of the land and at once feeling the walls shuddering above them, chunks of rock gunned down, so brittle for having so much weight, and a hundred feet into the half-dark the alleyway ended in a meteoric pile of rubble and they spun around.

"Here," the girl panted and they got in behind a massive boulder of concrete and lined their guns up atop it and readied themselves. The girl's shoulder hung limp and her face was white. The broken flats of concrete vaulted up in a steeple above them, sliced through with sunlight.

The first of the shots came and hit above their heads. A shadow blocked the light of the entryway to the alley and they saw the man's legs first and tried to gun him down at the thighs but he dove for cover behind another fallen slab. Outside was altogether too bright and the dust clouded the view. Bullets were biting into the dirt behind their heads but they had too little ammo to fire back without a target to aim at.

Two more silhouettes came into view, shadows advancing through the dust, the echoes of their shots blaring through the dark as they hit. Stone fracturing around them and the girl reloading in a fever and screaming in that animal call she'd adopted in the desert battle and screaming at Smith, "Shoot faster, man, take what's yours!"

He reloaded again, his ears blinding with the words. Shot again, shot again, reloaded, shouting with her but without words, and it became something like falling, something like

the death of rabbits and the death of grizzlies, and all of it
that rang out from under the ground and under the concrete
and under their hoofbeats and tiretracks, something like
flying.

He could smell the blood of her arm and the powder stick-
ing to his face from his gun and his finger stronger against the
trigger than all of the strength in his arm.

"Take what's yours!"

The girl was screaming something more at him in between
shots and he could not hear her. The black on her face smeared
with the side of her hand.

"Take what's yours!" This whole crazy violent world. And
he was pulling the trigger like she had pulled the trigger and
she had broken them apart but he had too and the blood, all
the blood had always been there, and you had to take it even
if it was broken, even if it was wrong and half gone, because
that was what was yours. And only yours, in a world in which
trilobites rode mountains for a million years then were carried
off in a teenager's pocket the same way she threw the bones
of men, where scores of fathers who came before you lost the
fight against the same land they raised you up to feed from,
where trees ran red with meat inside if you chose the right
ones.

He pulled the trigger again and another man went down
from his shot.

Take what's yours. And suddenly he was running through
the bullets out from the alleyway and up across the gravel
wash.

He saw Jackson and the other men in a blur and they were
climbing the concrete that formed the alley roof and drop-
ping gun-first into it as if leaping into the sea and they must
have seen him but would not take their eyes from pursuing the

girl. He kept running. And in front of the building there was a man taking the duffel bag of cash to the truck and Smith removed the back of his head with a blow from the shotgun and grabbed the bag and kept running.

He was at the mouth of the wooded path when he heard the alleyway collapse. He turned around to look. The dust rose in fragments like a fog of locusts, the mountains still pitilessly blue beyond it. When the rock had settled and silenced itself, the shooting had stopped. No sound save his own pulse. His hands wet with sweat on the shotgun.

He waited until the dust had faded, as if the air had been washed. Looked at his hands. Then went to his knees, counted out four thousand six hundred dollars from the bag of cash, put it in his pockets, and started toward home.

It took him two hours to get to the ranch. He had sprinted all the way down the dirt path and then down the road until he got to the truck and drove it north from there.

The road here was in among the trees, the asphalt a faint line in the green you could hardly see, and it felt like home. The screaming cicadas and the wet upon his face and he thought for a moment that he could smell cattle far off. The window open and the branches clipping the truck mirrors and he tore the cloth away from the empty eye socket and let the air hit it. The land, the land, and he didn't hate it. Sparrows lined the box elder boughs above his head and as the sun turned they made off for fields beyond to eat the grain.

And if you'd grown up that way, in the dark of the woods and under the stars that shivered in the sweat on your face beside the dog gnawing rawhide and the father chewing tobacco,

drawing blood to live and to breathe and chopping trees as if
they were made of the same stuff as cattle, then maybe you
could run through it, like coyotes or maybe even wolves, with
a shadow like the one cast from her skirts. You could run
through it and the trees might bend after you with the reach-
ings of the men locked inside, and they might break out of
there and they might not, but you'd have teeth to show them
or hooves to hurtle away, and the land would sigh and go back
to the slow decomposing it always had. But what was growing
old anyway, if not a decomposition, and if you could hold off
the land you could hold off that end forever. Be renewed, wash
the blood off your face, with a new spring of cattle and crops
again and again and again. He was home.

Lucy was standing in the kitchen and set down the pistol
when he walked in.

He took the cash from his pockets and laid it in stacks on
the counter in front of her as she watched him, then took her
hand by the wrist, upturned it, and placed the rabbit's jaw in
her palm.

She looked back at him, knew. Closed her fingers around
it.

He came around the counter to stand beside her and they
stared out the window, to where the ground by the hill was
closing now, five years after, like the hole healing in his arm.

Thank you to my agents, Jonny Geller and Chris Clemans—I am grateful every day for the privilege of working with you. To editors Maxim Brown and Cal Barksdale. To my Curtis Brown Creative classmates, who were there from this story's inception and saw it through to its final shape. To Julian Robertson and the Robertson Scholars Leadership Program community—the gift of your support, in all of its forms, is the foundation of my work. To my father, my first editor. To my sister and mother and my family, extended—I'm damn proud to be a DelBianco. To Julia Glass, Jim Shepard, Douglas Brunt, Joshua Ferris, Philipp Meyer, and Roger Reeves. To Joe Tam for woodworking what became the cover. To Coach Alex for teaching me, and by proxy the girl, how to fight. To Professor Victor Strandberg—had you not first taught me to be a reader, I could not have become a writer. To Professors Nancy Armstrong and Daniel Wallace. To my Tin House Summer Workshop family, for challenging and inspiring in equal parts. To Angela, for everything. To Jakob, Emilia, Marcus, Sebastien, Jaisal, Sterling, Nils, Margaret, Gene, Justin, Christina, Paul, Newton, Devin, Ashok, Marith, West; because we have scarce opportunities to put our appreciation of our friends in print, so I'll do it here. To the reading community on Instagram, for their unrelenting support. And to the one who opened her spare room and her life to me for the past three years so that I could pursue the novel—thank you chickie.